Allow Your Light to Fill the Darkness

A Primer to Living the Light within Us According to the Tao

DANIEL FRANK

BALBOA.
PRESS
A DIVISION OF HAY HOUSE

Balboa Press books may be ordered through booksellers or by contacting:

Balboa Press
A Division of Hay House
1663 Liberty Drive
Bloomington, IN 47403
www.balboapress.com
1-(877) 407-4847

Printed in the United States of America

ISBN: 978-1-4525-5773-1 (sc)
ISBN: 978-1-4525-5775-5 (hc)
ISBN: 978-1-4525-5774-8 (e)

Library of Congress Control Number: 2012915581

Balboa Press rev. date: 10/23/2012

I believe people are *as they* think. *The choices we make in the next decade will mold irrevocably the direction of our culture . . . and the lives of our children.*

—Francis A. Schaeffer

for my parents

Contents

Illustrations

Figure

Preface

All of us probably remember the primer, or first reader, that opened our door to reading. The word *primer* in the subtitle is meant to represent the central idea behind the Tao that opens our world to a vast array of possibilities, much as reading places a storehouse of knowledge at our fingertips. Reading was the dawn of our connection to the vast world of knowledge, past and present. It is our choice to make wise use of our link to this information. Likewise, it is our choice to understand the link and live the concepts portrayed by wisdom literature, such as the Tao Te Ching, and others, whose basic concepts mesh with modern-day scientific discoveries that are beginning to offer insight into the operation of our Universe. The sagacity of the Tao can be recognized within *each* of its fundamental characteristics, as revealed verse by verse, and can begin to be accessed through an understanding of the Oneness that is the Tao. The strength of the Tao lies in Oneness, not in the words that attempt to describe the nothingness that connects us all.

Dr. Wayne W. Dyer includes his personally selected translation of the Tao in his book *Change Your Thoughts—Change Your Life,* along with his essays that unclothe the wisdom within each verse. In the preface of his book, Dr. Dyer suggests that the reader do the following:

> First pursue one of the passages of the Tao Te Ching and the essay that follows it. Next, spend some time applying it, changing the way you've been conditioned to think, and letting yourself open up to a new way of conceptualizing these ideas. Finally, individualize the verse by writing, recording, drawing, or expressing yourself in whatever way you're called to. (Dyer 2007, xv)

Dr. Dyer's final suggestion in the previous quote fits well with my way of approaching new material. I began writing notes and making sketches to foster my personal understanding. As my appreciation for the Tao grew, my approach changed. I began to document my personal focus and understanding of the core message within each verse in both graphic and written form. The drawings that began as rough sketches developed into labeled graphics that represent what I conceptualize as a part of or *the* primary focus of each verse of the Tao as seen from my perspective. These illustrations attempt to capture and convey in real terms an aspect of the concise message each verse holds with not much more than a cursory glance. Although some of the commentaries in parts of the book are quite brief, I feel they are effectively complemented by the graphics, and together, are meant to illustrate the all-important message within each verse, or a key aspect of it that holds a parallel message of similar significance.

Because I am using Dr. Wayne W. Dyer's chosen translation of the Tao included in his book *Change Your Thoughts—Change Your Life*, along with his corresponding interpretive essays, making frequent references to his words and those of Lao-tzu feels essential to the process, since my comments and graphic illustrations build from there. In select locations throughout my writing, but particularly in the latter part, I draw on current reasoning from qualified, well-established, compelling, and credible authors of authority in the field. I have implemented these ideas into the gist of the verses that correlate, so as to produce an interflow with the main message of the Tao.

Therefore, for ease in reading, I have also taken the liberty to defy the rules for author-date citations, to allow for *page numbers only* after an initial author-date citation made earlier on the same page, instead of the established method, which accepts *page numbers only* after an author-date citation within the same paragraph. This means that quotes subsequent to an initial citation by the same author will be cited with only page numbers for not only the remainder of the paragraph but also for the remainder of the page, unless interrupted by a quote from a different author. This reduces the amount of author-date "clutter" on each page.

My comments focus particularly on the attributes of the Tao that I consider pivotal, and as well, I distinctly display significant detail in the labeled illustration. The way we think affects our decisions, which in turn affects our lives and the lives of others. The illustrations represent the gist, or a variation thereof, of each verse of the Tao and, in certain instances, may also help pinpoint behavior that might be wise to avoid. Although all verses of the Tao portray wise thinking, some verses are particularly significant. Too often, we don't recognize how our thinking affects our decision-making. Kindly forgive me for making "should" and "should not" statements throughout the pages of the book. They may tend to sound judgmental, but the intent is simply to convey what I consider a "good" way to work on accomplishing the "way of living" suggested by the Tao.

The project has almost taken on a life of its own. Stillness is the avenue—the conduit that connects our mind and opens our heart to whatever our predominating thoughts have surrounded and settled around on a continuing and evolving basis. Accepting situations as they occur opens us to recognizing things in our lives that serve to guide us. Gregg Braden, in his book *The Divine Matrix*, supports this thinking as indicated by the following statement. "Whether or not we recognize our resonant connection with the reality around us, it exists through the Divine Matrix. If we have the wisdom to understand the messages that come to us . . . our relationship with the world can be a powerful teacher." (Braden, *The Divine Matrix* 2010, 146)

Dyer masterfully unlocks the wisdom cleverly woven into the words of the Tao Te Ching approximately two thousand five hundred years ago. By applying this wisdom to our lives, we can begin to open to the world of all possibilities, because once we truly *get it*, the ideas are simple and can be brought into service through a realignment of our thought processes. A quote from the Chinese philosopher Confucius (BC 551-479) states that "life is simple, but we insist on making it complicated" (BrainyQuote.com 2012). The guidance available through the Tao opens us to our innate ability to implement changes that could lead to a life of meaningful purpose and virtue. We simply need to choose to avail ourselves to this offering by living the Tao. The simplicity of the idea is in direct opposition to our overactive, detail-oriented, controlling, and yet highly conditioned brain that remains very resistant to change.

It is appropriate at this point to include two quotes from Marcus Aurelius (AD 121-180), a Roman Emperor and philosopher. One quote reads that "the soul becomes dyed with the color of its thoughts," while the other reveals that "the universe is transformation; our life is what our thoughts make it" (BrainyQuote.com 2012). This reminds us that only we control our train of thought and that this invariably produces a significant part of our personality, which leads to the choices we make.

The use of the word *primer* in the subtitle has a second significant purpose that rests in its use as an acronym, reminding us that living a more meaningful life requires a change in thinking. The word *primer* might be seen as a reminder that a **P**ersonal **R**eality **I**ntervention (is the) **M**akeover **E**veryone **R**equires—PRIMER. The *decision* we make to implement the wisdom of the Tao into our lives allows us to begin the process of this all so important mind-makeover. The eighty-one verses of the Tao reveal what is needed to connect to our Source, as well as to tune into, and follow the intuitive guidance it offers.

This book is written from the perspective that because we all originate from the same Source, we are all in this together, hence the use of the first-person *we* throughout. I repeat: the commentaries are a merger of my portrayal of Taoist thought as arrived at through Dr. Dyer's book *Change Your Thoughts—Change Your Life* (Dyer 2007) blended with my personal contribution including illustrations. This leads to mentioning certain aspects of my book that make it somewhat distinctive. To use another author's book to justify a piece of writing may be considered by some as rather unusual. I concede that this approach is neither the commonly seen "bookstore style" nor the academic style of authoring a book. Although the following does not justify the process that I followed, it does suggest the high esteem I hold for Dr. Dyer, not to mention the other authors whose words and ideas I also respect and recognize as critically significant in promoting the change our world needs now. I refer the reader to a commonly used expression originating in the words of Charles Caleb Colton (1780-1832), an English cleric and writer, who said, "Imitation is the sincerest [form] of flattery" (BrainyQuote.com 2012).

A second unusual aspect of this book is displayed by the use of at least one illustration per section to help communicate the gist of each verse. The illustrations are also unique in the sense that a number of sentences are often used to clarify each illustration; and I have chosen to follow the principles of headline-style capitalization as if all labeling were part of the title. Another somewhat unusual aspect, but this time within the text, is the decision to capitalize words that I deem to be particularly significant to the main message, despite the conventions surrounding capitalization. Perhaps both examples of unconventional capitalization, as well as the other irregularities, can act as ongoing reminders, while reading the book, of the importance of changing many of the traditional ways we have been conditioned to think and seemingly forced to follow, without question. It is the ever-present awareness of the Tao, as it exists in us and everywhere around us that allows us to shift from our long-established beliefs by detaching from the pain of the past and the fear of the future, to live in the joy of life as it is in the present moment.

This project has roots that go back as far as 1978. At that time, a compulsion began to sprout within me from a seed planted by reading the book *How Should We Then Live?* by Francis E. Schaeffer. The book offers a remarkable analysis of the history of philosophical thought and the concept of God. It helped to unveil a deep need within me to seek out an alternate *and yet aligned* understanding to the Christian ethic that Francis A. Schaeffer offered in answer to this all-important question (Schaeffer 1976). My search clearly includes Dr. Wayne W. Dyer, and my increased familiarity with the topic is also grounded in other well-known authors. This describes the fourth atypical characteristic of this piece of writing—the use of a somewhat unbalanced number of corroboratory quotes.

I am a retired teacher with a BA and BEd. I *do not* have the university or college credentials or any other type of experience needed to be seen as qualified to propose scenarios like the following. For example, I suggest that the ever-present energy of the Universe that is the Tao may also be the *shared but previously unrecognized Source* that I feel played a part in the circumstances that were unequivocally involved in the formation of our many religions. I say this with the understanding that the ever-present consciousness or essence of the Tao has been part of our world throughout all time. This means it had to have been present at the time of, and in resonance with, the intention present within the founding participant(s) of each of the religions at their inception and, as well, at every stage along the pathway of development thereafter. Choices of integrity made by those in charge of decision-making in the growth and development of any religion keep its teachings as parallel to, and congruent with, the Tao, as ego, in its unrivaled urge to control, will allow. To my way of thinking, this universal Energy, or the "Divine Matrix," as Gregg Braden calls it, is integral in one way or another to the origin of many of the major religions of the world since it is the common thread of Oneness connecting us all. Because of the omnipotence of our Source, at no time in our history have the events in the lives of people been independent of their ongoing intentions. I also believe that all major religions are a product of the intentions of humankind interacting with Source through a level of consciousness higher than most of us can ever expect to experience. Our Source responds in resonance to the heartfelt intentions of any and all of us. This will have also been true at any point in history, including the occurrences at the wellspring of any one of the major religions where the participants of the time, such as Jesus, must have calibrated at a very elevated level of intention or consciousness.

Although the authors I quote later in the book may or may not be of a similar opinion on this point, I turn to those same trained and accomplished individuals to provide the required framework that I feel *melds* with the *idea* of the major world religions as having evolved from differing experiences of connection to Source, all having risen out of our shared Energy of creation, but each within the backdrop of a particular culture, as well as within the evolutionary history of the changing circumstances of the receiving personality or personalities. Certain of the wide array of possible variables within the realm of universal Energy are made manifest because of human intentions that exist(ed) as they did (and do) and gave (and continue to give) direction to the development of a religion by continually resetting the trajectory of the ever-evolving eventuality. I suggest that the level of intention of the founding participant(s), as well as that of the followers, resonated with the Source to manifest circumstances that were metaphysically disposed to set the stage for the development of the different religions.

There is strength in the collaboration of ideas. The harmonizing views of the authors that I quote endorse the idea of Oneness and help build an understanding within the book that serves to symbolically unite the overriding message of Oneness through a representation of the power inherent in the collaboration of ideas. This is not to suggest that more people saying the same thing invariably makes it true—it goes much beyond words; it depends on their individual and collective state of consciousness—and instead suggests that Truth has unraveled these ideas to those who have been receptive within their personal level of intention. People like Lao-tzu represent this thinking from his time in history while, for example, Deepak Chopra and Gary Zukav represent independent viewpoints that both, in their own ways, combine cutting-edge science and spirituality into individually unique and powerful voices that stand for living now, from the place of who we really are, spirit.

Bruce H. Lipton and Gregg Braden both pursue answers through science and discovery. Lipton, a stem-cell biologist focuses on the discovery of the energy factors that he says control our DNA (Lipton 2008). This is amazing science. Braden is "a leading authority on bringing [together] the wisdom of our past with the science . . . of our future" (Braden, *The Divine Matrix* 2010). His discussion of the connecting "energy" between our intention and our experience presents the idea of a "Divine Matrix" as the ultimate conduit of communication between all and for all. I believe that the ideas of these authors, as well as the ones referred to later in this book, embody the same fundamental thinking as is presented in the Tao.

Collaboration proves its strength in many differing scenarios where ideas coalesce to create a new solidarity of purpose. I am attempting to use the merging of ideas to support the message of the Tao by fusing it with what I consider illuminating and compelling ideas from the works of well-known authors in addition to Dr. Dyer. For myself and those interested, it is my hope to *coalesce* these *excerpts* of published ideas that refer to, and elaborate on, the integral part we play in the functioning and workings of our Universe, into a meaningful compilation—or *mass coupling*—of comparable concepts that complement and/or merge with the basic message contained in the eighty-one verses of the Tao.

While reading this book and always, it is important to remember that we exist as a soul of the Universe and will remain in the sea, or *"sky"* of universal Consciousness, the universal Mind— the Tao—God, Krishna, Buddha, Allah, or whatever we have chosen as the name for the Oneness that we all share. The terminology is up to us; it does not change the everywhere-existence of the Energy of the Universe. This decision too is a choice we get to make.

—Daniel Frank

In your light I learn how to love.
In your beauty, how to make poems.

You dance inside my chest,
where no one sees you,

but sometimes I do,
and that sight becomes this art.

—from *The Essential Rumi*,
translated by Coleman Barks
New Expanded Edition 2004
Harper Collins Publishers

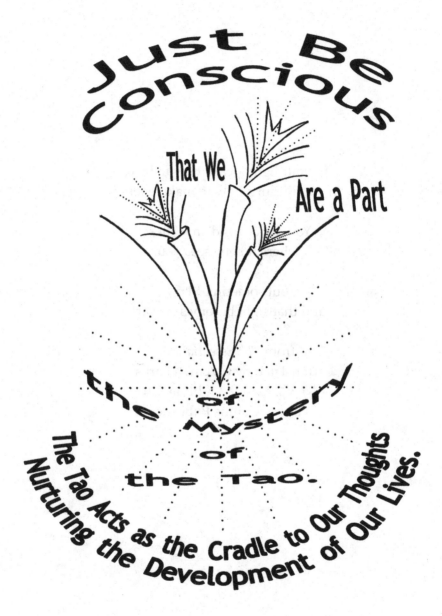

Figure 1: The Mystery of the Tao

Be Conscious
of the Indefinable Tao

1

In this first verse of the Tao, Lao-tzu refers to the mystery within the truth of the Tao as "the doorway to all understanding." Wayne Dyer encourages us to begin to live this mystery by progressing from our world of always wanting more, to gradually become more and more "desireless" (Dyer 2007, 2-3). We might begin the process by just accepting and allowing "the world to unfold without always attempting to figure it all out" (5).

Is it possible that the enigma Braden is describing in his audio presentation (Braden, no date (n.d.), CD1) *Speaking the Lost Language of God* as a "new science that has not as yet hit the text books" is the mystery of the Tao? Later on the first CD, he mentions that in the years between 1993 and 2000, "Western science began to establish the fact that we are surrounded by a field of what is called unconventional energy. It permeates all of creation." He goes on to tell us that, "In recent times this field has begun to be called 'The Mind of God'" (CD1).

Whatever the explanation of the mystery of the Tao, Wayne Dyer places emphasis on Lao-tzu's counsel that "letting go of trying to see the mystery" reveals manifestations of our desires but not the mystery itself. Besides suggesting that we "judge less and listen more," Wayne Dyer recommends, "cultivating a practice of being in the mystery and allowing it to flow through [us] unimpeded" (Dyer 2007, 5).

To desire that things change by first feeling the change within us may appear contradictory at first to Lao-tzu's recommendation of allowing and accepting things as they are, but reality lies in the strength inherent in the process of actually feeling as if what we want is already here. This allows us to let go of our attachment to our desires, be open to, and trust the Tao. All that there is, is of the Source. All we desire is in the part of the Source that is already in us. The doing is up to us.

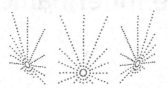

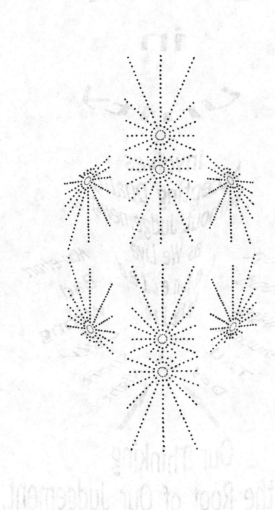

Figure 2: Accepting Duality without Judgment

Living in Unity

2

The judgments we make every day in our lives create the duality we see in our world. We discriminate between right and wrong, beautiful and ugly, good and bad, and so on.

Acceptance is the way of the Tao since it does not recognize variance within the Oneness or mystery that exists as a part of the material world, much as the lilies and bunnies in our backyard do not know about judging beauty and ugliness. We must accept the duality that we are. We are of the physical and of the Oneness of the Tao, and to live this acceptance is to live in unity by choosing to remain in contact with the Oneness in us.

Our physical body exists within material boundaries while containing something with no boundaries and no substance. It is infinite and formless.

Living in unity with the Tao allows for an influence on our surroundings far surpassing any amount of physical effort alone. We can hold thoughts of duality without succumbing to the idea of things like right and wrong. We need to allow the life we live to harmonize with our surrender to the formless energy within us, and to use the words of Wayne Dyer, this makes us a "living, breathing paradox" (Dyer 2007, 10).

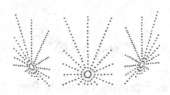

Our Thinking Drives Us toward Money, Power, Status and More.

We Feel Pressured to Fill the Hollow Fear within Us,
with the Things around Us.

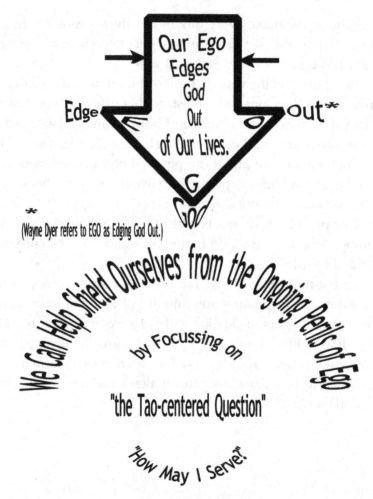

Our Ego
Edges
God
Out
of Our Lives.

Edge ────── out*

E
G
O
G
God

*
(Wayne Dyer refers to EGO as Edging God Out.)

We Can Help Shield Ourselves from the Ongoing Perils of Ego

by Focussing on

"the Tao-centered Question"

"How May I Serve?"

as Expressed by Wayne Dyer
in His Essay on Verse 3 in

Change Your Thoughts—Change Your Life.

Figure 3: Our Shield from Ego (Dyer 2007, 15)

Forgiveness Releases Fear

We bolster our ego with the repeated use of the ego-based thought processes of comparison and judgment. This type of thinking also commonly sets our mind on a path that focuses on wealth, power, and prestige. There is no real joy in the things of the external world because the satisfaction found in actions like these is always short-lived.

A quote from *Gifts from a Course in Miracles*, edited by Frances Vaughan, PhD, and Roger Walsh, MD, PhD, states that "nothing outside [ourselves] can save [us]; nothing outside [ourselves] can give [us] peace" (Vaughan 1988, intro 1995, 163). Nevertheless, in our search for peace, we keep making the same self-defeating decisions based on ego's drive for acquisition. We continue to judge ourselves and to judge others, often driven by ego's fight to be right, frequently through striving for or against a particular cause or point of view.

A second quote from *Gifts from a Course in Miracles* reveals that "judgment was made to be a weapon used against truth" (68). Judgment occupies our mind and steers our thinking away from the truth. Ego fears losing its control to truth and therefore uses judgment to maintain its position of power.

Wayne Dyer has said in his writing and television presentations that he sees EGO as standing for "Edging God Out." Our ego continues to refuse to look inward for the peace it keeps searching for on the outside.

A passage titled "To Teach Is to Learn," also from *Gifts from a Course in Miracles* (172), explains that since the things we have learned in the past have not given us happiness, we need to change direction and learn something new. When we begin to know and understand where peace exists, we can begin to apply it to our lives. We cannot teach what we do not know. The editors of the book referenced above tell us that the need to know the truth about peace motivates us to seek the truth. What and where is this truth?

A heart filled with fear sees mostly fearful situations in life. A heart filled with anger sees a world filled with anger. Feeling fear and anger invites more of the same into our life. Forgiveness releases the fear that fills our hearts and replaces it with love. A heart filled with the Love of God does not interpret the world and the happenings of life as fearful. Forgiving ourselves and forgiving others changes the feelings we carry within our hearts. Fear creates a feeling of hollowness within us that ego keeps trying to fill with external things. Fear blinds us, and only forgiveness can relieve us of this fear and free our hearts to reveal the Truth within us, the Love that we are.

No matter how many times we try, the things of the external world cannot buy our freedom from fear. This peace only comes when our motivation to find it dispels ego's need to judge and compare and we allow forgiveness to lead the way to the piece of God that we are.

The piece of God—the love that we are—can only radiate its light when forgiveness disperses the clouds of fear blocking our hearts.

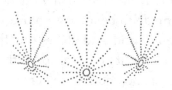

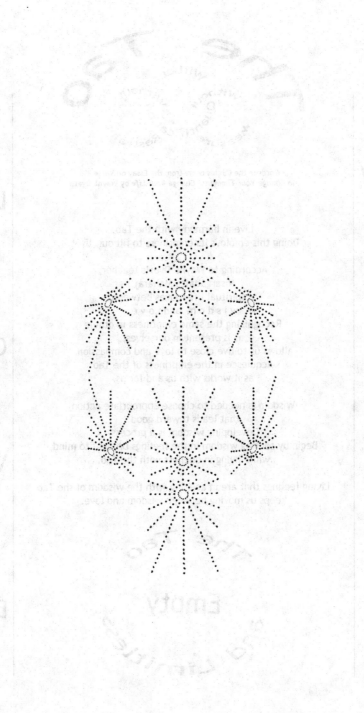

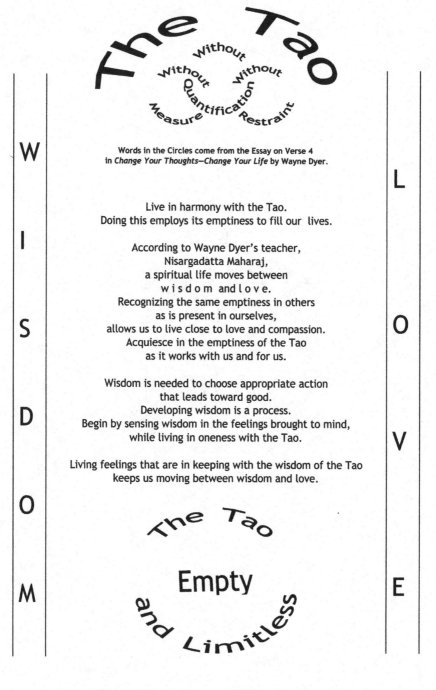

The Tao

Without
Without Without
Quantification
Measure Restraint

W
I
S
D
O
M

L
O
V
E

Words in the Circles come from the Essay on Verse 4
in *Change Your Thoughts—Change Your Life* by Wayne Dyer.

Live in harmony with the Tao.
Doing this employs its emptiness to fill our lives.

According to Wayne Dyer's teacher,
Nisargadatta Maharaj,
a spiritual life moves between
w i s d o m and l o v e.
Recognizing the same emptiness in others
as is present in ourselves,
allows us to live close to love and compassion.
Acquiesce in the emptiness of the Tao
as it works with us and for us.

Wisdom is needed to choose appropriate action
that leads toward good.
Developing wisdom is a process.
Begin by sensing wisdom in the feelings brought to mind,
while living in oneness with the Tao.

Living feelings that are in keeping with the wisdom of the Tao
keeps us moving between wisdom and love.

The Tao

Empty
and Limitless

Figure 4: Living Between "Wisdom and Love"

Our Infinite Source

4

Since the ego sees us as being strictly substance, what is the significance of the emptiness of the Tao that Lao-tzu refers to in this verse?

Anything that exists in the material world deteriorates and does not become revitalized and renewed with time. The same fate would befall us if we were strictly of the world of matter. Guy Newland elaborates on the idea of emptiness in his book *Introduction to Emptiness: As Taught in Tsong-kha-pa's Great Treatise on the Stages of the Path*. He indicates "that if we actually did have a very solid kind of existence" then "there could be no life—everything would be static and frozen" (Newland 2008, 7). A comparison he makes points out that "we can think of emptiness as like the clear, blue sky," and then he suggests that "our empty natures mean that there is no limit to what we can become" (7). The emptiness that is part of us, as it is a part of everyone, provides us with the unlimited freedom to develop and progress in the direction of our choice. This is phenomenal and is unknown in the world of matter.

Our ego is responsible for keeping our minds from even beginning to understand the nonpareil emptiness that we are. Instead, ego keeps our mind tied to the material by creating stories that provide reinforcement for its conviction that we are only matter. Guy Newland (Newland 2008) explains our tendency to "reify" many of life's happenings into more concrete and understandable chunks of information. By making things appear more tangible in our minds, we end up developing an overstated picture of ourselves, of our lives and of our beliefs producing either a positive or a negative spin. It often has little validity outside our imagination, but we keep living our lives as if these stories were true. Our thinking cloaks our lives in a denser and denser cloud of illusion. Behavior prompted by this confused way of thinking often leans on desperation, and creates the "twisted knots" and "sharp edges" in our lives that Lao-tzu mentions. It appears that our thinking is the influential variable responsible for our behavior and ultimately the determining factor in the path our lives take.

Wayne Dyer cites the following advice from his teacher, Nisargadatta Maharaj. "Wisdom is knowing I am nothing, love is knowing I am everything, and between the two my life moves" (Dyer 2007, 23).

Guy Newland reports from *Introduction to Emptiness* that spirituality involves the "balanced development of two factors: wisdom—which knows the emptiness of all that exists—and compassionate action for the welfare of other living beings" (Newland 2008, 8). The two factors just mentioned may describe the way life can effectively move between "wisdom" and "love," as noted in Maharaj's advice to Dyer. Newland goes on to elaborate that realizing emptiness increases our capacity for compassion because "there is no inherently existent difference between self and other," and that we all share "a fundamental nature of emptiness" (9).

If recognizing the emptiness in others opens our hearts to compassion, what can we do to enhance our level of wisdom? Newland tells us, "The way to begin to develop wisdom—or any virtue—is to reflect on the benefits of having it and the faults of not having it." He explains that this sorting technique "is already a sort of wisdom" (11). Wisdom is like our spiritual vision, guiding us toward what is good. Allow wisdom to grow and to move life down a path as near to that of love and compassion as our choices allow.

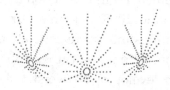

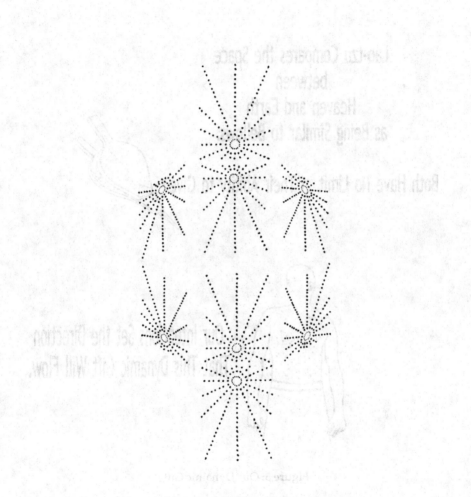

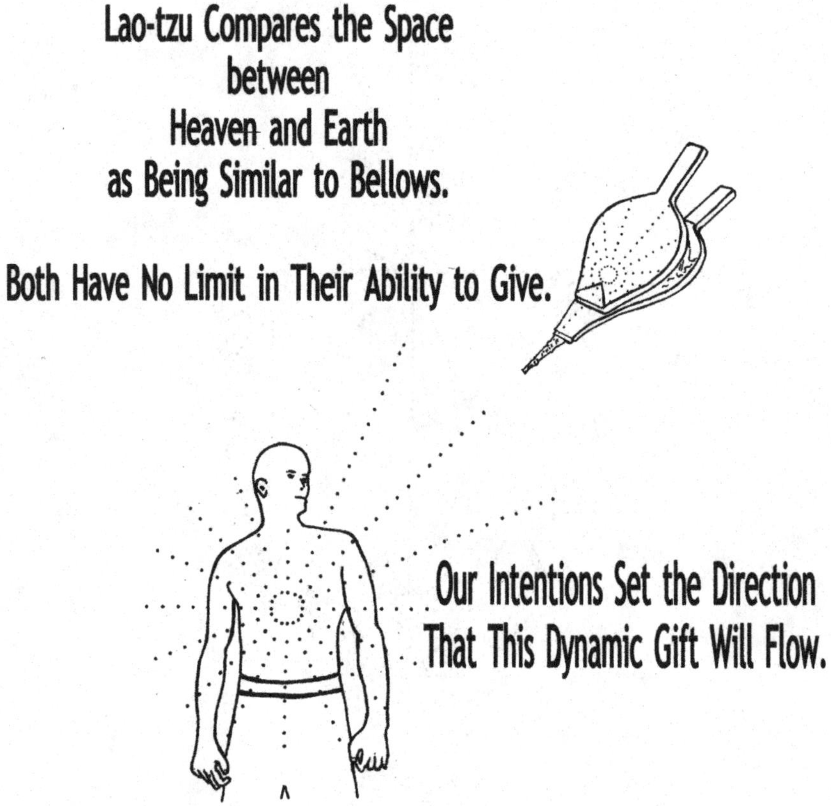

Lao-tzu Compares the Space
between
Heaven and Earth
as Being Similar to Bellows.

Both Have No Limit in Their Ability to Give.

Our Intentions Set the Direction
That This Dynamic Gift Will Flow.

Figure 5: Our Dynamic Gift

Don't Play Favorites

5

How do we present who we are to the world? The life we live moment by moment reflects our continuing thought patterns. When the choices we make in our daily lives demonstrate the goodness of the Tao, our connection to the Tao strengthens, allowing more and more of its inexhaustible vitality, power, and love to fill us and flow through us. It is through our intention that we place our signature upon this Energy of the Tao as it flows through us. Our internal nature, whether intrinsic or honestly and genuinely relearned, determines the spin our personality invests in this energy. If the character we display is in keeping with the virtue of our Source, our thoughts, feelings, and actions will represent a Tao-filled life. Our lives will favorably embrace the matters and situations life presents.

What does Lao-tzu suggest when he recommends we treat all as straw dogs? I believe that like this ceremonial Chinese object, we all have a significant purpose, but even so, none of us earn favor or disfavor in the eyes of the Tao. Wayne Dyer provides an explanation in Stephen Mitchell's translation of the Tao. I will paraphrase: straw dogs had a time when they were revered such as during their use in ceremony. This was followed by a time when it was seasonable to allow them to return to the Source because their purpose had been served (Dyer 2007, 25). The Tao does not play favorites, and we too should feel that everyone in our lives is an equal; none is better and none is worse, and all have their season. Since our Source is unbiased, our thoughts and behaviors should reflect impartiality.

The creator of all never stops giving. We need to look to the Tao as the ideal in which to strive. The worldly treasure we acquire is not ours alone; it is meant to be shared. Amassing untold wealth and property while setting out to prevent others from receiving will increase the likelihood of our experiencing shortages within our

15

own life. Respect and accept that all are deserving of the blessings of the Tao.

We are part of God, not separate from God or from one another. Our thoughts and intentions unite us when they are thoughts shared by God, our Source.

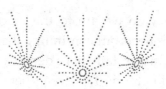

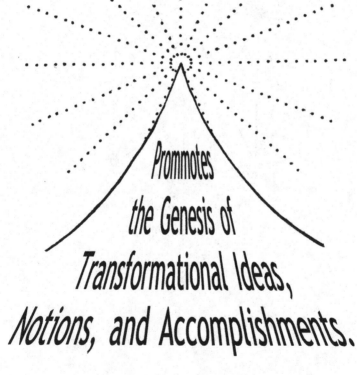

Figure 6: The Genesis of Ideas

Engage Your Creativity

6

The creativity of our Source rests in its infinite feminine capacity to bring forth new ideas. This unequalled strength is accessible to all. Of particular consequence is its ability to harmonize with us and to attract to us the same energy level at which we function, whether or not we recognize and accept its presence within us. We are all here as the perfect creation of our Source and live within its innovative and fertile female essence. When we are consciously aware of this creative femininity in and around us, we can routinely corral our stray thoughts. Our predominant thinking and action can unleash both good and insightful images into the realm of consciousness from the innermost perceptions of our hidden depths. When we reconnect to the Source from which we came, we feel the momentum of life as genuine acceptance of this reunion moving through our body. Our lives are intertwined within the eternal and indescribable feminine force of creation that continuously gives birth to new life and new ideas.

Figure 7: Gifts of Parity

Balanced Living

7

We are of the earth as we are of our Source. Our Source is without end; our earth sustains. It provides sustenance for its inhabitants by being a part of the balance of nature. Heaven and Earth are of the source of all there is, the Tao. Endlessly sharing the Love that is the Tao with all of existence is the Tao's eternal purpose. How does the earth maintain its role in this never-ending story? Since our earth and the balance of nature have both been established by our Source, nature balances our responsible use of the earth's resources with the ongoing provision of our needs. The equilibrium found in nature has had the cooperation of the earth and its myriad of inhabitants until the ego of man upset this balance through greed. Part of living in balance involves giving from the heart. The energy extended by a caring heart, along with thoughts, words, and actions, sets the level at which the piece of the Tao within us resonates. The rendering of the energy we put out is sent back to us, not according to what we want but in keeping with the lessons, we still have to learn.

Lao-tzu tells us that the sage is aware and can see the big picture. He observes that the uncharitable act of grasping at getting more for ourselves brings only temporary gain because there is not an exchange involving balance; it is one-sided.

Wayne Dyer comments on verse 7 and tells us that living from our ego keeps us constantly striving, only to have the desires we pursue elude us. He also suggests we live from our center, which is of the Tao (Dyer 2007, 35-37). Living with heartfelt feelings for others allows us to give without expecting anything in return. Giving that is genuine and wholehearted places our life in balance.

Living in awareness allows us to receive life's balancing complement in whatever form it takes, by paying attention to the clues and responding to them. This is living and accepting life in the present.

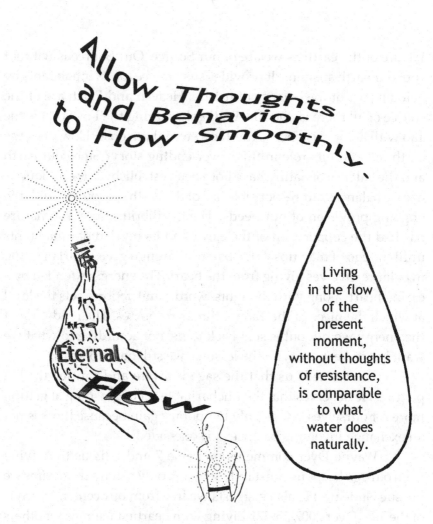

Allow Thoughts and Behavior to Flow Smoothly.

Live in the Eternal Flow

Living in the flow of the present moment, without thoughts of resistance, is comparable to what water does naturally.

Figure 8: Living in the Flow

Trust in the Flow

8

Allow life to just flow like water. Water does not have a plan; it does not predetermine its path; it rides the spontaneity of the moment. Like the Tao, it just flows. It is in tune with its environment and makes route selections in the moment. It has no list of places to avoid; all are options. Choices made within the parameters presented by the environment as it exists lead to a place of rest and tranquility. No matter the route taken, the goal and destination are the same: stability.

As we ride the rapids of life, they may be fast flowing; they may be smooth and calm; or they may be tumultuous. We too seek stability in our lives. In doing this, our ego often makes unwise choices because it thinks it needs to be in control. Even when present circumstances suggest otherwise, ego is reluctant to change. Although lack of clarity too frequently clouds decision-making, living in the awareness of the Tao helps direct our choices. The route we choose may not be the fastest, but it will provide the lessons we need to learn.

In his comments on verse 8, Wayne Dyer describes that water provides nourishment along its path (Dyer 2007, 41), and that we too can do the same for others. The ego's tendency to control can be replaced by communication in the form of acceptance, gentleness, and kindness. Dyer suggests that we trust in the eternal flow by allowing others to flow in the direction of their leaning, just as we remain true to ours. He reminds us that flowing water does not stagnate. When we manipulate ourselves into a placement sought by ego, the flow often stops; we lie dormant and become stale. All are equal in the Tao, and no one holds a station above others.

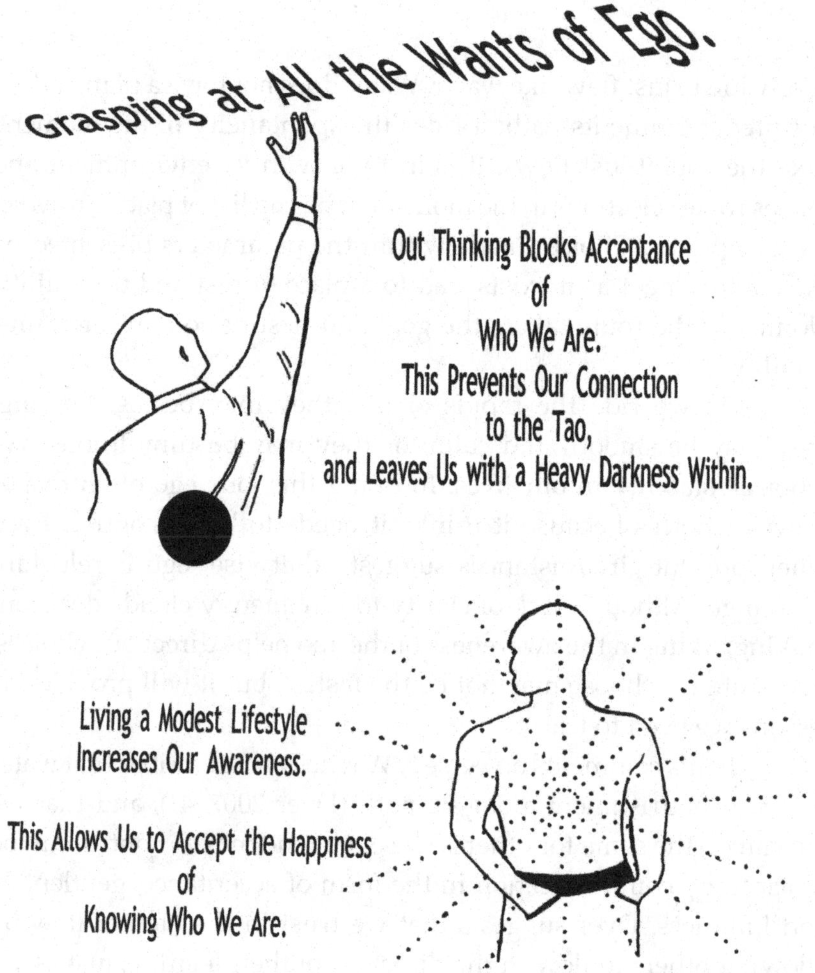

Grasping at All the Wants of Ego.

Out Thinking Blocks Acceptance
of
Who We Are.
This Prevents Our Connection
to the Tao,
and Leaves Us with a Heavy Darkness Within.

Living a Modest Lifestyle
Increases Our Awareness.

This Allows Us to Accept the Happiness
of
Knowing Who We Are.

Figure 9: Knowing Who We Are

Modesty
Helps Hone Our Awareness

9

How do we know if the drive we feel within is ego-based or stems from the part of the Tao in us that we are, seeking expression? The answer lies in our ability to communicate—in particular, our ability to receive meaningful communication meant to offer guidance.

Awareness is the true conduit through which genuine communication depends. It might be compared to the function of an antenna for cell phone reception. A signal that is not received cannot be conveyed to our ear even if the message is in the air space around us. Our decoding device needs to recognize and receive the signal. Only then can we process it and respond.

Using a cell phone in a loud cafeteria setting can be difficult, particularly when the reception is weak. Compare this to the endless demands placed on our attention by our ego. The ego's insistence can be stentorian in its ability to block any other incoming messages. Only stillness, like the silence of meditation, is able to momentarily sever ego's hold on our thoughts long enough to garner messages from the part of the Tao that we are, our true reality. The understanding collected in these moments helps us realize that the part of us that is real does not need ego's wealth, power, things, or vacations to be happy.

We just need to take the time to be still and listen. Tuning our awareness to our true self assures us that we do not need any more than enough to live comfortably. We must allow this idea to override the noise of the always-insistent ego. The stuff we amass controls us. Vanity urges us to gorge on the world's redundancies, leaving no room to receive seminal counsel. Modest living opens us and hones our awareness, allowing us to receive the wisdom of the Tao.

Living under the Weight of Feeling

separate

Why?

It is our thinking.

We all realize that thinking
affects the choices we make.

Many choices are made for us
that we simply accept without thought,
but these acquired choices
may keep us making
unthinking, automated decisions.

Living in the Freedom of the Oneness of the Tao.

Figure 10: Living in Freedom

Choose the Oneness
of the Tao

10

Referencing verse 10 of the Tao, Wayne Dyer describes our world as consisting of opposites, just as we consist of both body and soul. The world many of us experience is perceived as a rigid dichotomy of opposing cultures and religions.

At this point I will propose a greatly simplified scenario as to the possible formation of these differing cultures and religions. Every cultural group in history has evolved or adapted in its own way to meet physical and spiritual needs. Both the given environment and the time in history influenced how material needs were met. I will add that the unseen force of the Oneness of the Tao has always permeated all aspects of life in all areas of the world since time immemorial. Therefore, it might be assumed that experiences that appeared to fall outside of what was considered "normal" at the time needed an explanation. Consequently, unique belief systems probably developed by giving story to this unseen force. Over much time and much retelling, a seemingly separate religion with its associated culture developed out of the initial and perhaps subsequent interplay between the opposites of the physical and the formless. The impact of these stories that relate what is perceived as unusual occurrences can only be seen as gaining momentum with regular repetition. Over time, it is probably fair to say that a religion is born.

If our culture were paired with a different cultural group, the rigid dichotomy would also exist as part of this parallel existence. Seeing life from the perspective of *this* and *that* tends to divide rather than unite. When one cultural group is pit against another for whatever reason, the collective ego of each group tends to independently rule the behavior of the group in an attempt to

27

prove that they are right and the others are wrong. Religious wars in defense of tradition and accepted beliefs have been and continue to be the way of the world.

Dyer refers to the expression, "We are the world" in his essay on this verse. He tells us that the Tao is found in this "simple observation." If we are the world and our body is our only way of accessing the world, how can we affect change? Dyer encourages us to "feel the invisible energy that beats [our] heart . . . and the heart of every living creature" (Dyer 2007, 51).

As suggested earlier, at one time or another our distant ancestors will have set out to explain their experience with this same energy, and the set of beliefs that developed has been routinely revised and reshaped through the centuries, bringing us to today. This scenario probably applies to every major religion, in one way or another, each with its own set of experiences and circumstances making it real.

The following analogy will be considered by many to be based on a narrow outlook, but I will use it nevertheless, to help bring some perspective to the religious and spiritual traditions on Earth. Battles between religious groups could be likened to childhood squabbles about what makes the best pet. Each child's personal experience and training predisposes him or her to argue in a specific way. Repeated arguments establish thought patterns and reinforce the need to be right. Depending upon the expectations of the pet owner, be they children or adults, it appears that a number of pets might be a suitable fit for most people. Many pet owners will experience a feeling of satisfaction from caring for a living entity by giving of their time and effort, while also benefiting from a sense of comfort the pet's presence brings.

Personal preference and companionship aside, the choice of pet becomes subsequent to the underlying experience of giving. The giving of ourselves is the more significant factor, or the common thread affecting how we feel; the choice of pet may just act as a catalyst that makes the experience and companionship better for certain individuals, depending upon personal preference that probably hinges on past conditioning.

Now, to relate this analogy to religion and spirituality, we need to establish a common thread that ties most religions and spiritual traditions together. In my opinion, most are based on the inexplicable perception of a vital Energy that many people throughout history certainly sensed in themselves and in their surroundings. At certain points in time following this, they will have voiced and developed their own interpretation of these experiences. History has recorded these explanations and reports that the beliefs, customs, and traditions that evolved within each cultural group became so independently rooted that anything that was felt as a threat to these beliefs needed to be suppressed by violence or war in the defense of the faith. In my mind, this does not suggest that all religions and spiritual traditions are a sham; I will repeat; *it does not*—but *it does ask* us to look for the common thread that supplied the initial sustentation needed to spur each religion or spiritual tradition to develop.

I accept that the Tao is such a common thread, and as Dyer says, if we stop believing in opposites, even for a moment, the ego is surrendered, revealing the Oneness of the Tao within us.

We need to let go of our attachment to our thoughts about things such as traditions and instead enjoy life's flow, moment by moment. Dyer quotes Jesus from the gospel of Thomas, "the kingdom of the Father is spread upon the earth, and men do not see it" (Dyer 2007, 51). In the kingdom of which Jesus spoke, we all share the common Oneness (common thread) of the Tao, whether we believe it or not. If our choice of religious tradition (catalyst) means a lot to us, we may want to keep it and use it. It not only allows for the expression of our faith through our cultural traditions, but also could provide a shared Oneness with other major religions when we honor this commonality without myopically condemning the different directions various personalities have taken any given belief system. It does not follow that we agree with or condone any behavior within a given system that does not harmonize with the goodness of the Tao.

I believe the virtue of the Tao is the measure for this common thread. Therefore, behavior that steps beyond this goodness, of which

29

we are part, falls outside of the Love that is the Tao. A knowing within each of us can supersede ego's often-tyrannical measurement of right and wrong. This knowing is capable of recognizing integrity when our awareness allows us to do so.

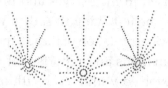

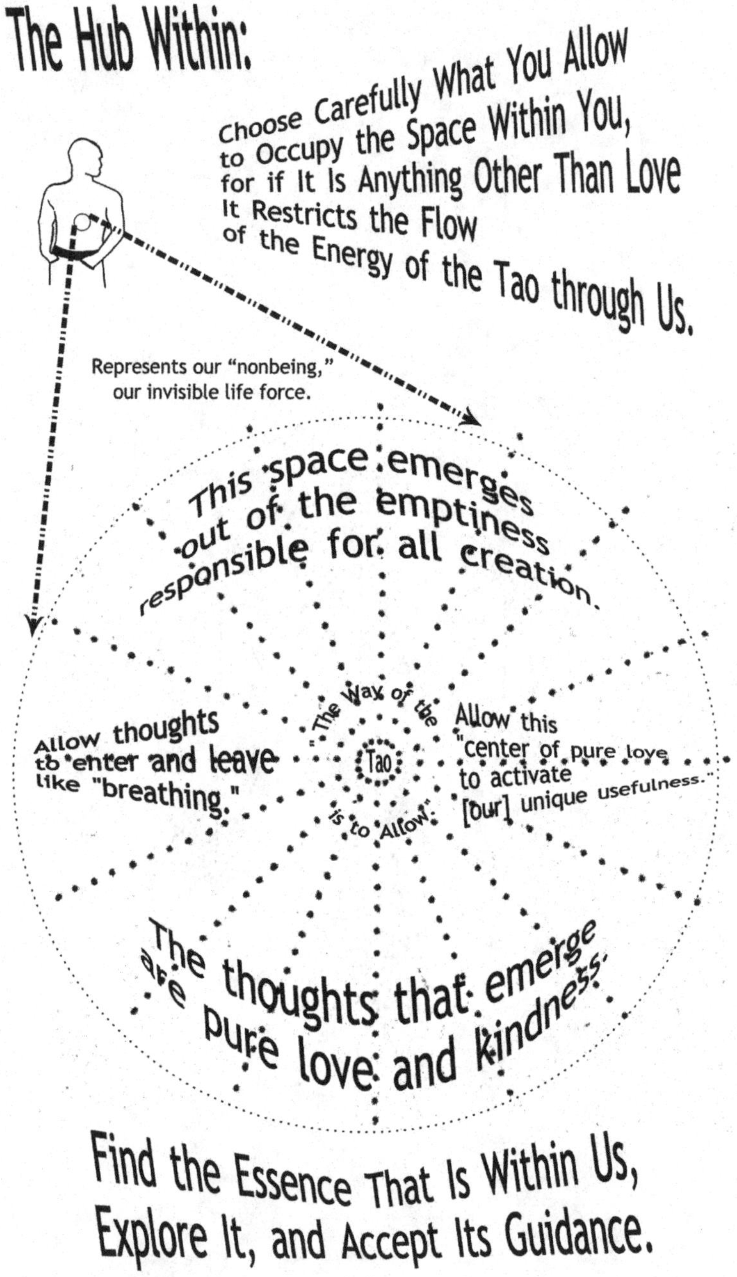

The Hub Within:

Choose Carefully What You Allow to Occupy the Space Within You, for if It Is Anything Other Than Love It Restricts the Flow of the Energy of the Tao through Us.

Represents our "nonbeing," our invisible life force.

This space emerges out of the emptiness responsible for all creation.

The Way of the Tao is to Allow.

Allow thoughts to enter and leave like "breathing."

Allow this "center of pure love to activate [our] unique usefulness."

The thoughts that emerge are pure love and kindness.

Find the Essence That Is Within Us, Explore It, and Accept Its Guidance.

Words in quotations above are from essay on verse 11 **in** *Change Your Thoughts—Change Your Life* by Wayne Dyer **(Dyer 2007)**

Figure 11: The Hub Within

Linking to the Nothingness at Our Center

11

"*I'll try*" is a commonly used phrase. What is it that we claim to be doing when we say we will *try*? Is it a continual effort at working toward a goal? Is it an intermittent effort? Is it an occasional effort just when it is suitable for us? Perhaps it is effort only when we think of it and want to. It may be some constantly changing combination of these ideas and more.

As stated by Wayne Dyer, "the way of the Tao is to allow rather than to try" (Dyer 2007, 54). Allowing, according to the Tao, can be compared to doing nothing. This, of course, sounds nonsensical because our worldview requires the implementation of effort to get things done.

Lao-tzu and Dyer both remind us that it is the nothingness within four walls that gives any room function, as it is the emptiness within our coffee or teacup that holds our favorite beverage. According to Dyer, a tree would not be a tree just as we would not be ourselves without the life-giving essence of the nothingness at our center or at the center of the tree. This invisible, intangible nothingness grants us the essence of our being and makes us a living part of the Tao.

Lao-tzu talks about the spokes of a wheel intersecting at the point of nothing at the wheel's center, giving it function at its hub (52). It is in this *hub within us* that our function lies as well. Dyer advises us to trust and allow our center of love "to activate [our] unique usefulness" (54). When we assume that whatever we want to "try" to accomplish is already here and really feel it as if it were present now, we will experience the emotions that go with it. Now the trust we have in the genuine feelings within us merges with the nothingness of the Love that we are. This leads us to do the things that are needed to accomplish our goal. We are allowing life to happen—not trying to control each step.

One definition of "try" in the *Sharp Oxford Electronic Dictionary* is to "make an attempt or effort to do something."[1] According to the wisdom of the Tao, things are accomplished by allowing life to happen, not by trying to control. We consent to life by accepting the choices that we make as well as those made by others, along with their ever-evolving consequences; for it is those choices that guide our lives in the direction that we allow our heartfelt feelings to lead us.

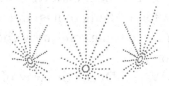

---

[1] Oxford English Dictionary, 2nd ed. (Electronic, PW-E300), s.v. "try."

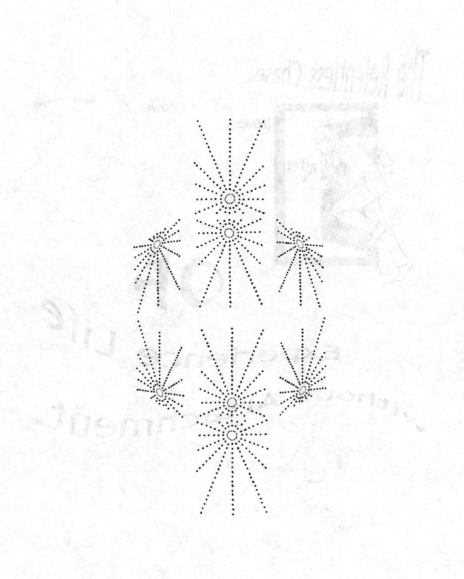

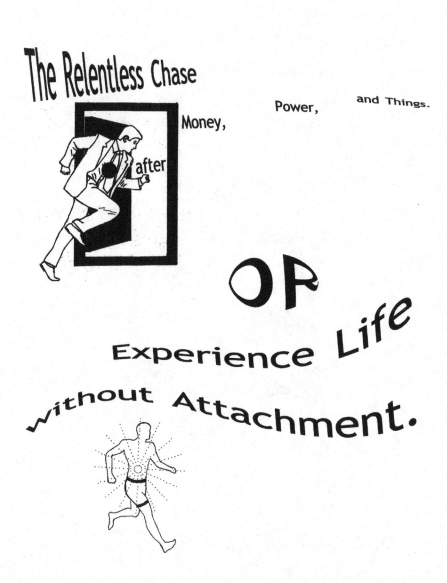

Figure 12: Life without Attachment

Look Inward

12

The ephemeral world of color, smell, and texture, according to Lao-tzu, entices us to give "chase" in an effort to acquire the accoutrements they offer. As we are drawn to these things that play to our senses, Wayne Dyer reminds us that our focus becomes restricted to these fleeting rewards. He goes on to tell us that we become unmindful by not recognizing the power of our creator and unconcerned about looking inward at our own creativity. Lao-tzu tells us that instead, we become caught up in "the chase" (Dyer 2007, 57).

The hunt for ego's endlessly changing desires captures our attention making us oblivious to the Energy of the Tao that exists in everything. Our attachment to the things of the sensory world shrouds the miracle of life from our perception. Dyer points out that the invisible force that turns a seed into a rose is the same infinite power that gives us life. Our being consciously aware of our Source, the animator of all and the creator of change, takes us to a place within that goes infinitely beyond the constantly changing world of color, smell, and texture.

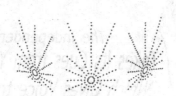

A Dependent Mind Accepts External Signals from:

People from whom you seek favor.

People with whom you fall in disfavor.

People who love you,

People who despise you,

The Independent Mind Takes Its Cues from Your Beingness, Which Gives Voice to the Inner You That Is Not Part of Your Body.

Figure 13: An Independent Mind

Remain Detached
from the Opinion of Others

13

Wayne Dyer's essay on verse 13 focuses on our "eternal self" and our "in-the-world self" (Dyer 2007, 62). Either we develop our "eternal self" on the solid footing of knowing that at our center we are part of the Tao, or we focus on our "in-the-world self" where what we think of ourselves is very much dependent upon input from others.

If we pursue the "in-the-world self"—the ego-driven-self— we demonstrate our physical body way of thinking. The opinion we have of ourselves is often heavily dependent on the impression others have formed about us now or in the past. This is not a stable or even accurate base on which to build. To paraphrase Dr. Dyer, when the primary notion we have about ourselves hinges on the beliefs others have of us who also judge from the point of ego, the validity of these second hand beliefs is tenuous at best (62). There is no inherent validity in this fragile contrivance of interpretation because there is no solid truth to build on. In addition, repeated reassurance is required to maintain even a false level of stability. Feedback from others is often time-sensitive, in both the meaning we think it may or may not carry as well the effect we allow it to have on us. The crumbling nature of these beliefs keeps us constantly seeking the favor of others.

A life built on the foundation of our "eternal self" has our true nature at its core. Building character through the essential quality that we really are, an independent soul within the Tao, releases depth and meaning to the goodness we represent as a part of the Tao. As our character grows through aspects of our world experience that are Tao-centered, the part of the Tao that we are is enriched, allowing us to live a more fulfilling life.

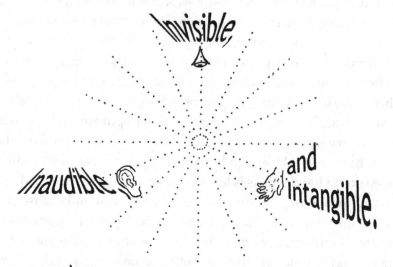

The Harmony of the Universe,
the Tao,
is

invisible,

inaudible, and intangible.

Live Life with Its Experiences in Form
in the Awareness of the Silent and Imperceptible Oneness
That is at the Source of It All.

Figure 14: Oneness: The Source of Experiences in Form

Experience Now
in Complete Awareness

14

Lao-tzu tells us that the harmony of all that is invisible, inaudible, and intangible "[is] present as one" (Dyer 2007, 64). In his essay (65), Wayne Dyer points out the importance of being aware that the form we see, hear, and touch is a manifestation of the imperceptible life force within all that exists, the Tao. Having this awareness as we progress through life allows us to perceive what he refers to as "the unfolding of God in everyone [we] encounter" (66). One way of helping ourselves do this is allowing our thoughts of acceptance to nurture our level of consciousness through our appreciation of the Oneness present in all. This helps us make and maintain our connection to this fundamental and formless "quiddity" that pervades everything, including us. As a feeling of serenity arises when we become still, we may momentarily experience within us a connection to the Oneness that has always been, as described by Lao-tzu.

Dyer tells us that this all-encompassing awareness reveals "the Way" and brings us peace and harmony (66). Keep the nameless Source that has always been and always will be in awareness, and embrace the infinite nature of the perpetuity that we are. Remain in awareness of this everlasting Truth by seeing an extension of God in those we meet, in the things we see, and in the experiences we have.

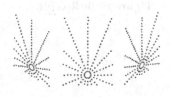

Lao-tzu Asks Us to be Receptive, Much Like "Un-carved Wood" Responds to the Cutter's Tool.

Figure 15: Be Receptive

Calmly Follow Life's Flow

15

In his comments on verse 15, Wayne Dyer recommends that we live life unhurried without the urge to rush or control. Allow an atmosphere of relaxation to reflect the calm within. This permits the stillness of the Tao to unfold the sprouting, blooming, and ripening of our life.

Remain alert and yield to the divine. Be filled with clarity; observe and allow life to flow, rather than making constant attempts to direct the course life takes. Wayne Dyer suggests that we "trust in the eternal wisdom that flows through [us]," instead of "trying to push the river" (Dyer 2007, 70).

Lao-tzu asks us to be receptive, much as "un-carved wood" (68) responds to the cutter's tool.

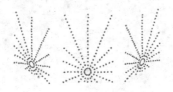

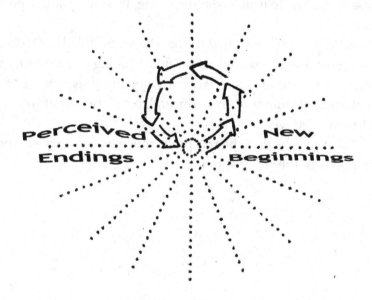

Nature's Cycle
(The Phases of Life)

Perceived Endings

New Beginnings

The Tao
(An Impartial Constant)
(Our Origin)

Figure 16: Perceived Endings

Accept Change
as a Constant of the Tao

16

Lao-tzu urges us to have a peaceful heart as we "observe how endings become beginnings" (Dyer 2007, 72). Cycles allow for change and the ongoing regeneration of life. Being in harmony with the nature of the Tao and its cycles allows us to experience the bliss of living the Tao.

Endings bring us back to what Lao-tzu calls our "root," which renews the cycle by ushering in what Wayne Dyer refers to as "what is to be" (74). He also tells us that this "root," our place of origin that is without location or name, is the "ultimate place of peace and enlightenment" (74).

Lao-tzu calls it "insight" to know that this cycle is constant, as well as impartial, and Dyer adds that "change is the only certain thing" (75).

Our purpose is to know and practice the Tao. The impartial constant that includes perpetual change and the phases of life is the source of all. New beginnings develop out of our perceived endings.

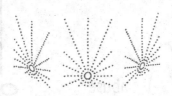

Our Level of Awareness
Affects
How We Interact with Others

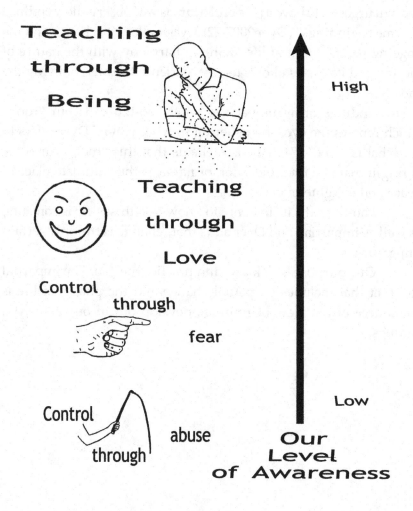

Figure 17: Leadership Styles

Teaching through Being

17

In addition to providing necessary instruction, sound teaching promotes the release of the dependence many learners have on others for incentive. A major part of a teacher's responsibility is to encourage motivation from within. It only happens when the learner's thinking begins to change in a way that prompts behavior to encourage and develop his or her distinct genius. Lao-tzu suggests that a superior leader's presence is rarely felt. Wayne Dyer tells us that such a leader "makes an enlightened difference" because he or she remains in the "background" and simply observes and allows by creating "space" for individuals to feel personally responsible. The "enlightened" teacher redirects any recognition received to the learner's own abilities (Dyer 2007, 76-77).

Dyer discusses three other leadership styles as portrayed by Lao-tzu. Because love wins over fear, offering love and commendation encourages others to learn and behave cooperatively. Sadly, this is effective only in the presence of the teacher, since much of the time the endorsement of the teacher is being sought. This keeps the learner dependent and not self-inspired (78).

Fear as a teaching style has no real merit. Threats control only while physical proximity keeps the threat real. Effectiveness dissolves in absence. Fear does not influence internal motivation (78-79).

Abusive actions control people with the consequence of hate and loathing directed toward the perpetrator. It also will likely affect behavior in a negative way in the future. When given the opportunity, the people that were initially denigrated and abused often inflict the same behavior on others (79).

Teaching through being promotes personal responsibility within the learner.

Our Decisions and Actions
Are Inspired by
the Love in the Part of the Tao
That We Are.

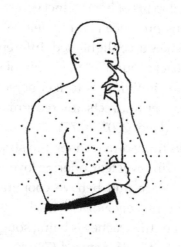

Feelings of Love and Kindness
Flow from Our Center through Our Heart
and Act on Our Mind.

Figure 18: We Are Love at Our Center

Alive on the Inside

18

Lao-tzu begins verse 18 saying that "when the greatness of the Tao is present, action arises from one's own heart" (Dyer 2007, 82).

If we do not allow the part of the Tao that we are to guide our choices within the parameters of the goodness of our Source, our ego takes control of our behavior. This includes behavior that stems from not learning the lesson that a previous experience had to offer. This exercises control over us by prompting us to repeat the same inappropriate behavior again the next time something similar happens.

According to Wayne Dyer's essay on verse 18, "*acting* virtuous is not the same as *being* virtuous" (85). As well, prudence stemming from a sense of duty is often prompted by the burden of obligation or the fear of consequences. Doing things out of habit because of feelings of indebtedness or the need to impress may appear to be the good and right thing to do, but in the overall scheme of things if it is not heartfelt, it leaves us with an empty feeling and perhaps worse, because it is not contributing to the fulfillment of our purpose.

In addition to self-imposed controls on our behavior, the society in which we live expects us to behave in particular ways in any given circumstances. If the laws, rules, and regulations that we have been exposed to in our lifetime were presented to us all at once, it would be a cacophonous echo of incomprehensible noise indicative of the vast size of our collection of dos and don'ts. We have been experiencing these dictates and directions over the span of our lives because of an attempt by those who know us, as well as those who do not, to control our behavior. When we were first exposed to this restriction on our behavior, whether rule by rule or in overwhelming numbers, our mind may have responded in synchronicity with the expectations that were in harmony with our natural tendencies. On the contrary, we may have rejected the rule(s) in favor of the wants of our ego, or perhaps even because of our better judgment.

Many people display little or no respect for others in the things they say and do. Rules are not honored. Why is this? It may be partly related to thought patterns that do not allow self-respect. When we do not honor who we really are, we also are not able to honor anything outside ourselves. The answer to this societal problem requires much greater input than simply implementing measures of external restraint like laws and regulations that are meant to improve society by controlling actions after they have happened, rather than preventing them from taking place at all. (The threats and/or the acts of punishment for various offences do not seem to be a deterrent.)

Fortunately, we have a natural control center on the inside of each of us. The onus is on us to first recognize it and then to ensure its function. The decision to live our lives in accordance with the goodness within us is ours alone. Knowledge about it leads the way, but it is only personal awareness that sets in motion the dynamic part of the Tao that we are. It is our responsibility to listen and respond to the guidance available to us through our awareness. Tao-inspired love needs to be the drive behind our actions, and it is up to us to keep it alive. Living the Tao results in actions rooted in goodness and integrity. Kindness, justice, and love are not sustained by rules. Living the expression of that which we really are allows these virtues to flow from our heart in close or nearly complete congruence with principled law enforcement, genuine religious piety, and honorable and right-minded rules of the workplace. This Tao-inspired love flows into our behavior and allows us to reflect kindness by guiding us to use polite protocol in the things we say and do. Living the Tao promotes decisions from within each individual that, generally speaking, should comply with, complement, and even surpass organization-based rules and regulations, making them superfluous.

Lao-tzu sees hypocrisy in rules and explains that "if [we] need rules to be kind and just . . . this is a sure sign that virtue is absent" (Dyer 2007, 82).

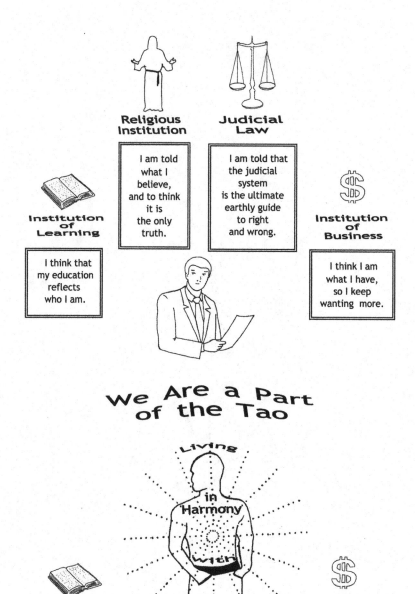

Religious Institution

I am told what I believe, and to think it is the only truth.

Judicial Law

I am told that the judicial system is the ultimate earthly guide to right and wrong.

Institution of Learning

I think that my education reflects who I am.

Institution of Business

I think I am what I have, so I keep wanting more.

We Are a Part of the Tao

Living in Harmony with

Institutions of Learning,

Religious Institutions,

Judicial Laws

& Institutions of Business.

Figure 19: In Harmony with Authority

Living in Harmony

19

We define ourselves through labels assigned by particular institutions. Wayne Dyer clarifies the areas of "sainthood, wisdom, morality, justice, industry, and profit," inferred by Lao-tzu in verse 19, as organizations to "renounce" (Dyer 2007, 88-89). For the sake of simplicity, these areas will be condensed into the categories in the accompanying illustration.

We expect an institution to determine and verify the authenticity and value of our qualifications. We allow institutions to lead us to what we believe as well as attach a code of conduct to it. We depend on institutions to make decisions meant to control our actions. Commercial marketing tells us that we can only feel complete if we have more and more money to buy more and more things.

Do we have the capacity to live a joyous and fulfilled life without relying so heavily on organizations?

Lao-tzu encourages us to "renounce" these institutions, and Dyer reminds us that we are "what [we] came from," and therefore, do not require artificial certification to become valid. He says we just need to "stay connected to the divinity of [our] origination" (91).

Imagine an idealistic world where we live from a place of harmony that has its origins in our very being. Laws and rules are not needed. Kindness, justice, and love are already present and are seen as individual responsibilities. When living from the Tao, institutional regulation and influence are not required because we choose to live from our heart.

On the other hand, these organizations are part of our world and it is important that we live in harmony with them while maintaining our connection to our Tao-centered purpose.

I'll Be Happy When ...

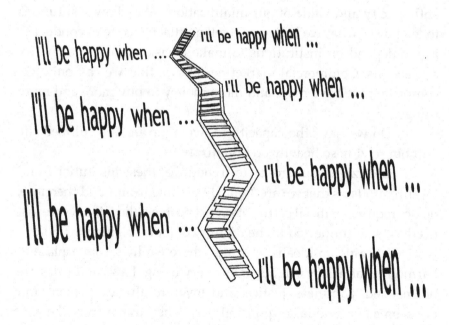

Figure 20: Be Happy Now

Free Yourself:
Decide to Accept and Allow the Present Moment

20

Why are so many of us preoccupied with endlessly climbing the ladder of success? We seem to have no heartfelt enjoyment about where we are in our life right now and little appreciation for what we have at this moment. Our mind is constantly wishing that we were elsewhere, enjoying a new collection of things and experiences. How can we free ourselves of this never-ending struggle with the present moment? Wayne Dyer tells us it is a "surrendering process" (Dyer 2007, 95). He also mentions that our freedom is found in our Source, the Tao, which is "the same source that has always handled everything" (96). Our connection to this Source provides the internal contentment that ensures that we are whole and perfect where we are and with what we have. This helps displace the hunger for more and the desire to be elsewhere. Many may interpret this as complacence, or simply as being unmotivated, but in reality it is how we see or understand the present moment that determines our happiness.

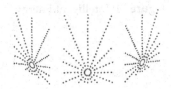

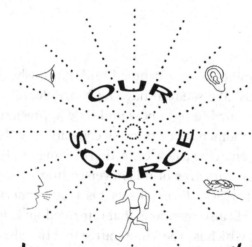

OUR SOURCE

Is the Intelligent Energy
That Makes Experiencing Our Planet
through
Sight, Sound, Touch, Speech, and Movement
a Possibility.

Figure 21: Intelligent Energy

Energy, Essence, and Life

21

What is it that allows us to see, touch, hear, and move? What is this essence of life that is found everywhere, in everything, and in us? Lao-tzu tells us that "the greatest virtue is to follow . . . the Tao alone" (Dyer 2007, 100). In turn, Wayne Dyer advises us "to find this nameless, formless force within [ourselves]." He asks us to "[see] it at work in all of [our] thoughts and actions." In addition, he suggests that we thank God for everything, a number of times a day (102). In the last lines of verse 21, Lao-tzu (100) calls on us to look within, to find the truth of the Tao as it has always been. The animation, vitality, and cognizance of life are made possible through the inexplicable Tao, which Dyer describes as "elusive and intangible" (102). The conduit of our own consciousness allows us to access the truth of the Tao through our awareness that the essence of life is a part of us, as it is a part of everyone. To follow the Tao is goodness of the highest quality. The enigmatic presence of the Tao remains elusive. To recognize it as a part of our very being identifies our body as a vibrant and dynamic creation of the Tao. Our body is not who we are; we are one with the essence of life. Our senses and our ability to speak and move allow us to experience life. We take this for granted but we owe this competency to what Dyer calls the "elusive paradox," an "invisible and formless energy field" from which particles emerge, according to Quantum physics (101).

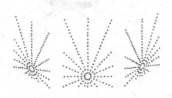

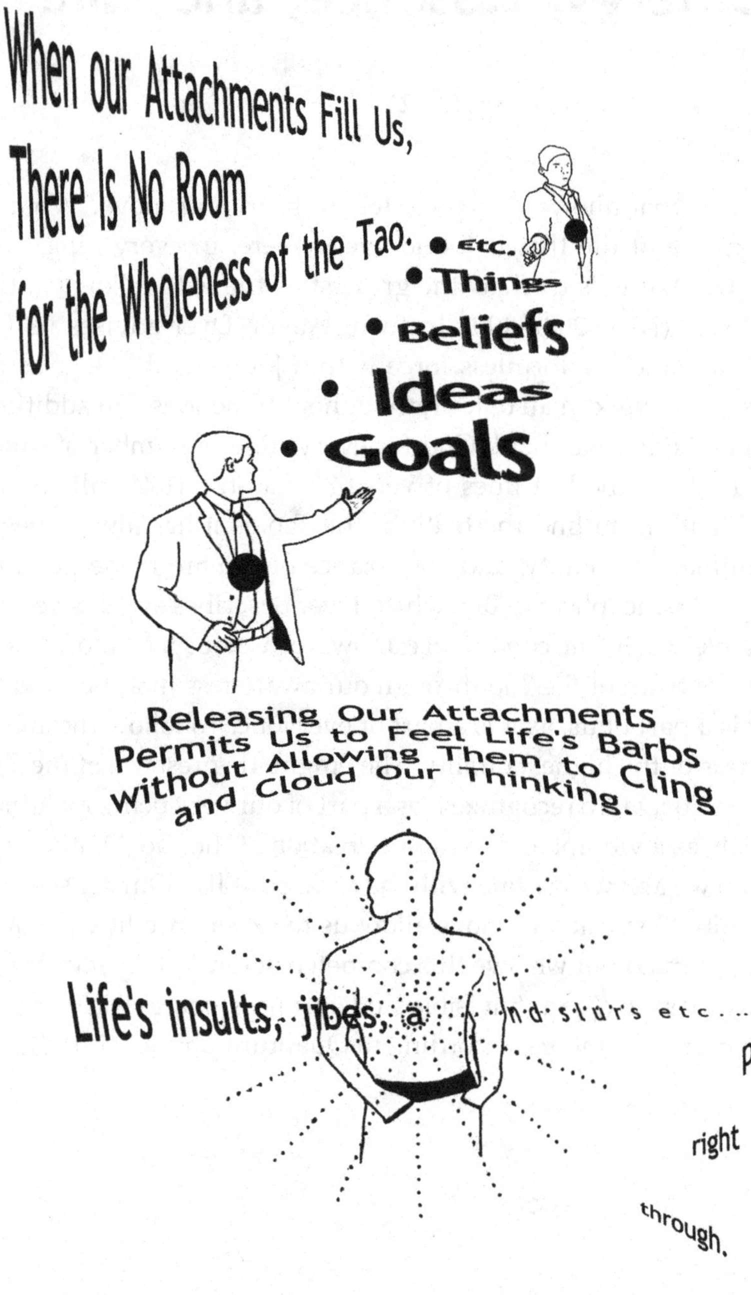

When our Attachments Fill Us,
There Is No Room
for the Wholeness of the Tao.

• etc.
• Things
• Beliefs
• Ideas
• Goals

Releasing Our Attachments
Permits Us to Feel Life's Barbs
without Allowing Them to Cling
and Cloud Our Thinking.

Life's insults, jibes, and stars etc. . . . . pass right through.

Figure 22: Releasing Attachments Creates "Space" within Us

The Answer is Within

22

In this verse, Lao-tzu reminds us that when we are filled with wants that we are attached to, we cannot attract wholeness into our lives. The Tao is nothingness, while at the same time it is wholeness (Dyer 2007, 104). Wayne Dyer advises us to "[trust] completely in the wisdom of the Source of everything" (106). If we are filled with attachments to particular outcomes that are related to our goals, our thoughts often become consumed by these attachments, thereby not allowing space for wholeness to enter our lives. Our attention and awareness is directed toward our attachments at the expense of genuine contentment. A cause, rigidly anchored, breaks. Attachments obstruct. Becoming fixed to beliefs, things, goals or ideas precludes the likelihood of our recognizing and accepting a perhaps much preferred possibility when it happens, all because we refuse to see beyond our fixation.

Ride out the troubled storms of life by relaxing, accepting, and allowing. Being centered in the Tao allows flexibility while remaining rooted. If the space within us is not occupied by our attachments, the part of the Tao that we are, emptiness, attracts wholeness into our lives, and those around us perceive this openness through the accepting manner in which we receive the presence and ideas of others. Dyer tells us (106) that when people feel acknowledgement from us for their points of view, they begin to feel a trust in us. When we finally reach the state of personal freedom from attachment, it is easier to keep the space within us open.

All too frequently storms of criticism, judgment, and dissent sweep through our lives almost systematically. This discord and dissension often revolves around the attachments of the ego. When the meaning we get from life depends on the things we are attached to, the barbs hurled at us, as well as the ones we direct at ourselves, are bound to get caught by one or more of our attachments. Since our identity has merged with these attachments, we experience pain.

Healthy resilience to the happenings of life is a byproduct of releasing our attachments. Dyer explains that it is the flexibility of the palm tree that keeps it "staying in one piece" in hurricane force winds when other trees are uprooted (Dyer 2007, 105). He suggests we "acknowledge the 'storm' . . . allow it to be felt in [our] body," and "observe without judgment" (107). We can experience flexibility similar to the palm tree by connecting to the emptiness of the Tao. Releasing the burden of our attachments frees our mind. This may make us more approachable and perhaps begin to direct us toward being more easygoing. People are able to see the expression of the light at our center when it is not obscured by the facade of ego parading as us. The image the ego has of us can become bent and even broken by the upheavals of life.

Accept knowing that we are not the front we too often project—comprised of ego-directed behavior defending a position. To help us do this, Dyer advocates that we "refuse to impose [our] position onto others" (107). Lao-tzu tells us that not knowing who we are in the eyes of the world allows others to see themselves in us. In my interpretation, I think the benefit camouflaged in Lao-tzu's idea of not knowing who we are might be the suggestion that we do not project our ego's false notion of our importance in the roles we play. I also believe that he advocates that we *live* who we really are, the light of spirit, by simply allowing sincerely felt good intentions drive our behavior. This allows others to see the goodness within us. This in turn may serve as a window that allows others become aware of that same goodness in themselves.

Lao-tzu also says that not having goals allows us to be ever-present to success (104). This advice appears to be totally inconsistent with what we have been taught and hardly seems to be a realistic approach to life. In our world, as dependent as we are on the things power and success bring, this comment flies in the face of what is routinely accepted as common sense. However, when a goal is seen and treated as an outcome that we are tied to, it is often attached to most every thought we have and every decision we make. The attachment to the outcome may become obsessive in that a regimental bond to the future dictates decisions from a single perspective. That does not mean that many of the decisions are not appropriate. They may be, but too often in our hurried single-mindedness we neglect the more important people and things in our lives.

On the contrary, living relaxed in the feeling of a goal *already realized* before it has materialized in our world allows us the freedom to accept things as they happen. Recently I alluded to this idea in a discussion with a long-time acquaintance that I had not seen in many years. The reply housed the typical response of not living in a make-believe world. On the surface, the idea does appear to promote living a lie. Conversely, the aspect that is so frequently and entirely overlooked in these circumstances is the importance of *where* we place our awareness. We are not to focus on the lack of whatever it is we seek. The hub of our intention should revolve around the pleasant feelings that a goal accomplished would engender. When we allow these types of feelings to drive our actions we are more likely to make conscious choices that lead us in a Tao-centered direction. I believe Lao-tzu's comment suggests that the problem lies in our *attachment* to the outcome of the goals we set, not in the idea or establishment of Tao-centered goals. Having goals is valuable. Attachment to the outcome is not. There is a fine but ever so critical line of discernment distinguishing the two.

Things do not always work the way we expect. When this happens it is the ability to redirect our thoughts, our intentions, and ultimately our efforts in a manner somewhat different or very different from what we had been doing previously that allows us to live detached from the outcome but remain true to the goal. Staying within the goodness of the Tao remains our strength and primary control. This involves living in the present, which allows us to experience the peace of mind needed to recognize and decide on a direction. Remaining attached to the outcome of our goals often sets our minds in a tailspin when things don't go in our direction. Because of our resistance to the *idea* of releasing our attachment we allow the formation of frenzied knots of energy to lodge within us and fill us with despair. This blocks the light of peace that naturally fills us.

Providing our goal was Tao-centered, it will have been and still may be valid even if we need to take an unforeseen turn in our lives. Our mental energy would be better spent connecting to ideas that blend with the goodness inherent in our desires. In time, this may lead us in a similar, or a different but equally worthwhile direction that we had not considered earlier. Attachment persuades our mind to resist certain things that happen that interfere with our accomplishments. We may blame ourselves. We may blame others. Either way we catch and cling to all the often oh-so-ready disparaging thoughts we have about ourselves, including any unfavorable comments made by others.

Knowing who we are while living in the present moment reveals the emptiness of the Tao that is part of us and allows the insults, jibes, and slurs to pass though because the attachments to which they are directed are no longer there.

Know that we are one with all there is.

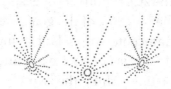

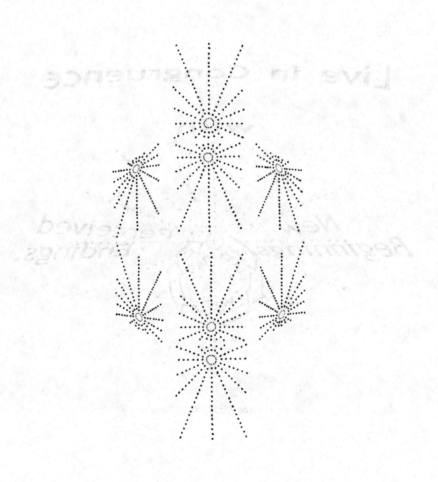

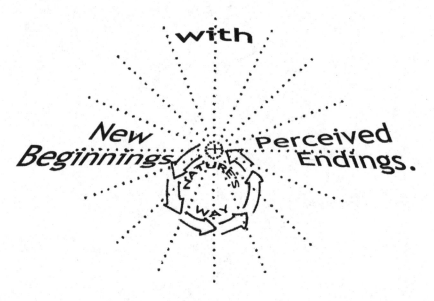

Figure 23: Natural Law

Choose Nature's Way

23

The ego tends to use force to get the things it wants and to resist what it does not want. Striving, manipulation, and force—together with concealed motives—seem to be the ego's continued choice of behavior because according to it, force appears to be the only choice to combat fear. The ego feels fear in many things, one of which is the fear of there not being enough—material goods and money—to go around, and another is the fear of losing its position of control. The Tao provides what is needed, when it is needed, but it does this according to nature's way, not using the constant exertion of force as preferred by the ego. Lao-tzu states it is not the way of nature to be extreme for extended periods (Dyer 2007, 108). Wayne Dyer reminds us that "all things on Earth are temporary," and that, we too "are part of this always-changing and always-decomposing principle" (109).

Make choices that are in congruence and consonance with nature. We can consciously share in the goodness of our Source by living in harmony and accord with the Tao. This is easier to do in good times. When circumstances do not appear in our favor, it might be better to allow the situation to run its course by navigating through it without resistance. Being aware of the present moment provides opportunity for inspired and wise decision-making.

Wise decision-making excludes using the ego-driven, forced resistance of what is because doing this prevents the wholeness of the Tao from revealing itself within us. Dyer explains (110) that "everything in nature is returning to its Source" and when we understand and accept this natural law of the Tao, we allow the all-creating power of the Source to flow through us.

In our quiet times, when we are keenly aware, we may perceive guidance that we recognize as choices that are wise and in keeping with nature's way.

My Ego
Needs to Seek Acknowledgment
for My Accomplishments
through Boastful Speech
and Behaviour.

My Spirit Knows
That These Accomplishments
Are the Work of the Tao,
through Us,
but Not by *Us*.

Figure 24: Accomplishment through the Tao

Be Thankful, Not Boastful

24

Lao-tzu describes boastful behavior as "odious and distasteful," and he may have thought of it as unacceptable, repugnant, and noxious since he compares bragging to a tumor (Dyer 2007, 112). Ego feeds the need to bolster a nagging sense of emptiness and inadequacy by engaging in the execrable behavior of much overstated exaggeration and self-righteousness.

Everything we do and accomplish comes to us from our Source. The only appropriate action for us to take is one of thanks and appreciation. Wayne Dyer prompts us to be thankful (114). He encourages us to say thank you when we begin our day, as our day progresses, and at the day's close. What we have, what we are, and what we have accomplished are a gift from the Tao, our Source, just as air, water, and sunshine are. Putting on airs, taking tributes, and gloating about our ego's apparent accomplishments are akin to personally taking credit for the air we breathe, the water we drink, and the sunshine that fuels plants (the "food factories" of the world). Dyer compares this type of behavior to weeds (114). Weeds, when left unattended, overpower the fruit-bearing plants in our gardens and leave us with very little to harvest. Similarly, the braggart has only his pomposity, and pomposity lacks substance. Selfish behavior severs our connection to the Tao. This removes us from the flow of energy.

Everything originates from our Source. To be a part of the abundance that the cycle of nature provides, we must follow the Tao. Say thank you for all you have. Say thank you for all you are. Say thank you for all your accomplishments. Thank you! Thank you! Thank you!

Figure 25: "Greatness" (Dyer 2007, 119)

Understanding "the Way"

25

In this verse, Lao-tzu asks us "to know the Way," by understanding the part within us that is timeless—the only part of us that has not changed and will not change our greatness (Dyer 2007, 116). Know the corresponding greatness that is constantly flowing throughout the universe, including heaven and Earth.

Connect to this greatness that Lao-tzu calls the Tao. Attract it. Greatness has an affinity for greatness. Become aware that the emptiness in us is greatness. Allow the ever-present, forever-flowing eternal greatness fill us.

When thoughts of our greatness within are routinely unwavering, our inner greatness acts as a beacon or guiding light that draws greatness to us.

Understand that to know "the Way" we need to acknowledge the everlasting emptiness, the always-present void within that is integral to everything and everyone in the universe.

"The Way" as described by Lao-tzu can be interpreted as the link that connects everything, including heaven and Earth. This link is our Source, the greatness that is the Tao. The humanity of Earth shares this greatness. Greatness is within all of us. In my mind, this knowing brings understanding to the concept of heaven. We too are part of the greatness that is the Tao.

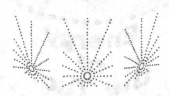

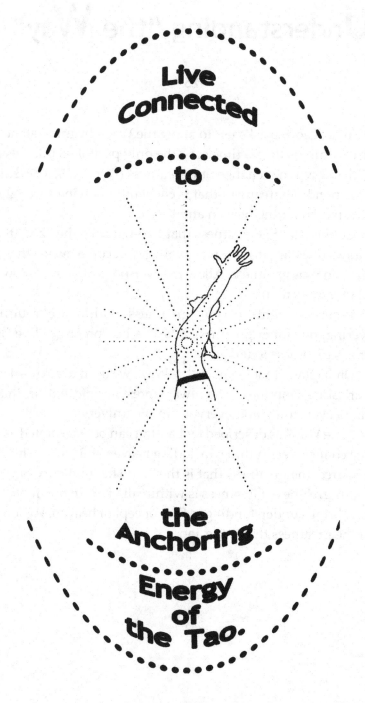

Figure 26: The Tao Is Our Anchor

Relax, Accept, and Allow

26

In the second line of verse 26 (Dyer 2007, 122), Lao-tzu reveals that "stillness is the master of unrest." One of the highlights in Wayne Dyer's comments emphasizes the moment-by-moment choice that is perpetually ours to make. He tells us "you can decide to be a *host* to God and carry around the calmness that is the Tao, or you can be *hostage* to your ego" (124).

When those around us reveal confusion and agitation and are lacking in rational focus, being able to demonstrate stillness, composure, and wise thought appears inconsistent but is truly a godsend that can only happen when we make the choice to find the stillness at our center. Dyer advises (124) that we take a few deep breaths to help us do this. A calm self-assured demeanor during the tumultuous times of our lives is an especially significant and welcome manifestation that a relationship with Spirit creates.

Along with the stillness, the light of God brings a stabilizing yet flexible force that functions like a root, anchoring us to the powerful energy of the Tao.

To share in God's grace, *relax* and know the Spirit that resides within us; *accept* the supporting and stabilizing hand of God, and *allow* the Spirit to guide us through the turmoil of life.

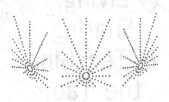

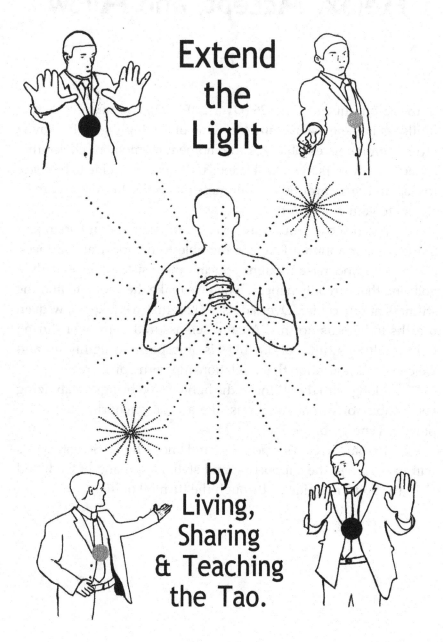

Extend
the
Light

by
Living,
Sharing
& Teaching
the Tao.

Figure 27: Sharing

Extending the Light

27

Be a teacher to all in need. Allow the light in us to recognize the light in those who see only darkness in themselves. Assume only the finest from others and gladly acknowledge what is offered. If that is not possible, at least accept the situation without resistance. Continue to expect good. Do not chronicle mental lists of indebtedness about those receiving your help or guidance. Live in the present. Take the *lessons learned* from the past to guide decisions being made now. Employ all circumstances that allow the Light of the Tao within us to contact others with the understanding that we are all one. Recognize and respond to all who are in need and appreciate those who extend the illumination of the Tao.

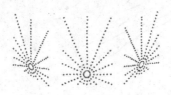

It is Our Choice!

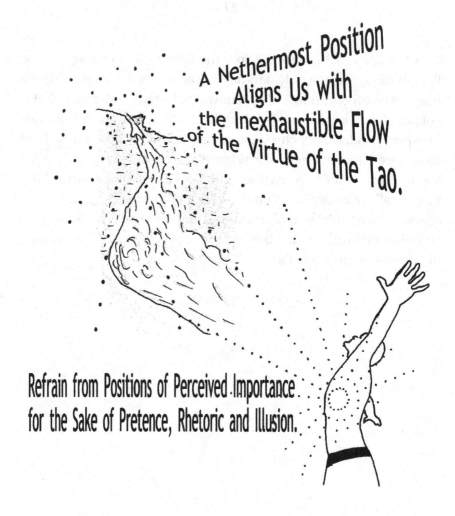

A Nethermost Position
Aligns Us with
the Inexhaustible Flow
of the Virtue of the Tao.

Refrain from Positions of Perceived Importance
for the Sake of Pretence, Rhetoric and Illusion.

Figure 28: Claiming an Unassuming Position

Get Down—Accept the Flow

28

In the twenty-eighth verse of the Tao Te Ching, Lao-tzu asks us to live a life of "virtue" (Dyer 2007, 132). In his comments, Wayne Dyer emphasizes the "four distinct images in this verse" (133). The first image is to "be a valley under heaven." Dyer compares us to "a fertile place of grace" a "place of humility" from which to observe and live "from radical humility" (134).

I will take this opportunity to express a part of my interpretation of Lao-tzu's frequent reference to water and how it could compare to the direction we take in our lives. Living our lives within the receptiveness of the Tao can be compared in some degree to the low-lying receptive nature of a valley. Its openness to accepting what is offered receives the energy of flowing water, the engineer of its formation. Just as the energy of the Tao, our Source, continues to prepare us for our return to Source, the energy within the flowing river prepares the path for water's return to source. Its course is cut by the erosive removal of matter, and the resulting fertile load of building blocks, holding seeds of embryonic life, is then carried and deposited for future growth and renewal. Flowing water is a part of God's natural transformation process and is powered by the force of gravity, a potency we participate in moment by moment without having a real understanding of how it works.

Compare this flowing energy to the energy of the Tao. It leads the river to its lowest level, its place of rest, its source, just as the Tao leads us in the direction of our feelings. Controlling actions originate in feelings of attachment, while the feelings of humility referred to by Dr. Dyer help us release these attachments. This allows us the clarity to receive and act on the subtle guidance offered along the path our lives take. It is the choices we make that affect the length of our journey.

As we navigate our personal river of life through a whirling maelstrom of life's twists and turns, how do we remain afloat? In Dyer's comment on Lao-tzu's second step to a virtuous life, "be a pattern to the world," he encourages us to "row [our] boat, and [our] life, gently *down* the stream" (134). When we do not resist things as they are, we are allowing the flow of the Tao to take the lead. This allows us to move through life with our minds free to be aware of seeds of opportunity that are germane to our situation, within the events of our experience, and to plant them in the fertile fields of life.

Know the many "ways of the world" as different expressions of the path of the Tao. Accept the many cultural interpretations of life, but know that following the goodness of our Source, irrespective of cultural tradition, keeps us focused and directly on course.

There is a force cutting and shaping a river valley, as there is a force creating all form, including us. The Tao is the source of all virtue, and Lao-tzu likens it to being "the fountain of the world" (132), while Dyer calls it the "third image for living virtuously" (134). This boundless force from which we came always offers its virtue and draws life's abundance to us. It is up to us to choose it. When we make the choice to live the Tao, Lao-tzu reminds us to remain humble.

Dyer quotes Jesus in his discussion of "the fourth image of living virtuously" (135), which Lao-tzu describes as "preserve your original qualities" (132). He tells us that these qualities referred to by Lao-tzu were the same qualities requested by Jesus in this quote from John 17:5 as taken from *Change Your Thoughts—Change Your Life*. "And now, Father, glorify me in your presence with the glory I had with you before the world began." Dyer tells us that these qualities are "love, kindness, and beauty" (135).

Remember who we are and where we came from. Right now our senses tell us that we are form, but from within we remain Spirit, a part of the Tao. Guidance originating from this place of Spirit comes from a place of virtue. Life's voyage provides endless opportunity that allows the goodness and Light of the Tao to flow through us.

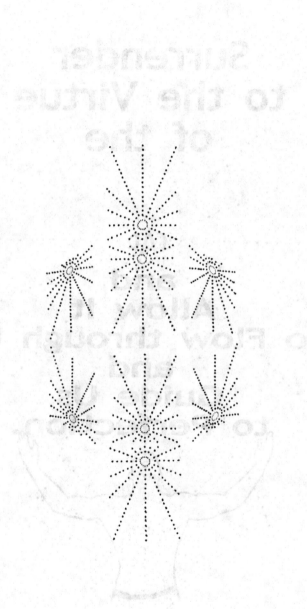

Surrender
to the Virtue
of the

(A)

**and
Allow It
to Flow through Us
and
Guide Us
to Perfection.**

Figure 29: Surrender

Allow Natural Law to Prevail

29

Both Lao-tzu and Wayne Dyer remind us that real control is not within the grasp of even the most demanding ego (Dyer 2007, 138-39). Dyer also reports that Albert Einstein believed that the "thinking and acting of human beings is an utterly insignificant reflection" in comparison to "the harmony of natural law" (139). Absolutely everything falls within the natural law of the Tao, not the human ego. The Tao knows precisely the lessons that we need to learn but we continue to have difficulty understanding the why and how of each lesson.

Where we are in our life right now is where we need to be. Allow and accept that ego-motivated control does not last. However, things that need to change *can be* changed when the desire for the change originates from our center of love. Tao-centered caring and concern is the only way to promote meaningful movement toward the idea of perfection.

Lao-tzu tells us that "everything under heaven is a sacred vessel" (138). We are among these "sacred vessels" on this earth, just as all things are objects of perfection. The Tao is the source of all reminders, both big and small, that help keep us on track to perfection. Our view of perfection and our personal input is not required; we just need to take our cues from Spirit. Both Lao-tzu and Wayne Dyer point out that we cannot exhale without first having inhaled. We live in a world of opposites. Our ego is convinced that we deserve only to feel good, but everything has its time. There are times that we perceive as good. Other times are seen as bad. All play a role in our journey. We more readily appreciate the good when having had an opposite experience. Do not judge. Instead we can choose to allow the energy of the Tao to flow through us. Accept and allow.

79

The Tao allows all "sacred vessels" in the universe to deliver perfect timing to the things that happen. Living from our center releases love. This Tao-centered love influences our world.

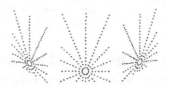

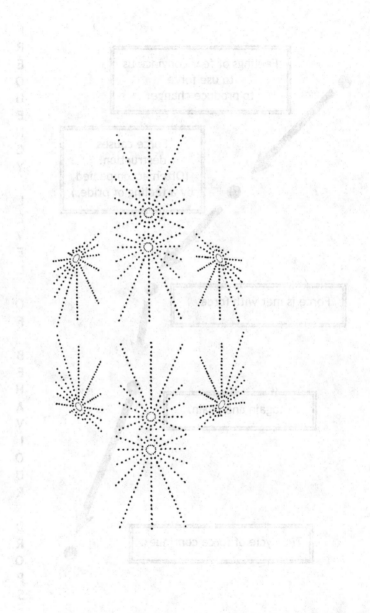

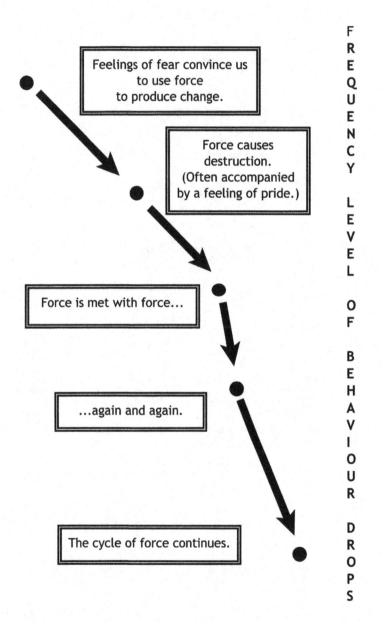

Feelings of fear convince us
to use force
to produce change.

Force causes
destruction.
(Often accompanied
by a feeling of pride.)

Force is met with force...

...again and again.

The cycle of force continues.

FREQUENCY LEVEL OF BEHAVIOUR DROPS

Figure 30: Our Behavior Style and Its Frequency Level

Control by Force
Invites Failure

30

Lao-tzu tells us that "[we] must never think of conquering others by force" (Dyer 2007, 144). How do people handle disagreements, provocation, or antagonism? Too, too frequently force is the chosen course of action. Sometimes acquaintances and family members resort to force, in varying degrees, when dealing with issues. Coercion is a common tactic in the workplace. Force, in whatever venue, can be present but remain invisible to the casual observer or can erupt into physical blows and much worse.

The course of action people use to force others to change usually returns to them in one form or another, with an equal or greater intensity. It is inappropriate but all too common for the ego to take pride in these temporary accomplishments of force.

Wayne Dyer reminds us (147) that a counterforce usually follows force. Vengeance is often perceived as unavoidable. It appears to be a requirement to show the other as wrong, and thus deserving of punishment. The harm done by force keeps replicating itself, creating more and more suffering.

Too many nations, societies, organizations, and groups adopt force, or a form of it, as an attempt to more quickly reach their goals when dealing with issues considered difficult. The cost is usually great at every level. As stated by Lao-tzu (144), the theater of war, with its origin in the ego of man, ravages the resources on which life depends. This decimation guarantees a demand by those affected to get revenge. Whether retaliation is immediate or long-standing, it makes war never-ending. Wars of varying intensity are fought at every level of society, within nations as well as between and among nations.

It is up to each of us to do what we can, within our circumstances, to change this inappropriate and overreaction to fear. Of course how this is done is up to us; but the most effective way involves the goodness of the Tao.

Wayne Dyer suggests we become "attuned to the Way." To help us do this he advises we "use less harsh language and to completely veer away from becoming physical in the resolution of any altercation" (147). Caring, put forward and delivered through a real connection to the Tao, offers, conveys, and provides the love and Energy of the Tao to those who will receive it. Whatever does not follow the Way of our Source will inevitably fail.

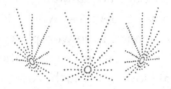

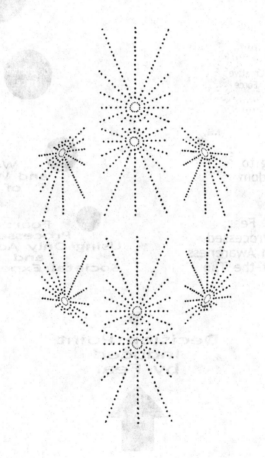

Decision
Points

 Life

 Death

 Creative Force

 Destructive Force

Connecting to
Divine Wisdom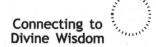

 Words
and Weapons
of War

Fear,
Processed
with Awareness
of the Tao

Fear:
Processed
Using Only Adrenalin
and
Societal Expectation

Decision Point
Induced
by Fear

The Happenings
of Life

Figure 31: Fear and Decisions

Decide to Help—Not Harm

31

According to Lao-tzu—the weapons of war "serve evil" (Dyer 2007, 150). Throughout history, weapons have been used by many cultures to defend their need to see themselves as separate and correct in their beliefs, among other reasons. All feel the atrocities of war, equally. To paraphrase Lao-tzu, the victor has necessity to mourn along with the defeated because all are connected to the same Source, or originating spirit (150). Harm directed to one is an assault on all humanity. Although "fight or flight" has its place, too many of us resort to adrenalin-driven decision-making that originates out of fear that favors the words and the weapons of war. Fear processed through awareness is much more likely to allow our thoughts to remain calm, perceptive, and able to receive the information that is needed to move *through* problems by using the creative energy coming from our Source. This promotes life.

Wayne Dyer encourages us to look at "nonphysical behaviors that are just as destructive." He tells us to notice "[our] language and demeanor" (152). To do this we will also need to change our thinking; it is our thoughts that control our actions.

Within the framework of our circumstances, our reactions are always parallel with the level of our consciousness. As long as we still have the power to think clearly and the ability to respond to these thoughts, our actions result from choices we make, even when some form of mental or physical assault on our person prompts our reactions. On the contrary, making rational, Tao-centered decisions under dire circumstances such as these may be very, very difficult, even nigh to impossible.

Making the right decisions during these times in our lives is vital, but it becomes extremely difficult when fear dominates our mind and clouds our thinking. It is at this point that we become vulnerable to societal pressure as dictated by the past actions of others and of ourselves, although there may be times when these are the only options open to us. Throughout history, force, violence, or even war has never solved anything; it may have resulted in a temporary benefit, but in the final analysis it only perpetuates problems. Violence and hate have proven to be worthless at problem solving. Perhaps understanding the plight of our "so-called enemy" might be a first step at solution. Communicating this understanding to the perceived enemy would be a vital second step. Offer compromise on a solid platform, built of understanding that is supported by the Love that is the Tao.

The aforementioned may appear to some of us as the right thing to do, but our feelings may only lean in this direction while we remain removed from an offending situation. When we are faced with what perhaps might be extreme, immediate, and horrific consequences, we are no longer functioning at a comfortable level. Even if what we experience is not nearly as drastic as the scenario suggested earlier, our feelings will probably urge us to react strongly toward removing ourselves from the circumstances, or removing the threat in whatever way possible, or both. The question remains: How do we steer our way through thoughts that arise in harsh and uncompromising situations?

To repeat, there may be times when quick and forceful action may be the best and perhaps only alternative, but in the majority of cases, it is not the best choice. We have been faced with a similar dilemma ever since we set foot on earth. Our survival as a species has been directly tied to controlling our circumstance and our environment through forceful measures. It obviously served our prehistoric ancestors to the degree that humankind survived the threats nature imposed. It is unfortunate that our survival has lead to the continued fighting and killing of one another, with increasingly more powerful weapons, while at the same time causing the destruction of nature, our lifeline, our support system.

Force and control are not working! It is causing our demise. We are killing each other on the battlefield and in every situation that life offers because we can't seem to think beyond the scrambled thoughts of control and revenge.

How is it possible to break free from the chains of fear that hold us to the belief that more pain inflicted on others will bring *them* to their senses and cause *them* to think as we do? Does the thought of experiencing pain at the hands of others create within us even the hint of a desire to respect and honor those responsible? The most it can do is temporarily force us to change our course of action in order to protect ourselves. The hate that the action instilled in us becomes dormant, to live another day.

What is it within us that continues to keep us thinking in such delusional ways? Is there anything that can bring us to our senses? Destroying our own kind, as well as many of our ecosystems and natural resources, is simply not logical.

On the other hand, logic according to ego demands control over things and people, in the thought that only *then* can our life be better. When this sought-after *"then"* has been realized, the emptiness within us continues to *scream* to be filled, much like a black hole devours what is near and remains totally insatiable.

Critical at this stage of the discussion is the realization that at our core we are all part of the Oneness, the Love that is the Tao. This realization allows us to make the necessary concessions. By conceding, for example, that even though our religious practices and beliefs differ from one another, we all share in the same originating Source, no matter what name for God is used or what story has been tethered to it. The Source is the same for all. A name is no more than a name; do not become attached to a name. Whatever we call God does not matter. It is just fine if we continue to use the name of God we grew up with and practice the parts of the culture associated with the religion or spiritual tradition of our choice, providing they are in keeping with the goodness that is the Tao. To have any hope that this type of thinking might slowly bring change to our world, we each need to go beyond ourselves, and our beliefs, to the shared space of creation . . .

It is not certain what response might follow gestures of acceptance such as this, but it is hoped that reciprocation in kind would gradually ensue. The uncertainty of diplomacy of this nature may be less of a gamble than the ravages of war that as much as guarantee failure in the overall scheme of things.

The answer has always been within the elusive Tao; therefore, it has also always been within us, as the part of the Tao that we are. Will enough of us, especially the influential among us, be able to release ourselves from the irrational behavior of ego, to get people worldwide to begin to think this way and initiate the surrender to Being that will unite rather than separate?

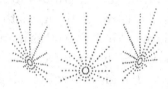

The All-powerful Source of All-Creation and Source of Harmony is the Nameless Tao

to Which Everyone and Everything Returns.

Figure 32: Our Nameless Source

Tao Goodness Brings Peace

32

Lao-tzu tells us the "Tao has no name" and that "all creation is born of the Tao" (Dyer 2007, 156). The Tao is whole, and part of this wholeness is represented or reflected by the form that we know as what Lao-tzu has called the "Ten thousand things" (156). All these things have names, and according to Lao-tzu, "there are already enough names; know when to stop" (156).

To me, this idea of "too many names" might also apply to the names given to God by the various religions that have developed over time. This *does not* suggest that the names are not appropriate or should not be used by those practicing the faith. These names effectively serve their role in telling their "God story." The reality, as I see it, is that the origin of all of them reflects the original nameless whole. However, to my way of thinking, they all share a part of the same Source. Does this mean that defending one particular God as the "true" God is the same as defending all of them?

The nameless whole, the Tao, is the source of all there is. Therefore, being at one with the Tao is like being at one with all people, all religions, all creatures, and the environment, which includes all things. The Tao remains the nameless Source, the source of harmony and the source of all. It cannot be overemphasized that everyone and everything is born of the Source and returns to the Source.

Ego wants to be in control, resulting in ongoing difficulties for individuals, groups, and nations; but the Source endures. Our ongoing awareness of the creative force of the Universe provides direction for our lives and allows peace to enter. Only the peace provided by our Source fills the emptiness that is in us all.

Lao-tzu calls the piece of the Tao in each of us "goodness," and he feels that if it would be possible to be "harnessed" the world would not need rules because "everyone would live in harmony"

(Dyer 2007, 156). Wayne Dyer advises that we practice "letting go" (159) and "ride this glorious wave of the Tao" (158) when making decisions and always.

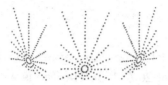

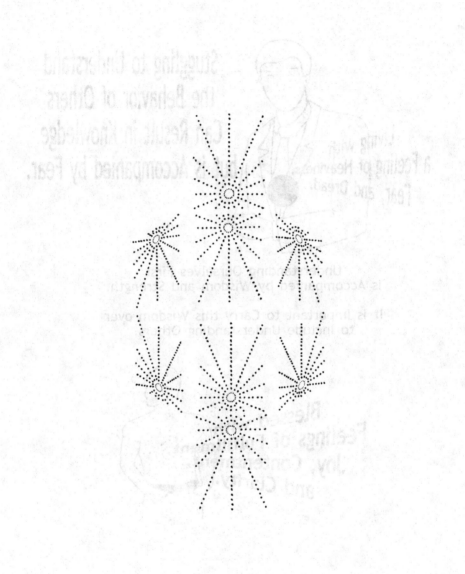

Stuggling to Understand the Behavior of Others Can Result in Knowledge but is Accompanied by Fear.

Living with a Feeling of Heaviness, Fear, and Dread.

Understanding Ourselves First
is Accompanied by Wisdom and Strength.

It is Important to Carry this Wisdom over
to Include Understanding Others.

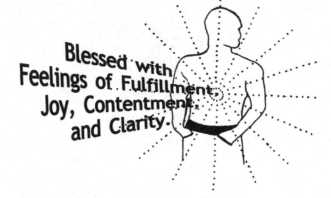

Blessed with Feelings of Fulfillment, Joy, Contentment, and Clarity.

Figure 33: Understanding Ourselves and Others

Understanding Leads to Wisdom

33

Not understanding the behavior of the people around us creates fear within us. We often question whether what others say and do is meant to hurt or harm us. According to Lao-tzu, our understanding of behavior gives us knowledge (Dyer 2007, 160). In his essay on this verse, Wayne Dyer explains that controlling events around us through things such as knowledge may promote "a long life," but "being in charge of [ourselves], offers imperishable wisdom and a ticket to immortality" (162).

What is it about learning to be "in charge of [ourselves]" and understanding the behavior of others that helps promote life? I believe that even being somewhat aware of the root cause of our own behavior and that of others can begin to help us live in the wisdom referred to by Lao-tzu. Perhaps taking a glimpse of what we already know about our behavior is a place to start. We know how fear of losing things precious to us such as people, material things, freedom, and so on prompts behavior meant to prevent things like this from happening. We also know that we use fear as power over others. Our fear also prompts us to instill fear in others in an attempt at control. It is easy to understand how recognizing our own fear and its effect on our personal behavior helps us to understand that others will be doing similar things because of the fear they feel.

Lao-tzu tells us that "one who understands himself has wisdom" (160). What more might Lao-tzu have been suggesting with the idea of understanding ourselves? When we look within we begin to observe just how often we simply react to others without thinking, instead of first being conscious of the real motivation submerged within our feelings. Allowing ourselves to see the reason for our behavior, within our feelings, provides the awareness needed for wise decision-making.

Also in his essay, Wayne Dyer tells us to understand that *we* make the final decision as to how we react in situations. No one else can make our choice unless we have given our power over to him or her. He goes on to tell us that now we are able to move forward with our feelings; we can step away from the control that others appear to have over us, and are able to move toward exploring and accepting our own feelings. When we accept our feelings and allow ourselves to feel them rather than deny them, they start to lose their power. Our feelings begin to be seen as something *we* control, not as something that controls us. Once we really get this and practice it, others begin to lose their power over our behavior. Finally, we begin to live our lives realizing that only *we* are in control of our actions. Dyer describes this state as being "suffused with the harmony of the Tao" (162).

Attach no responsibility to anyone or anything for the feelings we experience or for the decisions we make. Assume responsibility and accept what is, without resistance. This is strength. Combining this strength with the realization that we already have everything we need for life eternal contributes, in my opinion, to the consistency needed for the making of "wisdom." I believe that another part of the "wisdom" referred to by Lao-tzu (160), which comes with "understanding [ourselves]," is found in both the clarity that we experience when we know that we are a part of God and in the lucidity of the present moment in which we are able to recognize that behavior originating out of fear is not an appropriate choice. It is then that we override our fear and allow the "wisdom" of the Tao to lead.

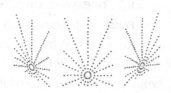

We Are All Born of the Tao, Our Source.

We live the cycle of our lives aware or unaware of our Source.

The Tao's Greatness is Present and Available to All That Will Receive.

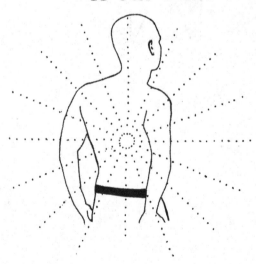

Figure 34: Born of the Tao

The Tao Is Greatness

34

Lao-tzu opens verse 34 by informing us that "the Great Way is universal" (Dyer 2007, 166). He also says that even though everything returns to the Tao, "it does not lord it over [us]" (166). Greatness is all around, up and down, near and far, and in the world and universe over. There is no direction, as there is no space, where greatness is not found.

Lao-tzu concludes that "the sage achieves greatness" (166) but does not claim it. In his essay, Wayne Dyer tells us that the worldview of personal greatness is domination by "those who stand out from the crowd" by "making the world a better place" (167). He goes on to explain that the Tao represents a type of greatness that is in direct variance to this way of thinking. He says the greatness of the Tao is so "all-encompassing" (167) that it is the Source of everything, but it "doesn't seek to dominate anyone or anything" and it "doesn't ask for recognition" (167). How can we even begin to emulate the Tao in our words and actions? The greatness of the Tao is our premier provider. Its flooding essence engulfs and fills all there is with greatness and the potential for abundance, without any form of expectation.

Accepting the truth in the ability of the Tao to produce and provide greatness allows those who hold this awareness within their being to release any attachment to any desired achievement, as well as to acknowledge singular gratitude to the Tao for all outcomes.

Part of the process is to allow the spirit of God, the Tao, to move through us and guide our life. Live a Tao-directed life, without self-proclaimed or outward tributes. Those that are filled with greatness will attract greatness.

Although the Tao is

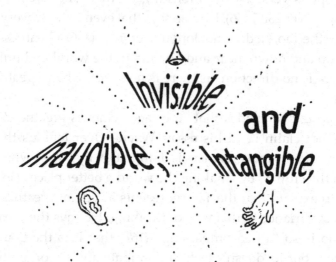

Invisible, Inaudible, and Intangible,

It is a Part of Who We Are.

We Are One with the Tao.

According to Lao-tzu,
It Is Our Source of
"Peace, Security, and Happiness."

Figure 35: The Tao Outshines the Physical

Absolute Contentment

35

The pleasures of this world that our ego seeks are available to us only though our physical senses. The places and people we see, the music and entertainment we hear, the food we love to eat, the things we own or use, and the physical closeness we enjoy all rely on our body's ability to perceive these stimuli. Lao-tzu describes these short-lived sensory experiences as "bland and insipid . . . when one compares them to the Tao" (Dyer 2007, 170)!

The Tao cannot be heard, seen, or felt. How then can our experience of the Tao trivialize our ego's desires to such a degree?

Our recognition and awareness of our Source, the Tao, reconnects the piece of God, which we are, with the One God, our creator. Lao-tzu tells us that those who "[keep] to the one" will find "peace, security, and happiness" (170).

To paraphrase Wayne Dyer, this peace transcends the transient pleasure of our earthly pursuits. The delights of the body come and go, but the inner joy and contentment stemming from our awareness of the reality of who we really are is the only way to fill us with the lasting peace we yearn for.

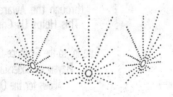

Take Note of Inner Responses as you Consciously Observe Your Interactions with Others, from a Position of Unimportance.

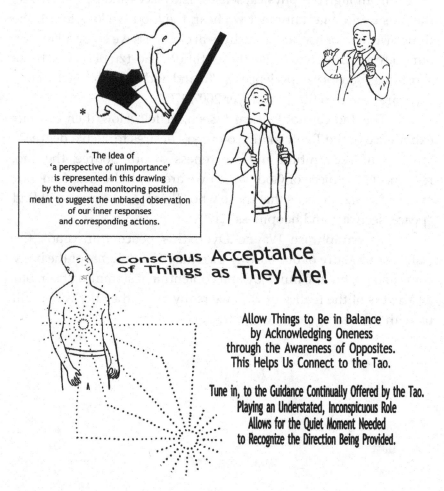

* The Idea of 'a perspective of unimportance' is represented in this drawing by the overhead monitoring position meant to suggest the unbiased observation of our inner responses and corresponding actions.

Conscious Acceptance of Things as They Are!

Allow Things to Be in Balance by Acknowledging Oneness through the Awareness of Opposites. This Helps Us Connect to the Tao.

Tune in, to the Guidance Continually Offered by the Tao. Playing an Understated, Inconspicuous Role Allows for the Quiet Moment Needed to Recognize the Direction Being Provided.

Figure 36: Our Conscious Witness

Observe from a Place of Unimportance

36

Lao-tzu begins verse 36 with advice in direct variance with the all-too-common haughty attack mode that we so often use to get our own way. With only slight provocation from a perceived adversary, many of us revert to our personally polished version of "control tactics" to dominate a situation. He says that whenever we have the need to reduce something, "[we] must deliberately let it expand" (Dyer 2007, 176). To do this, Lao-tzu goes on to say that we need to step back and allow whatever it is to thrive. This is contrary to those who feel they need to be in control and attempt to do so by displaying intimidating behavior to suppress others. They often tend to have their efforts collapse because they are leaning on false power, while those who look inward gain real strength.

Wayne Dyer makes the point in his opening comments on verse 36 that the lessons we learn as children teach us to strive toward standing out from the crowd for reasons of competition. Lao-tzu recommends "obscurity" instead of competition. Wayne Dyer tells us that "the idea of being weak grows out of having known what it is to feel strong" (178). In his essay on this verse, he uses a subtitle for one of the sections, which reads *Strive to Know Oneness by Seeking Awareness in Opposites* (178). This strategy of opposites guides us further into allowing what we want less of to become more. He also advises that we "stay in a state of Oneness," as we take note of any unwelcome, undesirable, or upsetting feeling within, by "[recognizing] the opposing feeling" in the following instant. He tells us that this provides for "a balanced sense of being at peace within [ourselves]." This Oneness allows the power and endurance of the Tao, which never divides anything, to awaken within us. Defensive attitudes and behavior coming out of selfish pride need to be discontinued if we want the benefits that Lao-tzu says are attainable by becoming inconspicuous and understated.

Conscious observation of ourselves interacting with life, from a "perspective of unimportance" rather than competition helps us to allow for the acceptance of things as they are. From this imaginary position in the "background of our minds" we can impartially observe our inner responses to the people, things, and events comprising our daily activities. We can learn to take note of how energy used unwisely in unconscious moments, such as in fits of temper or displays of pride, often lead to things worse than the need to apologize or to replenish the misguided energy. We can grow from events like these when we recognize and learn the lessons within them. Over time we can begin to remind ourselves to change direction as soon as we notice the need.

Being at one with the things that are helps to complete our connection to the Tao. Consciously accepting things that are happening now provides substance to the latent strength we already possess by allowing us to handle situations with a clear mind instead of one filled with thoughts of resistance. The daily practice of acceptance, combined with conscious observation, brings an understanding that engenders fullness of life. When the spirit within us connects to our Source, our strength grows without an outward display of might.

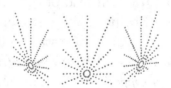

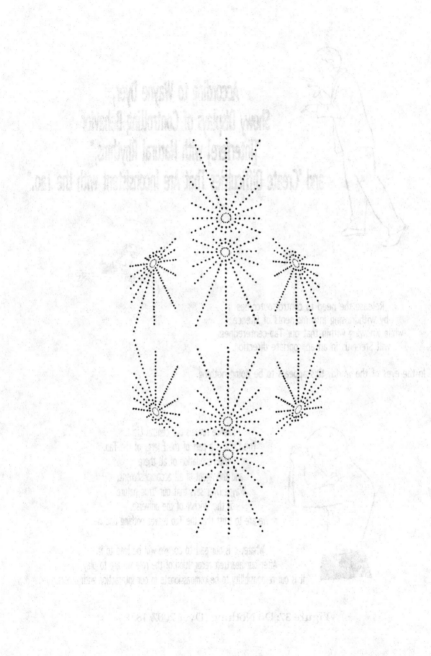

According to Wayne Dyer,
Showy Displays of Controlling Behavior
"[Interfere] with Natural Rhythms,"
and "Create Difficulties That Are Inconsistent with the Tao."

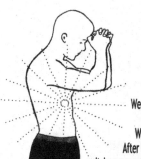

Release the need to control outcomes
by withdrawing into moments of Silence
while Knowing within that our Tao-centeredness
will Steer us in an appropriate direction.

In the eyes of the world, this appears to be doing nothing.

Silence reveals our central Light.
This Light is a part of the Energy of the Tao,
the Foundation of all there is
and the Agent of all accomplishment.
Wayne Dyer says that our "true nature"
is the "anchor of the universe."
We are to trust that the Tao leaves nothing undone.

Whatever is our part to do, we will be lead to it.
After our heartfelt recognition of the role we are to play
it is our responsibility to be compassionate in our interaction with others.

Figure 37: Do Nothing (Dyer 2007, 182)

Accomplishment through Tao-Awareness

37

Lao-tzu opens verse 37 with the words, "The Tao does nothing, but leaves nothing undone" (Dyer 2007, 180). Wayne Dyer opens his essay on this verse saying, "it obviously contradicts all that you and I have been taught" (181).

"Looking out for number one" is the mantra many of us live by in our daily lives. Attempting to steer our lives using actions that serve to control is perceived as one of the only options to effectively take care of our needs. Education and keeping ourselves informed can be vital "to living the good life" and allow us to function well within the multiple expectations placed upon us in our fast-paced, highly organized world. Unfortunately, problems often arise as we face certain experiences in our lives. As prepared as we think we are to face the issues of life, the events around us, together with the powerful influence of our often-misguided perceptions about those events, can provoke us to react in unthinking ways. Too often our ego's desire to gain or maintain power serves as a hair trigger that fires repeatedly when it feels threatened. Too much of life seems tied to appearances, which are often empty and too frequently deceive.

Our value as human beings does not arise from showy displays. Moments of silence and good deeds from the heart, done without pretence, invoke the Tao to work through us and for us. It is at these times that we demonstrate who we truly are. How can something that appears as doing nothing through the eyes of the world serve us? It opens us to the guidance of the Universe by helping to provide a personal mindset that helps produce the peace of mind required to recognize and be receptive to the options available to us. The reality is we are doing something much more effective than ego-controlled action. We are taking a quiet moment to step back and observe. It is from this vantage point that we can witness our ego's antics and recognize that bold and showy action may aim to impress and persuade but is not always presenting our concerns powerfully. Living in the awareness that we are a part of the Tao allows us to recognize Tao-centered action that is appropriate, influential, and potent.

Simplicity of action dissuades ostentation and escorts our mindfulness to our center, where wanting is not a priority. Silence reveals our central light. This light is part of the Energy of the Tao, the foundation of all there is and the agent of all accomplishment.

Wayne Dyer establishes that "as [we] alter the way [we] look at [our] own power and success, [we'll] begin to replace strong desires with calm contentment" (182).

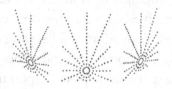

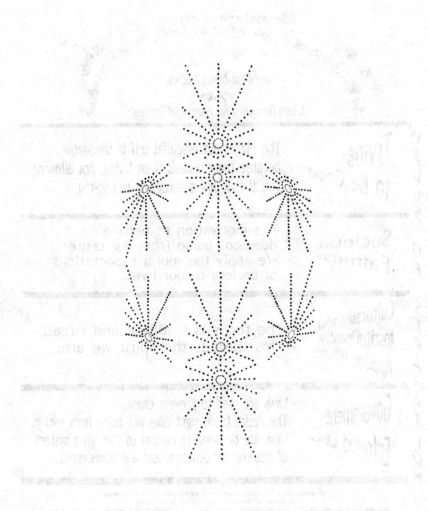

The Many Walls Separating Us from the Tao

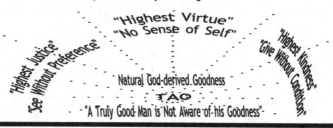

"Highest Virtue"
"No Sense of Self"

"Highest Justice"
"See Without Preference"

"Highest Kindness"
"Give Without Condition"

Natural God-derived Goodness

TAO

"A Truly Good Man is Not Aware of his Goodness"

W A L L S	**Trying to Be Good**	- This places our essential self in shadow because the emphasis is on trying, not allowing. - This is foolishness according to Lao-tzu.
O F	**Societal Fairness**	- The motivation to behave does not come from our center. - We apply the moral expectations of society to our lives.
S E P A R A T I O N	**Culturally and Institutionally Applied Rituals**	- The focus is tradition and ritual. - This shrouds the Spirit we are.
	Government Enforced Laws	- Laws are used to prevent chaos. - The desire to do right does not come from within. - Laws are designed to control us through a system of deterrence, consequences and punishment.

(The words in quotes on this page, as well some of the main ideas are taken from Verse 38
of *Change Your Thoughts —Change Your Life* by Wayne Dyer,
but organized in descending significance with respect to nearness to the Tao, as I interpret Verse 38 itself and Wayne Dyer's essay.)

Figure 38: Walls of Separation (Dyer 2007)

Follow the Goodness Within

38

Verse 38 begins with these words from Lao-tzu: "a truly good man is not aware of his goodness and is therefore good" (Dyer 2007, 186). Wayne Dyer tells us that the message in this verse does not agree with what we have been taught. We have learned to obey "the rules" to avoid punishment. This applies everywhere, from the home situation, to school, to the workplace, and beyond. Appropriate behavior is necessary for a pleasant existence, but from where does genuinely good behavior originate? A spark of God lives at our center, and only when the Oneness that this light represents is allowed to sparkle can its essence fill us. Oneness leaves nothing undone.

We are a part of the Oneness that is God, the Tao. However, because we think we are our ego we become firmly attached to outcomes that are seen as an ego enhancement, whether they benefit society or not. Throughout the years society has attempted to manage this chaotic nature of the ego through the development of various types of control.

Morality involves efforts made toward controlled behavior by following certain principles of conduct. It is a measure of restraint that is valued in a particular society but is not true goodness. Striving toward controlled behavior may also involve ritual as well as law. Practicing a learned protocol such as a ritual has the propensity to appease us and to leave us with the fleeting feeling of having done the right thing. In addition, many of us feel an *external obligation* to perform these rituals as well as to obey laws.

Rituals, laws, and moral codes are not a bad thing, as long as they do not keep us from recognizing and living the Truth. Unfortunately, truth can too easily be lost in the wrappings of effort. Too often the true goodness of the Tao cannot be perceived through the many layers of law, ritual, and moral code, all of which originate

113

out of ego's need for control. Granted, we all expect a civil society in which to live, and it is the intent of laws, for example, to maintain an acceptable level of civility. Laws are designed to control externally, but how are they going to affect how we function on the inside?

The true source of goodness rests in the Tao. We are each a part of the Tao at our core, so our genuine goodness comes from within. When the traditions we practice blend with the goodness that is the Tao (God), we allow our goodness to shine.

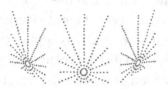

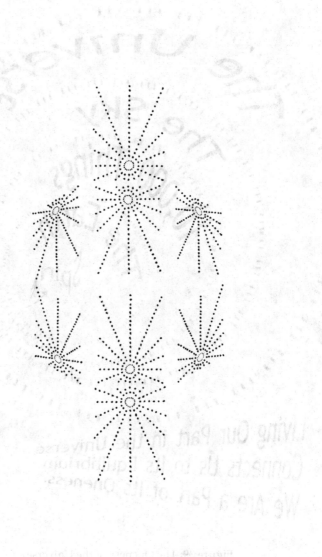

Figure 39: The Oneness of the Universe

Living in Oneness
with the Whole

39

Living our part in the universe without pretence and with a demeanor of self-effacement allows us to conduct ourselves in an insignificant and inconspicuous manner. It is precisely just such a sincere and unassuming manner that connects us to the equilibrium of the whole. This brings true purpose.

Lao-tzu says, "The pieces of a chariot are useless unless they work in accordance with the whole" (Dyer 2007, 190). Similarly, each key on the keypad of an electronic device must function in unison with the product's design if the invention is to perform to its potential. Just as each key has its own usefulness and has no independent merit, none of us should behave as if we are separate or disjoined from the whole. Congruence in purpose yields cooperation. Cooperation ushers in happiness.

Wayne Dyer suggests that we see in others the same portion of the whole that we also have within ourselves. Differences separate; so we are better off to seek out likeness in those we meet. Only by seeing through differences and recognizing similarities can the judgment inherent in this polarity begin to be neutralized. Dyer asks us to "live in the spirit of wholeness, knowing that [we] have a role as one of the parts of the Tao" (192).

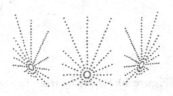

Yield
to the Tao
by Releasing from
the Control of Ego.

This Allows Us
to Connect to
and Be Filled by
the Spirit of God.

Figure 40: Releasing from Ego

Live Connected

40

Lao-tzu begins this shortest and what Wayne Dyer describes as "one of the greatest teachings of the Tao Te Ching" (Dyer 2007, 195) by telling us that "[returning] is the motion of the Tao" and that "the way" is to yield (194). With this, Lao-tzu is referring to the truth that we come from spirit. Conversely, our earthly experience here is directed mostly by *ego's* wants and desires, while the piece of God in all of us remains dormant. As Lao-tzu describes, we do not know when we will physically die and return to spirit, but an awareness of the essential being within us allows a connection to the power of spirit that gives us direction, right here and now, as we move through the journey of life on Earth. Lao-tzu refers to accessing this power while we are alive as "yielding" to the Tao (194).

However, our ego attempts to control of our lives. The ego part of us is drawn in by the barrage of new products available in the market every year. They can be thought of as many of the ten thousand things being recombined in new ways in an attempt to rekindle the feeling within us that our ego is in control. Our ego is convinced that these things will make us truly happy.

Happiness, triggered by any combination of the ten thousand things, is a short-lived experience. A hollow feeling inside soon follows the transient glee achieved by this consumption. When we enter into God's Love and yield to the grace of God, the piece of the Tao that we are prevails, and a connection to Spirit brings joy that fills the emptiness. Regular moments of silence maintain the connection we feel to the Spirit of God. Listen! Recognize! Respond! Live—a connected life!

Figure 41: Accepting the Lessons of Life

Thinking in Congruence
with the Tao

41

Keeping our thoughts consistent with the thoughts of God is the embodiment of living the Tao. Living "the Way" prompts ridicule from many because ego sees reality in the appearances projected by our object-oriented, ego-driven minds. Lao-tzu expresses that without ridicule, the Tao could not exist (Dyer 2007, 198). Wayne Dyer points out that the all-powerful wisdom of the Tao cannot be proven. Consider the previous statement in reference to the following quote.

> Modern scientists must accept the fact that quantum particles originate in waves of formless energy or spirit, without their ever seeing that infinite, all-creating field. (202)

The Tao suggests that there is power in passivity, but the ego sees this as frailty. The ego needs the impression of clear, hardworking, forward-driven, and visible action to be convinced of power.

Although the timing and nature of the solutions offered by the Tao as it unravels our worldly problems may not match our wants in the way we expected or meet our timeline, but it does carry through by meeting our needs and teaching life-lessons. To accept what is provided, while keeping our thoughts in consonance with the thoughts of God, may be seen by many as *a* backward, uninformed, and naive approach.

Conversely, the ego's attempt at power and control is based on the often much too detailed attempt at explication, or analysis of the happenings in our lives. Our ego also tends to be very quick to judge others, as well as ourselves. Much of this ego-centered behavior originates out of fear and keeps our often-anxious minds from moving beyond our unease.

Those who become wary of the folly behind this often superficial "über-thinking," with its time-after-time of unfortunate, drastic, or even devastating consequences, may begin to see the power present in "the Way." It unites the authority of the Universe with a mind in congruence with it. This takes life to a level much beyond outward appearances and definitely beyond controlling actions. Common sense, together with the experience gained from the lessons of life, provides some of the guidance upon which our daily decisions depend.

If we keep our mind in focus with the Tao, opportunities will manifest. We need to remain tuned to the frequency of the Universe, recognize the possibilities, and respond with grateful enthusiasm.

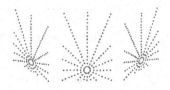

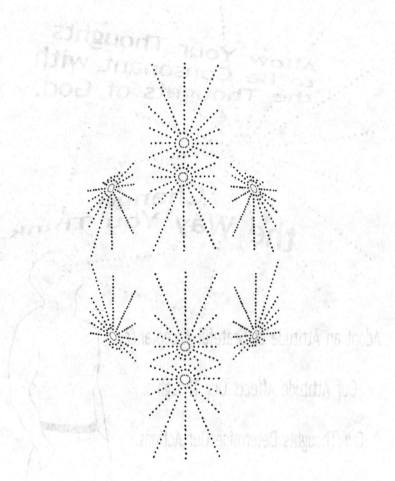

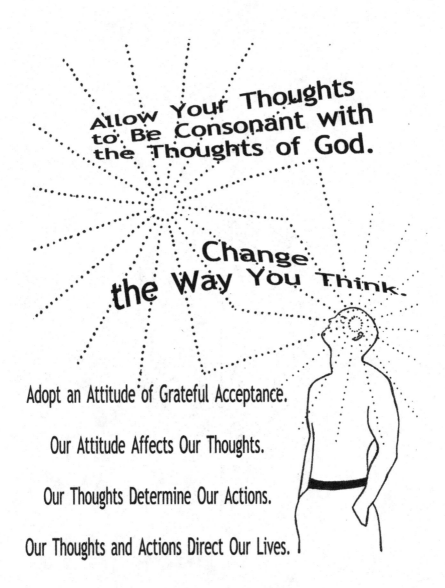

Figure 42: Changing the Way We Think

Thoughts Change Everything

42

In this verse Lao-tzu repeats the message that "one gains by losing, and loses by gaining" (Dyer 2007, 204). Wayne Dyer clarifies this in his essay on this verse that "you gain awareness of your Tao nature through the loss of the emphasis on the physical conditions of your life" (205). Feelings of resistance, anger, and mistrust while living day-to-day life serve to disconnect us from our Source. Feeling fear at the loss of anything we hold dear separates us further. Instead, live life with gratitude.

Dyer points out agreement in the many translations of two of the last lines of verse 42, with the translation he chose, which follows.

> The violent do not die a natural death. That is my
> fundamental teaching. (204)

I see similarity in the gist of what Lao-tzu is communicating to the common saying, "You reap what you sow." Furthermore, an obvious connection exists between this saying and the following verses from Galatians.

> Be not deceived; God is not mocked: for whatsoever
> a man soweth, that shall he also reap. For he that
> soweth to his flesh shall of the flesh reap corruption;
> but he that soweth to the Spirit shall of the Spirit
> reap life everlasting. And let us not be weary in
> well-doing: for in due season we shall reap, if we
> faint not (Gal 6:7-9, King James Version).

Although Lao-tzu only spoke of thoughts or actions of violence as promoting a violent death, Dr. Dyer believes that Lao-tzu felt the opposite is also true, as is also suggested in the previous quote from Galatians.

Our attitude changes our thoughts, and our thoughts change everything. An attitude of grateful acceptance allows us to move through our fear, by releasing the dependency we feel toward people, positions, and things. This leads to a deeper connection to the Source. The Source is the origin of all that is, and to paraphrase Dyer, this Oneness is the wellspring of our strength when we connect with it. It is the "nothingness" from which all life flows, and the architect of Lao-tzu's ten thousand things, which all, according to Dyer, "carry and embrace the opposites of yin and yang" (Dyer 2007, 205). Lao-tzu says that the combination of these feminine and masculine forces creates harmony.

As we begin to weave our peaceful thoughts and actions into this harmonic essence of the Tao, Dyer follows the lead of Lao-tzu and suggests that we "[loosen] [our] need for who and what [we] have" so that we are able to "melt into harmony with the Tao" (207). First it is our thoughts that must be consonant with the Tao. Our actions will follow our thoughts, and it is this blending of thought, in consonance with action, that attracts the harmony of the Tao into our lives.

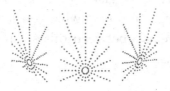

The Barriers We *Build* Around Ourselves and the *Groups* We Represent Prevent *Both* Communication and Compromise.

With God at the Focal Point of Our Lives We Are Able to Slowly Dissolve the Barrier of Fear That Has Taken Our Lifetime and Many before Us to Build. Changing the Way We Think is the Key.

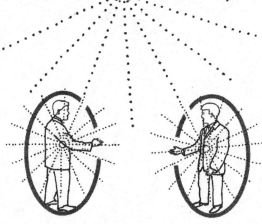

Figure 43: Breaking Down the Barriers

Centered Responses

43

Lao-tzu informs us that non-action is the way of the Tao and that "the softest of all things overrides the hardest of all things" (Dyer 2007, 208).

Gerald G. Jampolsky, in his book *Love is Letting Go of Fear*, explains that all our emotions can be classified as a form of fear or a form of love (Jampolsky 2004). Could this suggest that many of the problems of life, including those that are difficult to overcome, have their origin in fear? Is the way to solve our problems found in love? Fear has hardened our exteriors as a direct construct of our reactions to it. We project our interpretation of the cause of these feelings onto others—thereby feeding the feelings and keeping them alive.

Real or imagined situations continually evoke fear in us, making our reactions to fear ongoing. The barrier or psychological shield we construct around ourselves can also manifest physically as anger and hate, physical ailments, and can have countless other ramifications including an endless list of excuses. When these tendencies that we have as individuals merge at a societal level, the result is the world as we know it, with groups promoting hate and weapons of war. At any level of society, from the personal to the national, an inflexible resistance evolves that keeps all interaction at a superficial and often defensive level, many times with greed and selfishness as a priority.

Lao-tzu speaks of the softness of non-action as the answer in verse 43. Wayne Dyer uses the analogy of flowing water to represent both the softness and the power of non-action. A hand submerged in water senses the water's softness, while the Grand Canyon typifies its power. This strongly suggests that a soft approach used to conquer our fear will be effective; although, we can expect that progress might not be at the speed we might favor.

The discussion that follows is strictly conceptual, given the world in which we live. Some of the ideas expressed here go against the defensive approach that appears to be required for survival. Regardless, I feel it is worthy to attempt to build some sort of proposal and intention around goodness instead of around the power and greed that drives our world. Portions of the ensuing commentary about using a soft approach sound unrealistic, partially because the actual *how* remains hidden. It is my fervent hope that over time soft approaches will be able to replace the hard and often forceful actions of the past and present.

Even if the appropriate action needed and the essence of the operative force remain an enigma, I believe the key to the resolution of difficulties lies in the pursuit of Lao-tzu's suggestion of introducing a softer element to any situation. This includes those that may require compromise. For the purpose of illustration, the paragraphs that follow suggest the implementation of the stillness or softness of the Tao into our lives by comparing it to demonstrating behavior similar to the quiet and composed actions of an accomplished diplomat, but in this case one who represents the Tao. A sensitive, subtle, and discerning approach conforms to the softness of the Tao. It is also in step with the Tao to demonstrate an appropriate, sincere, and even-tempered demeanor in the delivery of any counsel requested, in any situation. Quiet and steadfast firmness is part of this expression, but all within the goodness of the Tao. Regrettably, this approach is best considered when circumstances and decisions do not present security or safety concerns. This does not mean to suggest that the approach does not work. It merely emphasizes that because things will progress at the level of consciousness within the situation, volatile circumstances may erupt into low-frequency events, despite a soft approach. Like many things in life, *timing is of the essence.*

I continue the analogy by suggesting that actions be derived only from Love and not from fear. The 360-degree ever-outreaching sphere in which we live includes the space all around and in us. It exists as an inescapable and omnipresent essence that Gregg Braden calls the "Divine Matrix" (Braden, *The Divine Matrix* 2010). At any given time it *symbolizes* a no-limit universe as well as *is* the world we experience. We are responsible for our own decisions. Furthermore, to continue the analogy, I put forward the idea that the choices we make that have their root in fear can be seen as forcefully intruding into our personal space within the 360-degree field of existence. The fear we feel inhibits our ability to flow in synchronicity with the goodness that is the Tao. Our fear acts as resistance and blocks our recognition of guidance from the Tao while it sets up a lower level of vibration, which the Tao will parallel. This is the invitation for low-frequency events to become part of our experience.

The intention behind the following analogy is to simplify the choice between Love and fear through visualization. Love might be thought of as the acceptance of the light that surrounds us in our multidimensional, 360-degree view. The visible light reflected from the events we experience portrays our life; the direction our life takes is set by our interpretation of these events in our lives. Fear swallows the light of Love in the heaviness of our resistance, allowing no light of hope to escape. The objective is to learn to discern between choices growing out of the light of Love all around us and the choices that bring us down because of the heavy darkness fear carries with it.

Just as Lao-tzu suggests non-action, I also believe he would not judge differences between cultures. Civility between and among people can only begin to happen when cultural differences are recognized and respected. This is more likely to happen if beliefs fall within the parameters of the goodness of the Tao. Unfortunately, in circumstances where this is not the case, the tendency to condemn seems to be our choice.

Lao-tzu advises us to do nothing and still get things done. What could this possibly suggest in this context? If it were possible to acknowledge somewhat of an understanding that includes respect for the origin of cultural beliefs that are foreign to us, perhaps that would be a first step toward a diplomatic solution. Without letting down our guard, we can offer to trust a potential adversary by extending acceptance and not rejection. This does not mean we overlook and excuse wrong action. Furthermore, I use the word acceptance in this context solely to recognize a particular action as one condoned within the backdrop of another group but not necessarily seen as acceptable by us. The way I am interpreting Lao-tzu's concept of doing nothing, I believe the point of non-action might be the juncture at which we recognize the viewpoint of another person or group as being valid despite not agreeing with the decisions being made. It is in moments like these that the door just may open to compromise. It is up to all involved to recognize and then act on the opportunity.

In the above speculative-role-play-scenario the function of a diplomat assumes that the stillness of the Tao is the only tool needed, in his or her "attaché case," to fuse with rational and right-minded thinking. The goal of any attempt at diplomacy would need to conform to the goodness the Tao represents. A soft approach to an issue is more likely to be our choice of action when our lives are not threatened or otherwise adversely affected. Difficulty in offering a soft approach begins to arise in the presence of more significant disagreement between individuals or groups. Impassioned division between religious, cultural, or other groups prompts fear to act as the driving force responsible for actions that we employ in an attempt to allay this fear.

It is not my intent to provide any advice beyond recognizing the significance of a soft approach to problem solving. From my point of view, the source of a possible resolution to these types of disturbing and often shocking circumstances starts with the recognition that we are not separate from others. The physical reality of the horror that can and does result from this fear is factual and cannot be denied. These happenings support our thoughts of being separate. Feeling separate leads to the justification of more and more conflict.

I might suggest that perhaps the very deep and underlying cause of conflict is often not what it appears to be. Because the outcome of conflict can be particularly damaging and often extremely disturbing, getting past the feeling of a need for revenge proves to be almost impossible. Lao-tzu suggests solving difficulties without actions, which implies without the use of force. If we consider the idea that we are capable of forgoing the idea of revenge, would we also be able to tolerate and accept that the culture and beliefs of others are as right for them as our practices are for us? I believe Lao-tzu's idea of a soft approach would hold this as a requirement. Acceptance, as it is used above, assumes that actions are in keeping with the goodness that is the Tao. Although the likelihood is remote, if it were possible for all of us to truly understand that at a fundamental level we are all spirit in a physical body with an ego that may often feel inadequate, there may be fewer decisions made out of fear. But, as it is, many of the decisions we make are predominately fear-based, often with overtones of greed and pride. Fear is an extremely powerful emotion. This is partly because of our mind's ability to paint spectacles of foreboding catastrophe. This way of thinking is reinforced by previous or present day calamity that appears to cement the accuracy of our fearful thinking. This solidifies the apparent need for forceful action.

Unfortunately, fear will continue to create a feeling of necessity for defensive action in unforeseen or unpredictable circumstances. That being said, we all share a part of the God Energy that some choose to call the Tao, while others choose to continue the use of the traditional name accepted by their religion or culture. There are also those who favor different terminology. This is all good. Distilling the nomenclature built around religions, spiritual traditions, and perhaps including some science based explanations reduces the seemingly separate phraseology into pure essence, the hub of the Source of all. To my way of thinking, recognizing the Oneness that we all share is at the core of an ultimately more powerful force than fear. It is present within all of us. We simply need to remain still. A moment of quiet connection may be enough for us to recognize this truth. It is then that we can begin to act on it.

Actions stemming from the recognition of our oneness do not focus on differences. Employing this truth in diplomatic discussions that examine things like cultural and religious differences could result in what might appear as temporarily setting aside our view of God in favor of another, but in my mind this is actually a step toward a 360-degree view of God. Each time we step back, recognize, and accept the view of another culture or person as having validity, we release another segment of resistance that conditioning has wedged into us. This frees that space to be filled with wholeness.

Because the Energy of the Tao is and always was everywhere, it is this very Energy that was present when each and every religion began to take form, or was first "realized." Consequently, if all religions share in the common Energy of the Tao at their Source, does it also follow that many religions will also share common values that work toward the development of goodness, the Energy of Love, which is God? When cultural beliefs do not harm and also fall within the scope of the goodness that is represented by the Energy of the Tao are accepted as valid by another culture, the perceived need for fear no longer exists because the basic tenets of both religions along with their cultures do not have to be defended. This would be the goal of a 360-degree view of God.

Issues that do not submit to the goodness of the Tao (God) will probably fall outside the parameters of acceptance of one, both or many of the groups concerned. These are issues that will require greater diplomatic discussion. If these concerns are approached without bias on one side as well as the other, the lead of the silent Love of the Tao may open us to compromise with all sides agreeing.

The previous comment sounds like an impossibility given the extreme situations our world faces. To have some semblance of this scenario become a reality, there must be an understanding attitude between and among religions. One way would be to first accept the concept of the Tao (or whatever descriptive term is preferred) as being the common source for our world religions. I believe that in the opinion of Lao-tzu, it is only with this common link that these ideas, even remotely, begin to be plausible. Throughout these types of proceedings, we must remain aware of potentially threatening situations.

I will continue on the assumption that a significant proportion of the world population recognizes a shared genesis, such as the Tao, as our universal Source. The softness that Lao-tzu speaks about includes the silence that does not judge the differences that fall outside of the goodness of the Tao, and instead opens the door to cooperation, concession, and perhaps recognition of another point of view. Forceful action is too often seen as the only approach, but force always prompts a counterforce. Although the concept of a calm discussion of the pros and cons of issues on both sides appears unworkable or even irrational, it is less likely to induce fear. Critics who scorn this soft approach will probably also assume that it prompts ridicule from the adversary involved in the negotiation, as well from onlookers. This could very well be true and serves to remind us that truthful communication is vital. Anything less is not Tao-centered. We cannot know whether negotiation is trustworthy and sincere or not, just as we are not able to rely on force to change things. In the case of force, history has proven that it has never worked long-term. This begs the question of the effectiveness of Tao-centered negotiation. Based on the historical record left by the use of fear to settle differences, softness is worthy of a lengthy trial period.

To get results, it may take a period of perhaps many more years than we would prefer of choosing Love over fear. In time, a view partially shared by both sides in a disagreement, may emerge. It is only from a mutual point of departure representing shared ideas and goals that understanding can happen; and progress for both sides can begin. This may slowly lead to accepting the idea of compromise. The greater understanding that develops over time—after genuine and repeated acknowledgement of the point of view of another—is able to undo the uncompromising attitude of condemnation that many people feel, when challenged by views other than those they have adopted.

Not understanding others promotes fear. Therefore, it is in our best interest and that of others to begin to understand those who differ from us. Only Love can overcome fear. Through a genuine immersion in our Source, we can hear the whisperings of God. Our unfettered response, when parallel with the thoughts of God, may peaceably lead us to conciliation through Love. The keen edge of consciousness created by a deep connection with our Source slowly and gently penetrates the hardened wall of fear that humankind has built around itself. When directed by actions that are both unified and God-centered and possibly represent a variety of people and nations, the Love of God may well-up out of the nothingness of consciousness and overflow, dissolving fear that has been passed down through the ages. This concept represents living within what I call the multidimensional, 360-degree view of God.

The antithesis of the Tao at its focal point is reaction based on fear, causing us to see ourselves as separate. This perpetual cycle of reactions, with fear at the helm, propels our world down the destructive path it is taking. Isn't it time to make a new and radical choice? Only the Love of God found in God-centered actions can recast our planet and produce transformation. As always, the choice remains ours, all of us.

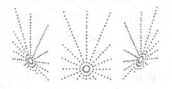

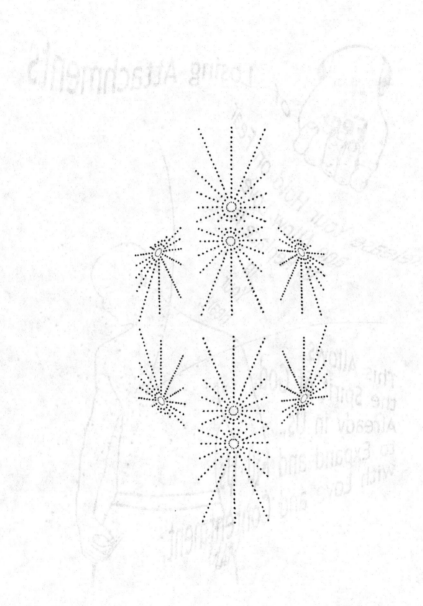

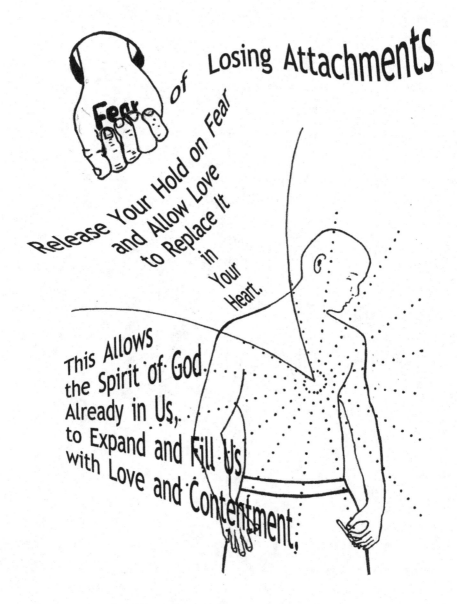

Figure 44: Releasing Our Hold on Fear

Stop Striving:
Feel the Love and Contentment

44

Lao-tzu tells us that "a contented man is never disappointed" because he knows when to stop (Dyer 2007, 214). Wayne Dyer explains that it is not the things or the desire for them that "keeps [us] from living a connection to the Tao—it's [our] attachment" (215).

Why do we not seem to know when to quit striving for more? Some of the things we have make us feel good but only for the moment. We like the feeling we associate with having things, so in search of that feeling we seek more and more things. Because positions of importance make us feel good, some people are always on the lookout for better and better positions of power and prestige. Money provides us with the things we need, and more money buys us the things we want. We are social beings, and because money impresses much of the populace, having money attracts social encounters. At one time or another we may have experienced the feelings of love, which we associated with the people in our lives at the time. We enjoy these feelings while they last, but unfortunately, many of us are not pleased with the constantly changing feelings we experience. Deep, lasting feelings of love are what we seek, not the passing emotions that leave us wanting and prevent us from knowing when to stop seeking a new job, more money, a new relationship, and so forth.

If only we were able to experience the sought-after feelings of love and contentment that we so desperately seek, without committing to the seemingly endless chase for wealth and prominence. Wayne Dyer tells us to experience "[our] connection to the Tao while [we're] still alive" (215), as has been mentioned earlier in the Tao Te Ching. Initiating the change required begins with releasing our *attachment* to the people, things, and power we think we need, as mentioned by Dyer in his essay on this verse. This speaks to the attachment only because situations with people, things, and power may be either enriching or devitalizing. Abandon that which is devitalizing. Although it is generally accepted that life's experiences are responsible for our feelings, only *we* have the ability to decide *how we feel*. Our response to any situation is always a *choice*, so choosing to feel *love* short circuits our ego's need to search for it.

Fear traps us in our thinking. We must release all fear that is connected to the attachments we have to people, things, power, and money. When we release our grasp on fear we are unshackled and free. Our thoughts can now begin to move away from our fears of separation. This provides space in our hearts for the Spirit of God already in us, to expand and create a deep feeling of connection to God's creation. Furthermore, in contrast to our sustained striving for more, giving of ourselves enriches our lives. Only when we truly *feel* from within our depth the joy of *sharing our love and what we have* with others can we experience the feeling of what we really yearn for, love and contentment.

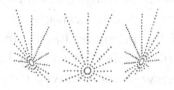

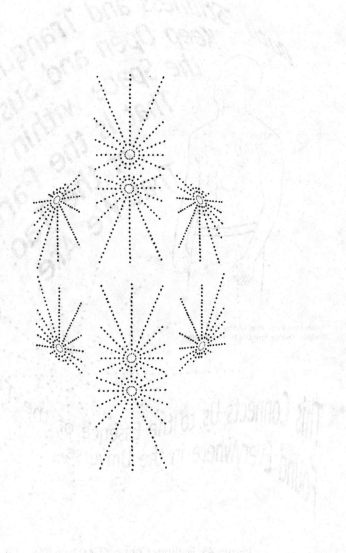

Figure 53. Feeling Confident (CTD©, p. 167)

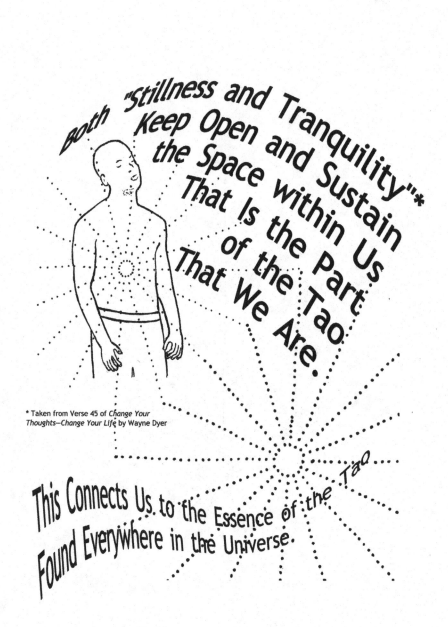

Both "Stillness and Tranquility"* Keep Open and Sustain the Space within Us That Is the Part of the Tao That We Are.

This Connects Us to the Essence of the Tao Found Everywhere in the Universe.

* Taken from Verse 45 of *Change Your Thoughts—Change Your Life* by Wayne Dyer

Figure 45: Feelings Connect Us (Dyer 2007, 218)

Honest to Go(o)dness Feelings:
Our True Connection

45

Lao-tzu concludes verse 45 with, "Stillness and tranquility set things in order in the universe" (Dyer 2007, 218). Many things in our daily lives need to be regularly set in order, so making wise decisions is critical; but unfortunately, our conditioning steers many of the choices that we make away from the Tao. Commercials, advertisements, and the junk info we collect electronically or otherwise help to convince our ego that happiness comes from gathering more knowledge and more stuff. Cultural conventions often dictate an expected style of conduct to match a given circumstance.

In addition, when we do not subscribe to the mores of society, whatever they may be, we often receive treatment designed to punish and bring us back in line. At the level of the society in which we function, our collective as well as personal ego is compelled to feel the need to control behavior that does not conform to society's expectations. We feel fear in the presence of what we consider offensive or condemnable behavior and this feeling fills us and therefore convinces us that control is required and is the only option to stop these actions. We all deserve a safe and nurturing environment and the reality is that the inspiration for appropriate behavior originates from the part of the Tao within all of us, not from the external controls that we think are the singular solution.

When we recognize the part of the Tao who we are, we are free to choose to live the Tao within the framework of almost any culture that honors the spirit of God within us. To live a life effectively connected to the Tao, it is best to recognize and respect the society in which we live, while honoring the Tao within. It is a particularly easy fit when our religious traditions mesh almost seamlessly with a Tao-centered life.

In the perfect and unparalleled emptiness of the Tao, doing less is the epitome of the application of the Tao in our lives. This quiet, gentle, and peaceful way, as inspired by the incomparable perfection of the Tao, appears at first glance to be a do-nothing approach and therefore considered counterintuitive by the standards of modern day society. The outward form of this (non)action suggests absence of direction, lack of effort, and general insufficiency compared to what is typically expected.

As Wayne Dyer stated in his essay on the previous verse, "The number-one priority in [our] life is [our] relationship with [our] Source of being" (217). Circumstances do not have to deter us from this connection to our Source. Another opinion expressed in the past by Dyer uses the analogy of comparing people to an orange. When the pressures of life squeeze us, whatever fills us comes out. This suggests that we are to love ourselves first so we are able to extend genuine feelings of love and compassion to others, despite the stress felt by circumstances. The "stillness and tranquility" of this action keeps open and sustains the space within us that is the part of the Tao that we are.

We are connected to the essence of God found everywhere in the Universe. It is this perfection, as simplistic and misdirected as it may appear to those driven by ego, that guides us past our rigidly set path and leads us instead in a new direction, perhaps bringing a clarity not seen or felt before. In the light of the aforementioned clarity, we are able to focus more acutely on intuition and thereby experience true fulfillment in the things we choose to do. As we continue to live our lives in connection to the Tao, the direction and guidance we may need is always available to us, if we *feel* fully aware of each life experience while it is happening. Honest-to-Go(o)dness *feelings* are our true connection to the Tao.

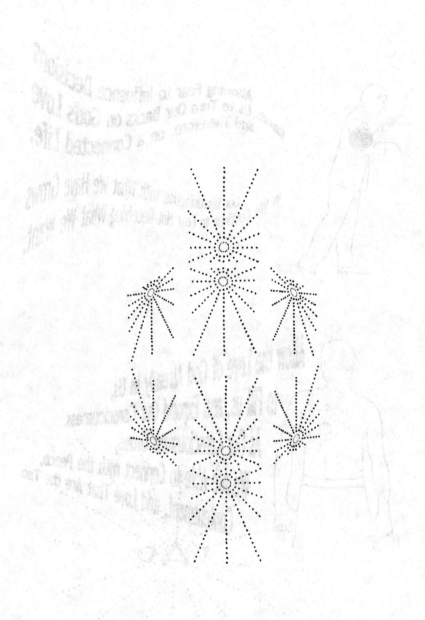

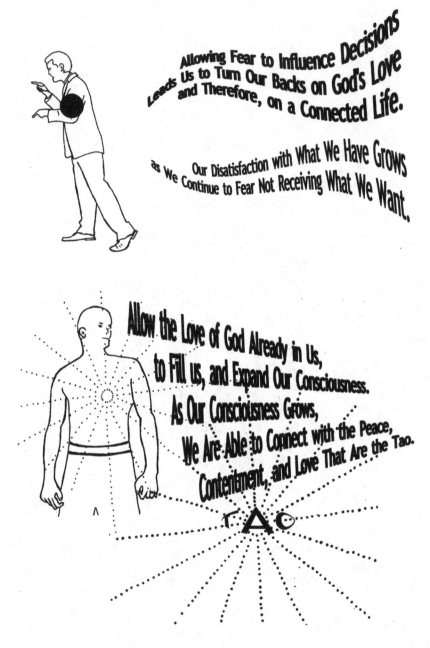

Allowing Fear to Influence Decisions Leads Us to Turn Our Backs on God's Love and Therefore, on a Connected Life.

Our Disatisfaction with What We Have Grows as We Continue to Fear Not Receiving What We Want.

Allow the Love of God Already in Us, to Fill us, and Expand Our Consciousness. As Our Consciousness Grows, We Are Able to Connect with the Peace, Contentment, and Love That Are the Tao.

Figure 46: The Tao: Peace, Love, and Contentment

Live Connected and Be Content

46

We all react with a varying degree of fear to circumstances that surround us every day. Many of our concerns fill us with fear, which becomes magnified by things, such as the hype presented by all forms of media, the projection of our own thoughts, or, perhaps our often-false interpretation of situations brought about by the choices we have made. Whatever we use as our excuse can be decoded as choosing fear over Love.

We fear not getting enough of whatever our mind has been persuaded to believe and accept as a necessity. The dissatisfaction with what we have grows, as we continue to fear not receiving what we want. A heart filled with discontent has no room for love.

Lao-tzu states in this verse of the Tao that there is "no greater tragedy than discontentment" (Dyer 2007, 224). The conflicts in the boardroom, the street corner, around the kitchen table, or the battlefield occur for the most part because people are not contentedly living the Way of the Tao.

In his essay, Wayne Dyer states that we should not base our achievement on what we have accumulated. He goes on to say that personal satisfaction, contentment, and inner peace are the true measure of accomplishment (225).

When our thoughts are not dominated by fear, discontent no longer fills us, and we can begin to feel the piece of God that is already in us. Only as this consciousness grows are we able to connect with the peace, contentment, and Love that are the Tao.

The good feelings we have when we get what we want are transient; we are part of the Tao, and the Tao is forever. Experience the Tao now; be content and live life connected to it.

Figure 47.1: My "Me Collection"

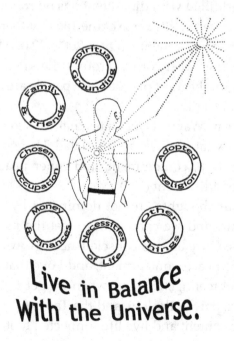

Figure 47.2: Balancing Our Collection

Just Feel It

47

In the forty-seventh verse, Lao-tzu tells us that the sage "does not strive and yet attains completion" (Dyer 2007, 228). We have all been conditioned, although in varying degrees, to strive to attain the things of this world in the pursuit of happiness. We aspire to get the things on our list. We constantly seek more. We struggle. We analyze and calculate. We collect this but not that. Our mind is in a whirl. We plan and present ourselves to the tasks and functions that we deem as opportune. Again we collect, or we do not collect. We misrepresent; we falsify; we distort and purposefully misstate—all in an attempt to gain position, to gain power and wealth, to gain or maintain friendships, or to gain "things." We do all this to finally attain happiness. We achieve many of our worldly aspirations and collect many of the things we believe will make us happy. We still do not feel happy; our struggle continues. We feel an untouchable emptiness within.

Nature conducts its business without prejudice. We are a part of nature. Wayne Dyer uses our heart "as a model for understanding and applying the lesson of living by being" (229). He tells us our heart "knows exactly what to do by virtue of its very nature" (230). Lao-tzu also tells us, and Dyer reminds us that the sage "does not venture forth and yet knows" (228). Dyer advises us that just as we surrender to the workings of the heart, we need to surrender to the Tao (231). Natural law is attuned to the energy of the Tao.

In all fairness, the Tao responds in the same frequency as the feelings within us that are truly felt from the heart. The similarity I see here between our lives and Dyer's heart model is how the feelings we have within ourselves almost instantly create a response in the rate of our heartbeat. Our heart does not question the feelings we are experiencing; it just responds appropriately. Panic increases the frequency of our heartbeat while a state of calm reduces it. Just

149

as the heart does not judge between a relaxed state and a frantic one but just beats accordingly, the Universe also does not judge affirming thoughts as better than those of dissension.

The feelings within us, whatever they are, simply attract more of the same. By choosing our feelings, we choose our life. This pathway is open to everyone, including all religious, ethnic, or linguistic groups.

It all comes down to perception. Know that the words we speak may be meaningful or may hold little or no meaning! It is the feelings that accompany our thoughts or words that have the power to communicate with God. The framework of most religions, as expounded by their respective scriptures, is able to accommodate wholesome confirmations from the heart that engender feelings of warmth, acceptance, and concern within the practicing parishioner and others. Thus understanding this conduit as a means of effective communication within the framework of perhaps all of the major religions serves to integrate and unify. Religion, on its own, has the tendency to separate because of the ego's need to be right. When working within this shared Energy of Love, which is the Tao, all religions can effectively be served by it. It unifies all these groups within the same functional understanding. In addition to this unifying feature, it allows the aspects of the culture of each group that fall within the parameters of the goodness of the Tao to remain intact. Thus, the cultural integrity inherent within each corresponding religion can be maintained, for the most part.

Only by living the Tao can we know without first seeking or attain without a long struggle.

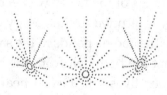

Figure 48: Trusting the Wisdom of the Tao

Seek Nothing of this World; Just Be

48

In verse 48 Lao-tzu tells us that "the practice of the Tao consists of daily diminishing" (Dyer 2007, 234). Wayne Dyer refers to ownership as coming complete with "an element of imprisonment" (236). Wanting bigger homes, recreational vehicles, and boats, along with faster cars, brings us only short-term expressions of object-dependent happiness. These things end up placing us in servitude since our lives are controlled by them for a variety of reasons, including the effort, time, and money needed for their care and protection. Too often, burdensome debt is also part of the duress we choose for ourselves, through the apparent ownership of things.

Lao-tzu tells us that "learning consists of daily accumulating" (234). Dyer clarifies that "learning is about accumulating information and knowledge; the Tao is about wisdom" (235). He goes on to say that wisdom is not about knowledge and information; it is about "living in harmony with [our] Source" (235-36).

We already possess many of the "toys" we think we need, as well as the necessary knowledge and information. Are we happy? True happiness does not come from things, position, or knowledge. If we focus on our attachment to these things, the Universe will likely not respond with happiness and contentment because our feelings are focusing on the fear of loss instead of the joy of being. Releasing our attachment to any of the manifest world, including giving away things that have particular value to us, as Dyer suggests, helps us live connected to the Tao and will set the part of the Tao within us free, allowing this nothingness to fill us with the love of God. Our connection to our Source nurtures the piece of the Tao that we are, bringing comforting warmth and contentment to us. We must remember that the feeling we seek can only begin to be realized when we no longer allow our lives to be commandeered by the things we think we need to have. Genuine contentment grows as we make changes in our lives that reduce our apparent need for things.

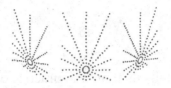

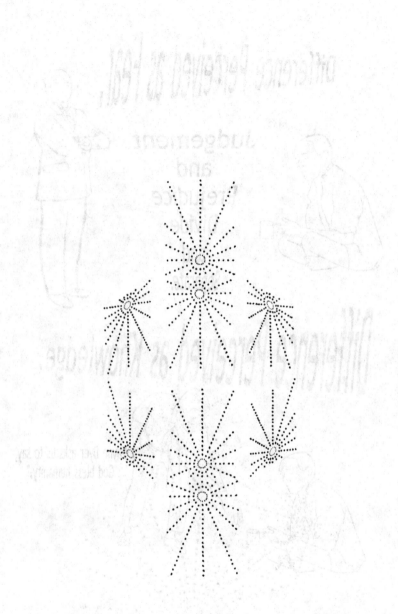

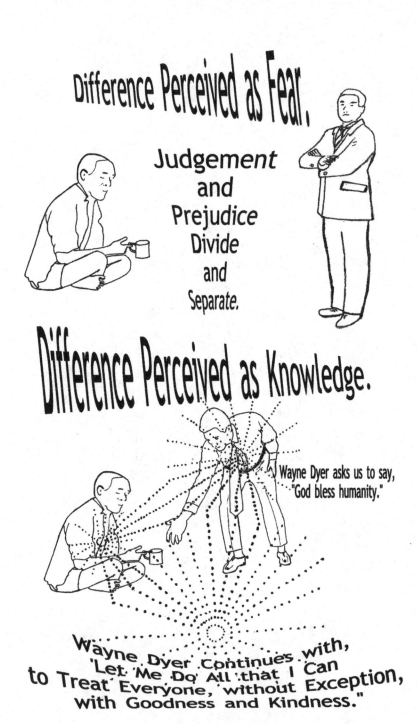

Figure 49: Perceiving Difference as Knowledge (Dyer 2007, 240)

Childlike Acceptance

49

Lao-tzu reveals that "the sage lives in harmony with all below heaven" (Dyer 2007, 238). The majority of us, on the other hand, have become experts at judgment and prejudice, the opposite of harmony. It is in our homes, in our schools, on the streets, in our shops, at our place of work, in our houses of worship, and in political systems. Differences between cultures are particularly targeted. Wherever we go, it is there. One can only speculate why judgment is so insidious.

On a personal level, we refuse to accept many aspects about ourselves. Maybe one reason we judge so readily is the recognition of behaviors or traits observed in others that we consciously or unconsciously see in ourselves but refuse to acknowledge. This may make us quick to judge in an attempt to hide this truth from others, as well as from ourselves. At the same time, judgment of those around us bolsters our own ego. There may be as many perceived reasons for our faultfinding as there are judgments made. Whatever the thought process, the common thread appears to be convincing ourselves that we are better than our targets, and we lay blame on them, thereby stroking our own ego. In addition, too often we listen as others judge an absent third party, and too frequently it is for the sole purpose of shoring up our own ego for social or political reasons. Many times we join in and share in the ego building instead of moving on to another topic as quickly as possible. This is almost a daily ritual practiced by many and has no utilitarian value.

The judgment that happens on an individual level also happens between and among groups, not only at the level of community, state, or province but at the national level. The major difference is that the stakes are higher, and the devastating consequences affect more people.

There is only one solution. Choose love over fear. Something perceived as being different is feared. Do not focus on what is different. Accept differences as knowledge. Wayne Dyer asks us to "[notice] instead of [judge]" (241). Unless there is definitive reason to think otherwise, knowledge treated at the factual level need not be feared, just accepted. Once accepted, we can look past the differences and choose love.

When we are observing from the position of love rather than fear, we are better able to allow the goodness in us (we *all* have goodness) to see past the behavior and appearance that the society in which we live deems inappropriate. This *does not* condone the behavior, it simply allows for a new beginning, without which improvement in behavior cannot be expected. Beyond the physical in all of us lies the goodness of God's creation that we all share. Recognizing our connection to one another in this realm is the ultimate act of goodness that goes beyond any help we may offer at the physical level. Dyer refers to the Sanskrit word "Namaste" that he tells us "roughly translates to, "I honor the place in you where we are all one" (241).

Approaching humanity from the narrow vantage point of a predetermined perspective arrived at through things such as religion, appearance, inappropriate actions, social status, and so on does nothing but divide and separate.

Lao-tzu asks us to "love everyone as [our] own child" and to "[behave] like a little child" (238). Childlike acceptance unifies. At the level of our Being, we are all One.

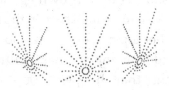

Fear of Death is Our Most Burdensome Fear.

We Choose Fear and Claim it as Our Own.

FEAR

Clinging to Fear Inhibits Life.

Choose Love over Fear
and Release Attachments to Life.
Allow Love's Radiance
to Fill Your Heart.

Recognizing and Accepting
That We Are Immortal Spirit
Allows Us to
Truly Experience Life
and Avert the Fear
of Death's Grasp.

Figure 50: Choosing Love, Not Fear

Choices

50

In verse 50, Lao-tzu explains that one person out of ten feels "sure of life," and later adds, "[because] he dwells in that place where death cannot enter" (Dyer 2007, 242). Wayne Dyer clarifies that 90 percent of us perceive ourselves "solely as a physical mortal" (243). As mortals, we are attached to many things in our fast-paced existence. Our world is obsessed with acquiring a steadily increasing number of gadgets and other paraphernalia, along with the wish for more and more types of experiences. We are attached to the things and experiences we enjoy; and therefore, to life itself. Having all this "stuff" available to us is just fine. The problem arises when we decide to become attached to them. We fear losing these attachments. The ego thinks that *it* is who we are; and the coda of death is its greatest fear. Thus, we choose to live our lives with fear because we are afraid of losing our life, and with it, our attachments.

Instead, we could choose Love and be thankful for each moment that life provides for us. Expressing heartfelt feelings of gratitude and appreciation for every moment of every day will resonate with the Universe and attract experiences of a similar uplifting nature. So why not choose love? Beyond our physical makeup and our experiences, we are Spirit. *This* moment, the moment we experience right now, is *all* we have. It is our choice; we can appreciate the moment by experiencing it through love; or we can reject it by choosing to feel fear, by harboring anger about a concern from the past or the present, or by feeling anxiety about the future.

As we live our lives, we choose how we spend the moments that we collect in our memory. The many choices we make each day play a major role in determining whether we will experience light and loving moments or heavy moments filled with fear. The choice is ours. When we release attachments to life with all its physical adornments and accept the idea of our physical death, the essence within us is set free to live. A feeling inspired by love grows out of our depths, and if we regularly choose Love over fear, it becomes apparent in the way we live our lives. Hearts filled with love's brilliance radiate warmth, compassion, and caring and avert the fear of death's grasp. We are able to successfully step over life's edge and enjoy living from our innate Being before leaving the physical plane, by realizing and accepting at our very core, the Spirit, which we are.

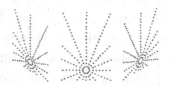

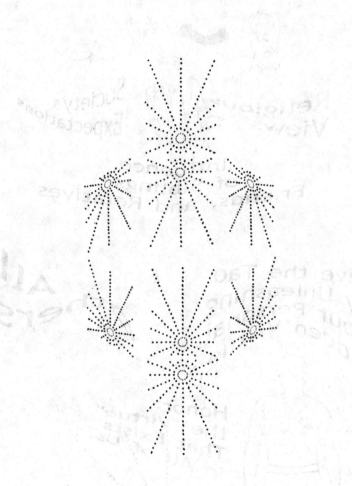

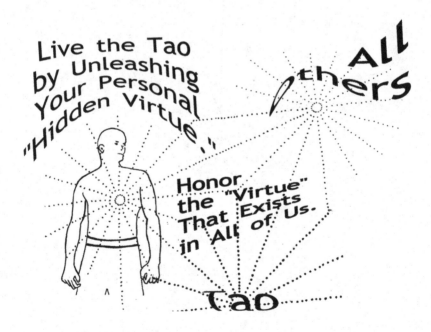

Figure 51: Unleashing Our "Hidden Virtue" (Dyer 2007, 246)

Live by Giving of Yourself

51

In verse 51 Lo-tzu begins by saying that "all living beings [connect] to their Source," and later explains that "all beings honor the Way and value its virtue" (Dyer 2007, 246). Each of us is a piece of God. In his essay (247), Wayne Dyer tells us that we are much more than the merging of parent cells that brings forth only one aspect of us, our physical form. Along with our legal registration as the child of a given set of parents, our physical existence is initially tied to their care. We learned to take our cues from them and theirs, and knowingly or not we often continue to do so, even later in life. Many of us have been raised to meet specific familial expectations as well as those of society. This creates pressure on us to achieve certain goals. These hopes may or may not match the dreams that originate from our Being.

The "Spiritual Spark" within has always been part of us and is who we really are, but unfortunately our ego works nonstop at concealing the presence of part of the Tao in us—the hidden virtue. It diverts our attention to the constant need for the gratification of the ego with money, power, and possessions in an endless effort to fill our emptiness, instead of recognizing this space as Oneness, the Spirit that we are. In our quiet moments we may become aware of the hidden virtue within us. The direction or guidance it imparts may take many forms, including the words we hear, the examples we see in our physical world, what we think are coincidences, and much, much more. It continues to provide, support, and direct us to what we feel we can contribute to make our world a better place. It is up to us to recognize this guidance and respond to it; the guidance does not look for compensation.

It has been often said that life's lessons should be viewed as opportunities, but I will add that these may be opportunities to live from the "hidden virtue" within us. These happenings may bring into action our dormant personal expectations of ourselves or those others have of us. They may or may not be in keeping with the Spiritual Spark within us that needs to burst its light freely in a direction only *we* are able to feel to be true; so it might be wise to respect, be alert to, and perhaps consider ideas gleaned from family, friends, and acquaintances. If a suggestion rests within the goodness of the Tao, it may resonate with our "hidden virtue"—the unparalleled part of us that knows unequivocally how to recognize inspiration that rouses us to spotlight our energy on helping others, which in turn transports the goodness of the Tao into life experience. We must not opt for activities that do not contribute to goodness. When we live our lives from the perspective of our hidden virtue, we are able to give of who we are. One way we can do this is to recognize an activity of virtue that brings us fulfillment and then give of ourselves without wanting in return.

Everyone shares part of God in a body generated by a physical miracle. The freedom brought by this shared parentage is released through this spark of "hidden virtue" in all of us. It allows us to have success, our way, without the need to possess, or be possessed, by others.

Live by giving, without expecting in return. Gently reaching out and connecting to our Source honors the "hidden virtue" within us all, including ourselves, by realizing and understanding that who we really are is not our body; we are all one in Spirit.

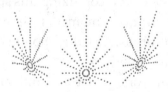

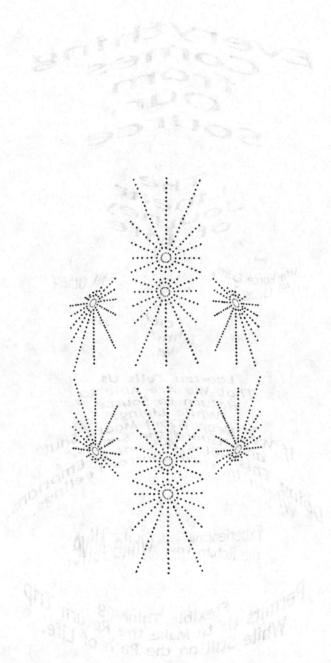

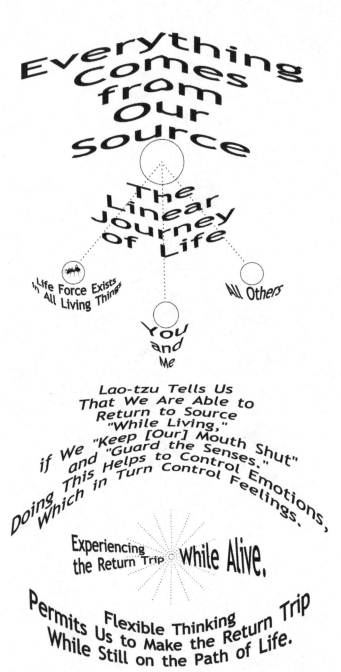

Figure 52: Living the Return (Dyer 2007, 252)

Live the Return to the Light

52

Lao-tzu begins verse 52 by saying "all under heaven have a common beginning." He calls this "the Mother of the world" (Dyer 2007, 252). Wayne Dyer tells us that if we "decide to know and honor her," we "will view all of the ten thousand things as offspring of the Mother" (253). Both Lao-tzu and Dyer see a full life as more than being a linear existence from birth to death. The choices we make are critical in enabling us to enjoy reunion with our Source prior to completing the linear path.

We spend every moment of our lives interacting with one or more of the living or non-living ten thousand things, and this presents us with choices that only we can make. For example, we need to think before we initiate, listen to, or take part in discussions that badmouth someone, whether or not they are in our presence. Choose not to take part; walk away; or gently try to redirect the conversation. Decisions like this fall into the realm of forgiveness and are in keeping with the Love of Spirit.

Decide to see the splendor in everything created by our Source, from the vast expanse of a starry night to the imperceptible microorganisms responsible for our morning yogurt. All that exists is of the Source, and the more we consciously recognize even the small, seemingly insignificant things in life and truly appreciate the part they play, the closer our connection is to our Source. We also need to be open and accommodating in our relationship with all the people with whom we share our world. Physically, each of us appears different, but we all are, and will remain, part of the Tao. At the center of our Being, we are all equal—One; we all share a piece of the Light of God, which is our common Source. It is to this Source we must return. Our choices are able to lead us closer to our Source.

The following incorporates my interpretation of what I consider pertinent information to this topic accessed from a CD recording by Nightingale Conant titled *Speaking the Lost Language of God* by Gregg Braden (Braden n.d., CD#7), together with my understanding of verse 52 of the Tao and the accompanying essay by Dr. Wayne W. Dyer. My brief interpretation of the merging or synthesis of these interrelated ideas follows.

It is our responsibility to filter our emotions wisely. Our irrational reaction to fear plays a major role in producing the lingering feelings of discomfort that we carry within us. These feelings often affect us directly and immediately on the level of our physical well-being. At the same time, at the level of our spiritual Being, the frequency level of our feelings that form within us hold the preparedness to communicate with and to attract that which vibrates in resonance with the energy we put forth. We are the ones who make the decision whether to channel our emotional responses in the direction of love or in the direction of fear.

When we hear disparaging comments, we often allow ourselves to react verbally in opposition, and then just as was alluded to in the writing of Lao-tzu, our mouth and ears tip our emotions toward fear, creating anxious and often distressing feelings that encourage us to quickly slide away from our Source. The fearful feelings will begin to manifest physically and keep us on a strictly linear path.

Conversely, when our emotions channel our thoughts into loving feelings, an exceptionally powerful attraction develops that peacefully draws us closer to the Light of God, our Source that resides within. In time, the love we feel in our hearts toward others is returned in a meaningful but perhaps unexpected way. The feelings we genuinely experience at the depth of our hearts is our liaison with Spirit. Being consciously aware of this connection brings us closer and closer to our Source.

Lao-tzu and Dyer speak of flexibility. Flexibility allows us to move away from linear thinking. This freedom in turn allows us to recognize all around us as being part of the same life force that exists in us. This includes, for example, the life force in an insect such as an ant at our feet. From this new perspective, according to Dyer, when we allow ourselves to truly comprehend the interconnectedness of our world, "we gain this clarity, which is the return trip [we're] encouraged to take while alive" (Dyer 2007, 255). We are able to enjoy reunion with our Source while being allowed to complete the linear path of our lives in a more fulfilling and rewarding way.

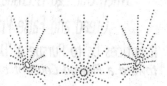

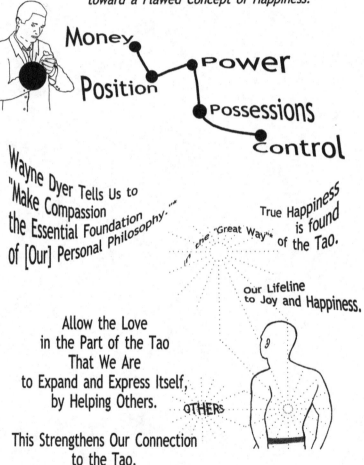

*(Taken from Verse 53 in *Change Your Thoughts–Change Your Life,* by Wayne Dyer)

We Remain Closed to the Tao
When Our Ego is Ensnared by
Greed and False Pride.
It Entices Us to Pursue a "Devious"* Path
toward a Flawed Concept of Happiness.

Money

Position

Power

Possessions

Control

Wayne Dyer Tells Us to
"Make Compassion
the Essential Foundation
of [Our] Personal Philosophy..."

True Happiness
is found
in the "Great Way"* of the Tao.

Our Lifeline
to Joy and Happiness.

Allow the Love
in the Part of the Tao
That We Are
to Expand and Express Itself,
by Helping Others.

OTHERS

This Strengthens Our Connection
to the Tao.

Figure 53: Our Lifeline (Dyer 2007, 256)

Right-Mindedness and Integrity

53

Lao-tzu reveals in verse 53, "The Great Way is very smooth and straight, and yet the people prefer devious paths" (Dyer 2007, 256). Why do we veer from the simple path that leads Home and instead endure an unprincipled and often deceitful and stress-filled path that leads to a misguided, uncertain, and what oftentimes proves to be a spurious destination? Is it because we feel there is not enough to go around? Is this our fear? Do we really think that we need to amass more and more in order to ensure that we "get ours"? Perhaps our relentless search for more is really a sign of our unhappiness despite what we have. Do we think that more food than we need to survive, more clothes than we need to live comfortably, and larger, over-equipped homes and cars will really fill the void that keeps us from feeling happy and fulfilled? The quickly passing emotions of ego gratification keep us lusting for more and more.

In his essay on this verse, Wayne Dyer refers to us as being part of our environment (258). Concern for our environment, as we go about racking up stuff, is often only given a passing nod through the mind-mollifying use of such eco-pacifiers as fluorescent lightbulbs and carbon credits, which do have their merit; it just is not enough. Our life of today, with our hurry and hurry hard mentality and our "I-want-it-now" attitude appear to be strictly fear-driven.

The moment-by-moment choices we make too often have fear as their guide. When we feel motivated by fear, fear will also be the ultimate outcome, even though we experience brief periods of pleasure that act as the bobbing bait before us that we keep chasing.

Our ego also takes us down the path of "I'm not good enough the way I am, *but* if I have *this, that, or the other thing*, then I will be happy." Yes, we feel elated during the quickly passing moments when we think we have arrived, only to be told again by ego, often with the help of society, that we still are not good enough. This twisted path keeps us searching and searching again and again. The path toward our Source is straightforward. The Way does not involve the accrual of the latest gadget, convenience, or fashion, stuffed into our homes for exhibition, or the accumulation of more and more money, or even the acquisition of positions of prestige, with the power to control others. This is not to say that those of us who live the "Great Way" do not have access to these things; it simply means that we are not attached to the idea of having these things, but if we do have them, one of their primary uses should be to help others.

The strength of the Great Way lies in its simplicity. It is in the clarity of this simplicity that we find the joy we seek. Following this path provides an unswerving avenue where we can use the things of the world to support us as we attend to or assist with the needs of others, especially the disadvantaged. Helping others by doing something we enjoy and love brings us all the joy we seek.

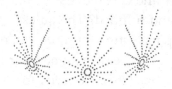

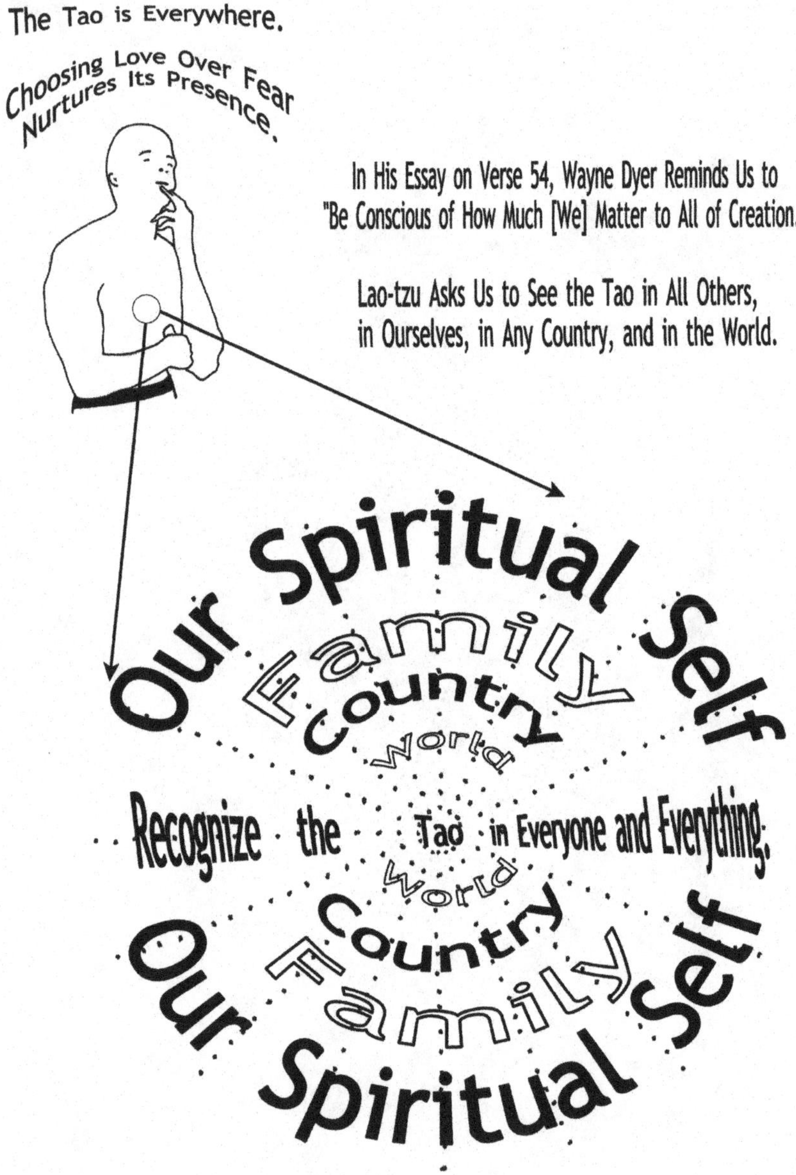

Figure 54: The Tao: Oneness with All (Dyer 2007, 262)

Choose to Live Life
Nurtured in the Tao

54

Lao-tzu reminds us in verse 54 not only that "the Tao is everywhere," but also that "it has become everything." At the end of the verse, he asks, "How do I know this is true?" His reply is "by looking inside myself" (Dyer 2007, 262). If we would genuinely look for the truth, which is in us, we would recognize that we too are Spirit, but *is* this where we place our priorities?

Ego is convinced that we are our physical bodies and so directs our thinking to obtain "nourishment" only on the level of the physical, fully expecting that this will provide all we need. However, the everlasting part of us is Spirit! These roots must seek "sustenance" through the Love of God for our spiritual spark to flourish. In his essay on verse 54, Wayne Dyer clearly emphasizes the gist of this verse as being that the way we live our lives influences the world, and therefore we should live with that in mind (263). In our moment-by-moment choices, it is wise to be genuinely grateful for the physical experience we are having. As difficult as it may be to do, it is equally wise to accept others even if we perceive that the choices they make do not come from a place of love.

The choices we make each moment of each day measure our true appreciation of and our ability to experience life on the physical level. Choices that show honor and respect for others and ourselves come from love, while choices involving judgment of others or ourselves stem from fear. Our lives become as vibrant and fulfilling as permitted by the new choices we make every moment of every day. Choosing Love over fear is one of the best ways to show thanks to the Tao for the life we live. We can choose to *live* with appreciation or merely to endure life through the eyes of judgment.

177

Seeing the Tao in all we meet and everything we encounter brings the connectedness and Oneness of our world to a more recognizable level, even though we may not comprehend the how and why behind all happenings. It is important to bring the Love of the Tao into all the choices we make. As more people recognize the Spirit that they are, the greater the rectitude or integrity that is embodied by all of humankind.

Many of our actions convey a message with an integral influence often hidden within the effort. Each of us who sincerely lives the Tao acts as an exemplar for Tao connectedness. The heartfelt feeling engulfed within our actions guides our spiritual essence and sets the direction for any ancillary influence our actions may engender.

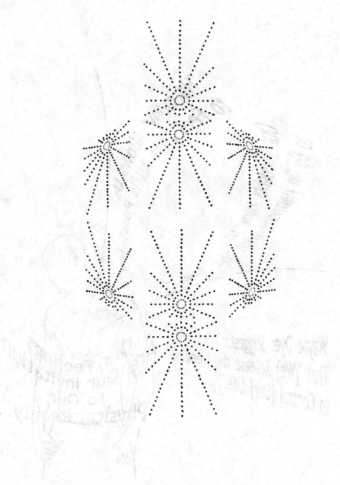

Our Connection to the Tao Fosters "Harmony."

This Encourages No-Limit Thinking, like That of a Child.

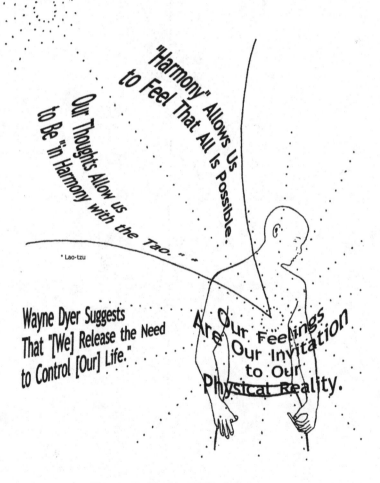

"Harmony" Allows Us to Feel That All Is Possible.

Our Thoughts Allow us to Be "in Harmony with the Tao." *

* Lao-tzu

Wayne Dyer Suggests That "[We] Release the Need to Control [Our] Life."

Our Feelings Are Our Invitation to Our Physical Reality.

Figure 55: No-Limit Thinking

Relax and Trust the Tao with No-Limit Thinking

55

Lao-tzu begins verse 55 by saying that "he who is in harmony with the Tao is like a newborn child" (Dyer 2007, 266). Unfortunately, the majority of us, as adults, do not take the time to recognize the part of the Tao that we are. We simply follow our ego, thinking it is who we are and allow it to control our behavior. Our attachment to our preconceived notions persuades our ego to work toward coercing others to comply with our expected outcomes. We expend too much of our energy rejecting the present when it does not conform to these attachments. Even more energy is required when we continue to attempt to force things in the direction of ego. We condition ourselves when our ego-driven state of fearful discontent is periodically punctuated with fleeting instances of joy brought by things of the world. A predisposition develops to keep repeating the same behavior.

Young children do not feel any limitation in their abilities. Children have had limited exposure to years of training and habituation and consequently may feel a closer connection to Spirit. They may innately realize that they are a piece of God; after all, the Spirit of God is within them, as it is in everyone. The mind of a child, at this point, has not yet been "conditioned" to believe that because we are partnered with our physical body, the observer within us is not who we are. Our children make statements that suggest that they feel anything is possible. Too often in our concern, we respond in an effort to protect them from future disappointment by convincing them that their dreams are outside the realm of possibility. By so doing we may assist in curbing their dreams and in severing their innate ties to Spirit, the Observer within them. This may help convince the impressionable child that he or she is alone. Further feelings of separation may develop.

Ego drives our feverishly paced workaday world. The relaxed state of the connectedness felt by a child appears impossible for us to achieve. It does not have to be this way. Wayne Dyer tells us in his essay on this verse that "you attract the cooperative power of the Tao when you release the need to control your life" (268). We are able to return to that connected state, by realizing that who we are is the Spirit within us. Truly believing that we are a part of God ignites a spark at our center. The resulting connection to the Tao enhances the possibility of experiencing what we genuinely *feel* within us as the direction we need to take to live a connected and fulfilled life. Trust in the Tao acts as a powerful agent that offers both protection and guidance in our life.

We Attempt
to Persuade Others
to Help Us
Confirm and Establish
Our Attachments.

Silently Connect
to the Tao
Knowing
That Its Peace
Will Release Our Attachments
and Fill Us with Love.

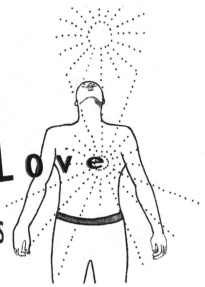

Figure 56: Connect to the Love

Feeling Peaceful Awareness

56

As stated by Wayne Dyer, verse 56 begins with words that make it "the best-known verse of the Tao-Te-Ching" (Dyer 2007, 271). These words are:

> Those who know do not talk. Those who talk do
> not know. (270)

What motivates people who tend to expound their point of view by going on and on? Dyer points out that it is "almost always tied to an attachment" (271).

In our seemingly endless yearning for this or that appealing attachment we like to build purposeful connections with people of power and success. Part of this involves our showy displays of knowledge while in their presence. Because of our attachments we also use our collection of masterful ways to control circumstances with the use of clever verbal communication or whatever our preferred control tactic. Some of us also like to embellish our ego through a performance of our often only self-perceived superior knowledge. The temptation to lecture others about truth as we see it is seen by ego as an opportunity not to be missed.

Lao-tzu infers that all the exploits and maneuvers we employ to control and manipulate others are stilled by the "primal union or the secret embrace" (270), which is our connection to the Tao. Dyer suggests that "living in silent knowing" (Dyer 2007), reveals that all the games we play in our lives are unimportant and actually insignificant to our real purpose. He also tells us that the approval of others becomes less and less important to us. Lao-tzu informs us that knowing about connecting to the Tao "is far beyond the cares of men yet comes to hold the dearest place in their hearts" (270). When we connect to the Tao, we develop a peaceful awareness that allows us to live in synchronicity with the Universe.

The awareness of the part of the Tao within us transforms into a feeling of good that emanates from our heart. This feeling emits precisely that which we know in our hearts to be worthy, admirable, and true. Living with love exuding from our heart attracts more of the same to us.

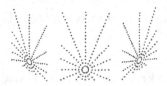

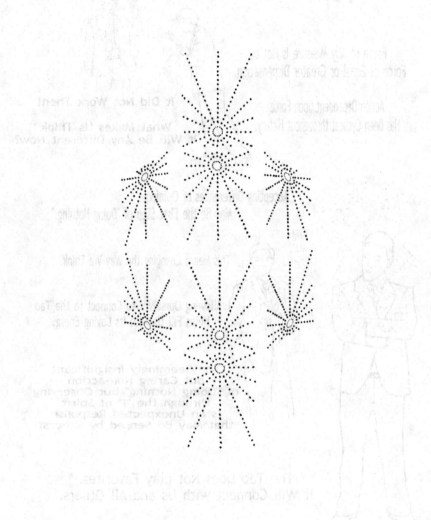

In Almost Every Situation, Force is Not the Answer.

Force of Any Measure Is Met by Force of Equal or Greater Dispensation.

Action Dependent upon Force Has Been Cyclical throughout History.

It Did Not Work Then!

What Makes Us Think It Will Be Any Different Now?

Accepting Differences of Opinion May Be the First Step of "Doing Nothing."

This Means Changing the Way We Think.

Allowing Ourselves to Connect to the Tao Helps Fill Us with Its Loving Energy.

The Seemingly Insignificant but Caring Non-action of "Doing Nothing" but Observing through the "I" of Spirit Is an Unexpected Response that May Be Sensed by Others.

The Tao Does Not play Favorites. It Will Connect with Us and All Others.

Figure 57: Observing through the "I" of Spirit

Feel the Change— the Rest Will Happen

57

In verse 57 Lao-tzu talks about the importance of the statement "stop trying to control." He concludes the verse with, "if I keep from imposing on people, they become themselves" (Dyer 2007, 274). One main purpose of the ego appears to be to control others. Why are we not able to be more accepting? Are we able to change? Where might real change in any of us, and all of us, originate? What does it take to change? Not everybody, in any society, is convinced by words, rewards, actions, rules, the laws we encounter day by day, or even by incarceration.

Typically, the actions of humankind in most places on the planet demonstrate the varying but often very limited success that these types of attempts have had in controlling human behavior. Households, communities, religious organizations, educational institutions, and, paradoxically, even regional and national law enforcement agencies have not found a common means, method, or mode that serves as a universal language that effectively communicates the inner goodness needed within each individual to form a society not reliant on the external control of behavior. Whatever the approach, it needs to promote cooperation and understanding for the betterment of society and our world.

Phrases such as the "war on terror" or the "war on drugs" create a mindset opposed to cooperation. Force and violence in almost any form have been used since the beginning of time as a means to gain and an attempt to maintain control of individuals as well as groups. Temporarily enforced compliance is all that has ever been accomplished using power and might; yet most all sectors of society continue to endorse its use when *they* deem circumstances warrant action. Why? If behavior classified as inappropriate by a particular society's beliefs and values is not held in check, our conditioned brains appear to be oriented toward exercising control. Deviating from this mindset is usually not even considered by the majority. To many, retributive justice is expected because it is thought to be the *right* thing to do. This type of thinking leads us to *believe* that it is the most appropriate response. Actions growing out of fear continue to get the same undesired result. Taking negative steps to control others promotes the return of an even more negative reaction.

People can be forced to comply, and only continued coercion keeps conduct controlled. Each cultural group places demands on its own people as well as others, according to strict standards usually influenced by custom and tradition. Cultural ties run deep. People's thinking patterns regarding what type of behavior is deemed appropriate are usually established quite early in life. Change requires a very real and major shift.

We need to expunge our fear-based thinking that clings to force as the most effective way to effect change and supplant it with the radical idea of doing "nothing," as suggested by Lao-tzu. We are almost constantly in thought. It is something we seemingly cannot stop. We tend to dwell on the things we do not want, but by doing this we help to bring what we do not want into our lives. These things, after all, are constantly in our thoughts and feelings. The practice of clearing our thoughts regularly, each time we are aware of fear-based thinking, moves us in the direction of the power of God's Love.

Wayne Dyer comments that the main thrust of verse 57 is "to *allow* rather than *interfere*" (275). The first step in changing, really changing, is to revamp our thinking by coming to the understanding that who we actually are is not our ego; it is Spirit; it is that within us that allows us to observe or witness our own thoughts, actions, and behavior. Our determination to control behavior and the need to see consequences for inappropriate behavior is fuelled by ego. Conversely, when our feelings grow out of a caring attitude, and our will receives guidance from the silent observer of all our actions, our Spirit, we do not feel the obligation to control. From a place deep within our heart, the Love that is Spirit grows and emanates into our world. How can we keep returning to this place of peace and live our lives as an example—although imperfect—of living from our Center, the part of the Tao that we are?

As we participate in life, we continue to experience life's vicissitudes, along with the corresponding emotions. Accepting situations, both good and bad, allows us to feel the matching emotion in its fullness. In the instance of negative or undesired emotions, accepting them and allowing ourselves to thoroughly experience the feeling allows the feeling to pass because we are not resisting it and thereby feeding it, keeping it alive, and even allowing it to grow. Realizing that we are a piece of the Tao, the Energy of Love, reminds us that we have nothing to fear in the first place. Our conscious awareness, in harmony with the Spirit that we are, truly represents the change that we seek within ourselves. Is this realization possibly the universal language that connects us to our inner goodness? Will practicing awareness gradually realign our attitudes with the thoughts of God?

As more and more people consciously perceive and observe this feeling of acceptance, the change the world needs will begin. When increasing numbers of us present this shift in thinking to our children, consciousness will grow and grow, causing the changes we feel to seek form in a renewed and truly God-centered way of life. One might apply the above scenario as a possible interpretation of the words of Lao-tzu near the end of verse 57, where he tells us what a sage would say: "I take no action and people are reformed."

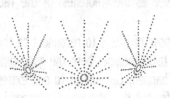

The Wholeness Of Our Life

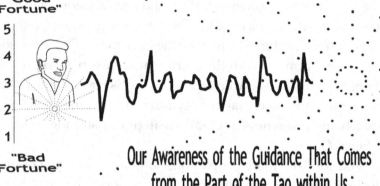

"Good Fortune"

5
4
3
2
1

"Bad Fortune"

Our Awareness of the Guidance That Comes
from the Part of the Tao within Us
Can Be Used as a Directive for the Choices We Make.

Lao-tzu's view of our journey in life
paints a picture showing both good and bad fortune
as a part of the wholeness that makes up our lives,
as well as the wholeness of the Tao.

The purpose of life is to reconnect to the Tao.
The path our life takes includes both the good times and the bad.
Unforeseen events happen, carrying us to one extreme or the other.
It is all part of life, but it is the way we respond to these events
that determines the next shift in our path.

Figure 58: The Wholeness of "Good and Bad Fortune"

Accept the Wholeness of Life

58

In verse 58 Lao-tzu describes the good and bad times of life as each having both good and bad states constantly present with one or the other dominant, while the opposite one prepares to emerge (Dyer 2007, 278). Wayne Dyer sees this verse as describing "another way to see the world" so we are "untroubled by good or bad fortune" (279). He describes the "good" as being "the other half" of "bad" fortune, and together they produce wholeness.

What guides the wholeness of our lives? Do we allow ourselves to believe that we receive guidance from the wholeness within us, which is part of the Tao? In our humanness, we are convinced that we are ego; consequently, we usually do not recognize the guiding light when it is offered. Could the choices we make play a key role in the part of wholeness that comes to the fore in our lives? Pure wholeness, which is exemplified only by people like Jesus, would keep our lives in perfect balance, meaning our lives would be neither "good" nor "bad." Life would run on an even keel and would function on the *straight and narrow* path toward the wholeness of the Tao. But the reality is that our humanity experiences major emotional U-turns, and when we feel we cannot accept them, we make choices meant to change our direction. It is our level of awareness that keeps shifting our path by opening or closing our perception of inner guidance, causing our life journey to weave and, figuratively speaking, cross over the *straight and narrow* regularly. These self-made adjustments, or what sometimes appear as impromptu fluctuations, keep us shifting our path back and forth over a place of balance, thereby opening us to the experience of varying allocations of the "good" and "bad" aspects of life. Our present moment choices keep redirecting the trajectory of the journey our life takes. There is no singularly correct path; all paths lead home. Some just take longer.

In the conclusion of verse 58, Lao-tzu describes how to "serve as an example" (Dyer 2007, 278), and in Dyer's words, to be an example is to "be pointed, straight, and illuminating without piercing, disrupting, or dazzling" (280). We can help ourselves to be an example to ourselves and others if we allow our keen awareness of the Tao's guiding light to direct our path, by recognizing and responding to signs that prompt us to change our course.

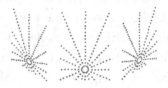

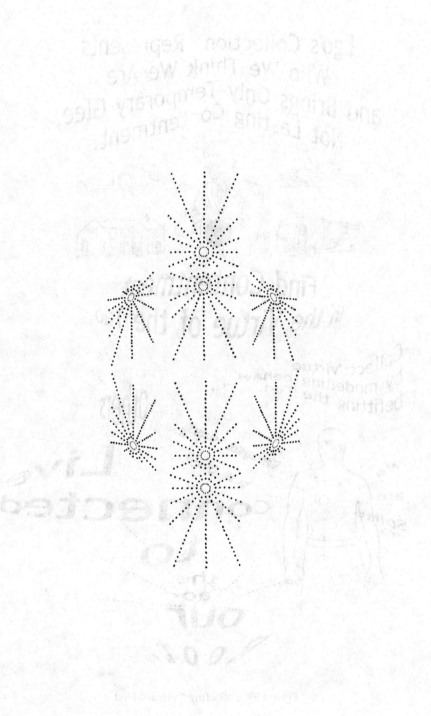

Ego's Collection Represents
Who We Think We Are
and Brings Only Temporary Glee,
Not Lasting Contentment.

Find Contentment
in the Virtue of the Tao

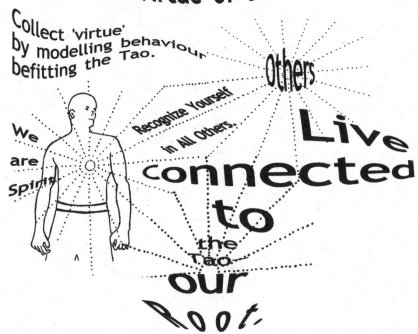

Collect 'virtue'
by modelling behaviour
befitting the Tao.

Others

Recognize Yourself
in All Others.

We
are
Spirit

Live

connected
to
the
Tao

our
Root

Figure 59: Collecting "Virtue" First

Focus on Thoughts of Virtue

59

Lao-tzu opens verse 59 with the idea of living our lives with "restraint" while filling ourselves with "virtue" (Dyer 2007, 282). Wayne Dyer elaborates on a life lived without "practicing conspicuous consumption" and the role it plays in gathering "virtue" (284). If we place the emphasis of our lives on the prestige, power, and things that our ego prizes as goals to achieve and objects to accumulate, the collection we end up with is comprised of a quickly deteriorating, superficial, and ultimately meaningless representation of who we think we are. On the other hand, as mentioned by Dyer in his essay on this verse, if we anonymously give of ourselves and our accrual of things material to others, whether our collection is large or small, we will begin to "gather virtue points" within our being. Collecting things, power, and prestige does not bring virtue. Instead, the greed and false pride these things encourage camouflage the virtue that exists within us.

Could virtue and happiness be related? Our actions, good or bad, greedy or generous, wasteful or thrifty will most likely affect and influence other people. Hidden within our actions exists a plea for happiness. We think happiness is linked to attaining wants, but real happiness changes according to the stability of our personal footing. What do we use as our anchoring root? Internal joy is not dependent upon anything or anybody. Although money is able to provide a certain level of freedom, too much attention given to things and worldly wants leads our thoughts in a direction that creates limits, by restricting our intention to a focus primarily on physical wants and desires.

Our intentions develop from our thoughts. When our thoughts are consistent with who we really are, pure consciousness, the virtue in us that ongoing and right-thinking represents, allows us to rejoin the ever-expanding light of our Source, while the intention that we feel within us follows in harmony with the Universe and influences the direction of our life experience.

As Lao-tzu states at the end of verse 59, virtue accompanies a life that is "deeply rooted and firmly planted in the Tao." He also says that with virtue "nothing is impossible" (Dyer 2007, 282). Being virtuous brings the joy of Spirit into our lives.

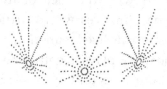

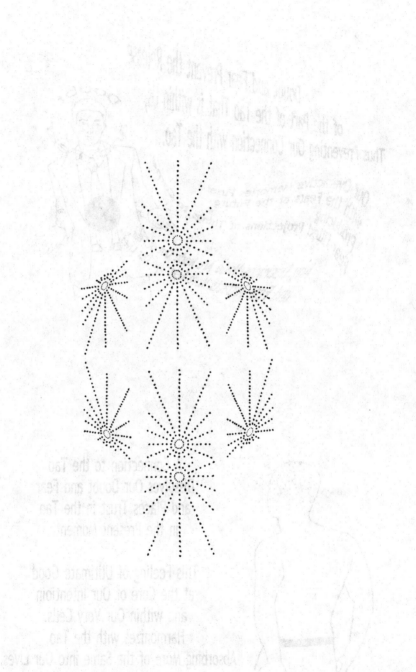

Doubt and Fear Prevent the Release of the Part of the Tao That is within Us, Thus Preventing Our Connection with the Tao.

Our Overactive Memories Fuse with the Fears of the Future producing Fear-filled Projections of Things to come

Any Decisions Made Are Made Out of Fear, and Fear Attracts More Fear into Our Lives.

Doubt and Fear

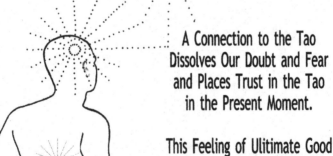

A Connection to the Tao
Dissolves Our Doubt and Fear
and Places Trust in the Tao
in the Present Moment.

This Feeling of Ulitimate Good
at the Core of Our Intentioin
and within Our Very Cells,
Harmonizes with the Tao,
Absorbing More of the Same into Our Lives.

Figure 60: At the Core of Our Intention

When More People
Begin to Trust the Tao ...

60

In verse 60 Lao-tzu clearly expresses that a connection to the Tao offers protection (Dyer 2007, 286). Wayne Dyer adds in his accompanying essay that the Tao "gives sustaining energy to everyone, without exception" (287). Lao-tzu also refers to interference in our own lives and the lives of others by using the cooking analogy of spoiling a small fish with too much "poking" (286). This suggests the idea of needing to trust in the Tao without intrusion. One way to live and evince trust is to be intimately conscious of the here and now while applying the lessons of the past, thereby experiencing the fullness of the present moment. To avoid too much "poking" only offer input if the situation warrants intervention because of valid safety concerns, or if deemed necessary, but only if an opinion is requested.

The only opportunity we have to engage with our own composite of reality is right now. When our thoughts stray from the exclusive moment we have, the moment that is life, doubt, and fear intricately entwine and fuse with our overactive memories of the past and our concerns about the future. The confused judgments emerging from these commingling thoughts are then meticulously projected by our anxious minds into an anticipated and often disquieting picture of our future. The probing and prodding of each moment of the present by the insidious prongs of doubt and fear confounds our perception of our present circumstances in life with unreal trials and suffering.

To truly trust in the Tao to protect others as well as ourselves requires conscious awareness of the present moment. A genuine understanding of the motivation behind the actions of others is required to make appropriate, clear, and firm responses that upon necessity may involve protective measures but not retaliatory maneuvers. This way the aggressive behavior of individuals as well as of groups or countries will more likely be lessened or perhaps even stopped over an extended period.

Focusing our attention on the present connects us to the Tao and helps divert and often subdue our seemingly indefatigable doubts and fears. Allow and accept the present as it is. This provides the mind-space we need to welcome as well as feel the ultimate good that needs to be held at the core of our overall intention. It is then that we are aware of our connection to the Tao and experience the consciousness of which we are a part. The key to all this is *acceptance of what is*. As soon as we deny what is, our thoughts become cloudy and congested, and we are consequently unable to recognize, welcome, or receive what is available here and now.

Dyer expands on Lao-tzu's comments in the last part of verse 60 with the following: "[Hurtful] behavior [can] be rendered impotent if enough people [are] willing to live in ways that encourage cooperation and a spirit of love in place of competition and revenge" (Dyer 2007, 288).

Clearly focusing on the present brings perspicuity to the moment and allows us to sense within our cells the goodness carried by our intention. According to Lao-tzu, as clarified by Dr. Dyer, if we trust our Source as described above, our mental energy that is focused on "receiving only Divine love" serves to protect us (289). This is true for all who choose to trust in the goodness of the Tao.

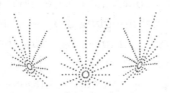

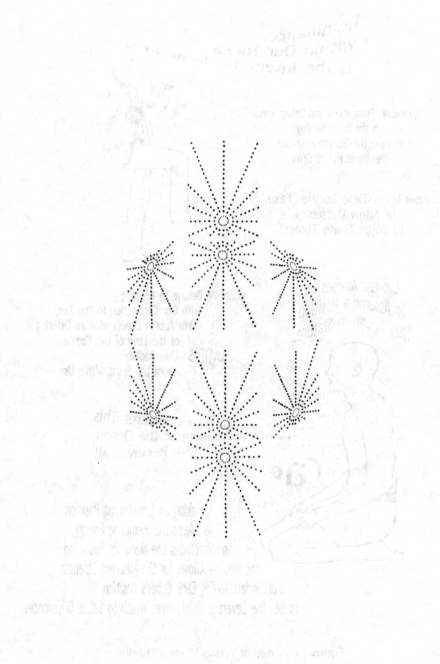

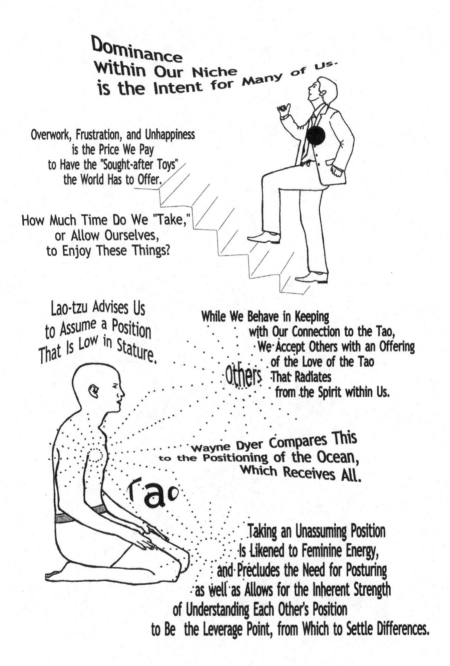

Dominance Within Our Niche is the Intent for Many of Us.

Overwork, Frustration, and Unhappiness is the Price We Pay to Have the "Sought-after Toys" the World Has to Offer.

How Much Time Do We "Take," or Allow Ourselves, to Enjoy These Things?

Lao-tzu Advises Us to Assume a Position That Is Low in Stature.

While We Behave in Keeping with Our Connection to the Tao, We Accept Others with an Offering of the Love of the Tao That Radiates from the Spirit within Us.

Others

Tao

Wayne Dyer Compares This to the Positioning of the Ocean, Which Receives All.

Taking an Unassuming Position Is Likened to Feminine Energy, and Precludes the Need for Posturing as well as Allows for the Inherent Strength of Understanding Each Other's Position to Be the Leverage Point, from Which to Settle Differences.

Figure 61: Arrogant Versus Modest Thinking

Trust
from an Unassuming Position

61

In verse 61 Lao-tzu talks about a country stooping and remaining low, so "it is the reservoir of all under heaven, the feminine of the world" (Dyer 2007, 290). Wayne Dyer points out that "countries are made up of individual men and women," and that as a country, "we need to become a critical mass of individuals," who live the "wisdom" of the Tao (292). As indicated in the opening of Wayne Dyer's essay on verse 61, many, many people have learned to strive to be the best and to have the most. We have learned to push, pull, prod, and manipulate. Too frequently, our ego's domineering behavior and lofty posturing easily overshadows any desire for peace and trust that may exist in us. Ego has the need to dominate all aspects of our lives and often the lives of express individuals and groups. It especially focuses on creating the persona we wish to present to others, which at times may differ profoundly from how we really perceive ourselves. The manipulative maneuvering of the ego too frequently leads us down a path of frustration and despair. For all our trying, we regularly fail. For the times we do succeed, the tendency is to take the credit personally. Doing this places pride between continued success and us. Pride, of this sort, only invites harm.

How can we bring our human failings into balance? Lao-tzu suggests that we lower ourselves rather than feign greatness. The pure and meaningful acceptance that we all are part of the same Source serves as our personal entry point to the humble and unpretentious position that Lao-tzu suggests for us. This leads to a consciousness that connects to and emanates truth, understanding, and compassion. The loving Energy that this represents exists in all that is, and when we *know and believe this*, we are able to receive Love in a variety of forms all around us. Conscious awareness allows us to assimilate this singularly important Truth. Now we are able, in all modesty, to reach out and offer Love to all we meet. The feeling of wholeness that we experience by recognizing and accepting this reality guides us in a direction of balance and trust. When we position ourselves in an unassuming role, we all share part of this infinite strength, vitality, and never-ending presence, which is our Source. This ongoing presence allows for change, and it is the feelings we have come to know within the core arena of our trust that give direction to this change.

However, too often, whether we are male or female, we direct our trust into what is often termed as a testosterone-driven, "forceful-fist" path. Those who receive our bullish and too often hateful and injurious conduct often magnify the behavior when they direct it back at us. This often causes ongoing feelings of contempt on both sides for the people deemed responsible, and frequently leads to a concatenation of disputes that seem to have no end.

We must identify the things that we need to change and do differently—things that are not perceived by the ego as appropriate but in their absence of control attract improvement into our circumstances and the circumstances of others. Clearly focusing on these changes is the next obvious step. While we offer the Love in us that is a part of God, to all involved in any of the roles that we play, it is our responsibility to keep the multidirectional pushes and pulls of life balanced. This will help to keep the conduit connecting us to our Source open.

Trust adds what could be seen as a truly powerful feminine energy and direction to life that has typically been perceived and represented as both weak and ineffective. Contrary to this long-established way of thinking that continues to this day, trust is an energetic force unto itself and stands immune to any form of categorization. Put very simply, it involves being absolutely aware of who we are. The beauty of this consciousness lies in the freedom it allows. It releases us from the need for grandiose posturing in an attempt to validate our strength. With this release, it gives us permission to take an unassuming position that initially may appear unguarded. We realize and present our true strength when we accept things the way they are and genuinely feel the things we want before they arrive, through the part we play, and the part we are in our seemingly insignificant and yet vitally momentous lives.

Close to the conclusion of Wayne Dyer's essay on this verse, he says that "as [we] see [ourselves] as that low, patient ocean, [all] those who wish to tower above [us] in conquest will ultimately flow down to [us]" (Dyer 2007, 293).

The attitude and general feeling we bring to the table of life determines the menu served as well as the possibility of dished and delicious dessert. All is good, as it is meant to be, and is in keeping with the always watchful Oneness of the Tao.

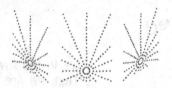

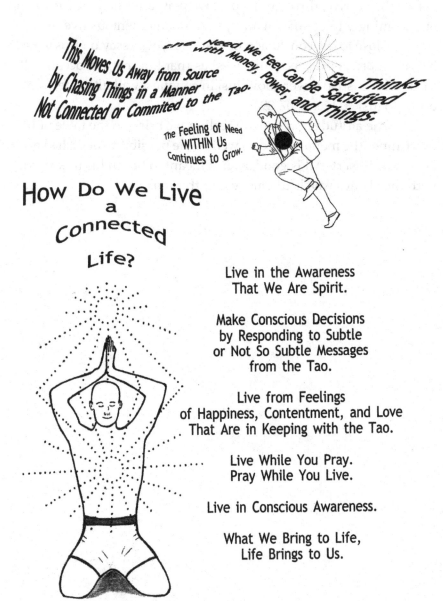

This Moves Us Away from Source by Chasing Things in a Manner Not Connected or Commited to the Tao.

...the Need We Feel Can Be Satisfied with Money, Power, and Things,

Ego Thinks

The Feeling of Need
WITHIN Us
Continues to Grow.

How Do We Live a Connected Life?

Live in the Awareness
That We Are Spirit.

Make Conscious Decisions
by Responding to Subtle
or Not So Subtle Messages
from the Tao.

Live from Feelings
of Happiness, Contentment, and Love
That Are in Keeping with the Tao.

Live While You Pray.
Pray While You Live.

Live in Conscious Awareness.

What We Bring to Life,
Life Brings to Us.

Figure 62: Praying While We Live

Accept the Gift
and Offer It to Others

62

Lao-tzu opens verse 62 by saying that "the Tao is the treasure-house" and "the secret Source of everything" (Dyer 2007, 294). Wayne Dyer opens his essay by asking us to "imagine" a locale where we can "commune with the sacred Source of everything" (295). Where is this place?

Whether we have a street address, live on the street, or own it, we remain in a state of yearning that probably waxes more frequently than it wanes. Our varying vulnerabilities and changing personal and financial circumstances set the stage for a great many things and situations that pose as being our answer that may lead to filling the void within. The company we keep, the institutions we support, the power we hold, the knowledge we have, the things we collect, and the money we enjoy can provide strength, comfort, and support for a time, but these things cannot purge the undertone of emptiness, the ache of separation felt especially at our Center. In his essay, Dyer explains this type of behavior as energy moving away from its Source. All these things serve as a transient pacifier only, because their pursuit is not Tao-centered.

The truth of what we pursue to fill this void remains indefinable, intangible, and ever-elusive. We need to be fully conscious that what we really seek is all-encompassing and everlasting.

Anything so vital, so precious, and so sought after must surely be concealed in a very special and most secure treasury. However, where do we go to find the "treasure house" of which Lao-tzu speaks? The answer is *anywhere* and *everywhere*; yes, it is everywhere. On numerous occasions, Dyer has stated that there is nowhere it cannot be. Moreover, accessing it is as simple as accepting it as our reality. What could possibly be everywhere at the same time? Why is it nigh to impossible for us to find this treasury? Could it be because recognition of this elusive Stillness in everyone happens only after we are *aware* of the intangible and long-sought-after treasury within our own being? If what we seek is everywhere, we need to accept that we are not separate; we are part of this all-encompassing Presence.

But we tend to consider ourselves as separate, set apart from all others, and as a consequence we don't recognize that those same others could claim their part of the same Oneness of the Tao that we share and not affect our unlimited dispensation one iota.

In addition, when our awareness of the Presence in this treasury within joins to become one with our genuine feelings of love and caring, it yields the pure potential that we are, and we begin the journey of connection.

How do we direct this potentiality, held so vibrantly in every cell of our body, when it is denied so vigorously by our ego? The ego is the "I" we are convinced we are. Our ego steadily and undauntedly tries to reassure us, often forcefully, that it is our only reality.

However, ego is not our answer; what we are seeking is awareness, a consciousness that who we really are is Spirit. Being consciously aware of the Spirit that we are can fill our void. To be convincing in its role, ego needs to feel in control, but real control rests with our everyday, ongoing thoughts. Planning now, by using the past as a guide, for a future that is in keeping with the Tao is a well-grounded application of thought. Worrying about past or future events is fear-based, wasteful, and not of the Tao. Thinking about what we do not want stems from fear. Enjoy interaction with the happenings of the present, whether it is passive or active. Quite simply, right now is all there is. Thoughts that we keep thinking are after a time accepted by us as our version of truth. The conclusions stored in these truths produce feelings that consummate at our core. These feelings prove to be either a powerful ally or an agonizing burden, depending upon their veracity, or lack thereof.

It is in our best interest to truly feel the Tao-centered experience we aspire to before the event actually occurs. It is also prudent not to dwell on what we do not want. Heartfelt emotions, no matter the content, will produce a sensation within our Center. This tends to affect every cell in our body. The Universe responds to whatever our persistent emotion happens to be. To have this knowledge is a gift, a gift to be shared with all. Awareness of this all-important understanding allows our consciousness to lead the way. Consciously we need to choose to live our lives in the present. Conscious decision-making allows us to be more receptive to the subtle guidance of the Tao. We need to be mindful of all we have and appreciate it. Remaining thankful makes it easier to maintain an outlook that brings about the feelings associated with what we desire. Living consciously is comparable to living what we pray. The way we live is what we become.

Thinking that is generated by Love allows our light to shine. Perhaps it might be thought of as a "bubble of energy" being released around us, a living radiance, that attracts the nourishing and creative energy of the Tao. Since we do not really understand how the Tao, or God, really functions, a simple visualization may be helpful as a way to imagine a connection to Spirit. How things really happen within the reality of the consciousness of the Tao is probably beyond our understanding, but it is our grasp and appreciation of the concept, regardless of how it works, that allows us to connect to Spirit. The bottom line is that Spirit moves at making our feelings a reality, even if to our way of thinking it is ever so slowly.

To be aware of the relationship between the "treasure house" within us (who we really are) and our heartfelt feelings is a gift more valuable than any earthly treasure can provide. Living in harmony with our Spirit within our "treasure house" brings awareness to our being. The consciousness, in which we live each moment, provides us with the assurance that the knowledge and practice of this gift of awareness is the gift we need to give to all who will listen.

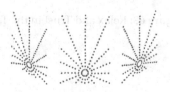

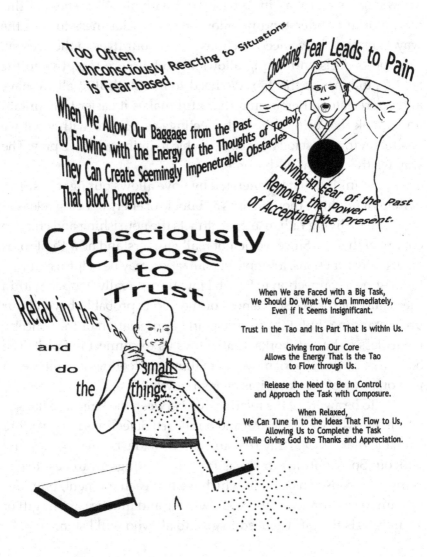

Too Often, Unconsciously Reacting to Situations is Fear-based.

Choosing Fear Leads to Pain

When We Allow Our Baggage from the Past to Entwine with the Energy of the Thoughts of Today, They Can Create Seemingly Impenetrable Obstacles That Block Progress.

Living in Fear of the Past Removes the Power of Accepting the Present.

Consciously Choose to Trust

Relax in the Tao and do the small things.

When We are Faced with a Big Task, We Should Do What We Can Immediately, Even if It Seems Insignificant.

Trust in the Tao and Its Part That Is within Us.

Giving from Our Core Allows the Energy That Is the Tao to Flow through Us.

Release the Need to Be in Control and Approach the Task with Composure.

When Relaxed, We Can Tune in to the Ideas That Flow to Us, Allowing Us to Complete the Task While Giving God the Thanks and Appreciation.

Figure 63: Relax and Trust in the Tao

Trust More—Fret Less

63

Lao-tzu asks us to "see simplicity in the complicated," in verse 63. He concludes the verse with, "the sage always confronts difficulties, he never experiences them" (Dyer 2007, 298).

When life presents its challenges, each wearing its unique coat of seemingly impenetrable armor, either we can feel held hostage, unable to respond appropriately, or we can simply trust. When we live our lives believing from one moment to the next that we are in the place in our lives where our previous thoughts have directed the Universe to lead us, we live a conscious life of trust. No matter the situation, we should attempt to avoid choosing fear over Love, which inevitably leads to pain. The universe grows in the direction of our thoughts and focuses on what is good when Love is the choice that we make and goodness is at our center.

We need to release the baggage amassed from earlier incidents in our lives. It entwines the energy of our thoughts into often-undetectable obstacles within that prevent us from moving forward with the purpose of our lives.

We must first allow ourselves to be flushed free from our past and brought fully into the present. The assumption that what happened in the past remains in the past, forgotten and discarded, can be as untrue as the apparent vanishing of the mountains of garbage that we dispose of. The refuse that does not completely decompose in a landfill site continues to exist and may remain as a putrid mass for an extended period or endures inert and intact. In some ways the way we treat our Earth is similar to the way we treat ourselves. The rubbish is comparable to the past unpleasant events of our lives that either dissipate without another thought or remain festering within us only to reappear, revealing an existence potentially more menacing than the original. Placing our trust in the Tao carries us through what could have been a hellish pit of misery, to a place where living one moment at a time helps close the door to the past because we have realized that the present is all there is, ever was, and ever will be. The past only has the power we give it, each time we dwell in it.

The universe will continue in its emergence whether we exercise our trust in it or not. Our repeated and ongoing thoughts evolve into intentions that provide direction for our life, but the true *course* and actual *events* that happen are the domain of the Universe. In hindsight, after examining actual events that occurred, we will find oftentimes that the events were in fact in keeping with our predominant mindset, the things we really believe, despite the words we may have spoken. If we consciously learn from our past, the parameters of acceptance for our own words and behavior will be regularly reset. Either we use the connective force always available to us or we keep *reacting unconsciously* instead of *consciously responding*. A conscious response implies the implementation of thinking that prompts appropriate action *for the purpose of good.* We need to trust the Tao to grow in the direction of our good intentions, instead of reactively fretting about the future, for whatever reason, including fear of repeating the past.

When confronted with an issue, we first need to recognize that to trust in the power of the Universe, we need to trust in ourselves, in common sense and in the lessons of life. To help us do this we need to *give* of the potentially powerful life force within us. We do this by accepting situations as they are while feeling within our core the sincere emotion associated with our Tao-centered desire. Over time, the Universe attracts the development of scenarios that round out our issues and bring each to a new beginning. Giving from our core opens up a space within us that allows for the all-encompassing power of the Tao to move through us and guide us to the next step. Our moment-to-moment job is to commit to heartfelt, conscious, and inspired input until the Universe renders a transient resolution. The outcome may or may not be recognizable as a manifestation of the intention we *thought* we were living; however, it *will* be consistent with the true nature of our lives as made evident by the clarity of our presence. The beauty in the workings of the Universe lies in simplicity. The saying *less is more* is particularly applicable when it comes to allowing the Tao to provide ideas that lead us to the actions we need to take. Our awareness of messages from the Tao becomes more keenly refined when we release the need to control each step we take. When we surrender control to the Tao, our awareness may become more attuned to it, and our personal load may begin to lighten, just as a load lifted by a lever feels lighter. When we place less emphasis on our personal control of things and place more in our trust in the Tao, it appears easier to get things accomplished because we have released our attachment to the outcome.

Feeling less inclined to control contributes to relaxation. An appropriate corollary that might follow this type of thinking could conceivably be the granting of permission to ourselves to endorse a less "clenched" and less intense approach to life. When we relinquish the need for total control and allow composure to be our natural state, we feel ready to relax and trust the Tao.

Wayne Dyer asks us to "change [our] notion of 'thinking big' to 'thinking small and getting big things done'" (Dyer 2007, 301). He encourages us to do what we can right now.

With calm and trusting presence of mind, we can approach the issues of life in full consciousness and take the first step toward a possible resolution. Continued moment-by-moment consciousness will allow for the awareness we need to be more receptive to a notion that otherwise might be overlooked by an unconscious, preoccupied mind. It is our awareness of a notion or idea that may lead us to the next and the next appropriate step. Living this way allows us to do more by doing less, without experiencing difficulties, as Lao-tzu tells us.

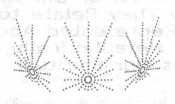

We Are Here to Grow and Learn in the School of Opportunity.

(Our Portal to the Tao)

We Face Directives from Various Sectors of Society through Ego, Often Via Fear and Drama.

Spiritual 'I'

Stage for the Dramatic Performances of Our Ego.

These Instances Often Prove to Be the Lessons of Life That We Need to Learn.

This Continues as We Move through Life.

**Awareness of Our Actions
and How They Relate to the Tao
is Represented Above,
Metaphorically,
as Our Spiritual 'I.'**

Figure 64.1: Our Performances on the Stage of Life

Do Nothing

64

In verse 64 Lao-tzu asks us to "act before things exist; manage them before there is disorder" (Dyer 2007, 302). Wayne Dyer tells us that the essence of this verse rests in the idea that "every goal is possible from here" (303). "From here" might be interpreted as *from where we are in our lives right now.* I would also like to think of it as our *portal* to the Tao. When we position our present circumstances together with the idea of a portal to the Tao, we can see that the Tao can be accessed from anywhere at any time because it is everywhere, including "here." Awareness, intention, and heartfelt communication might be considered part of what is elemental within the connection we need, to open ourselves to the flow of Energy, which is our Universe. I believe it is "from here," our portal, that the process of what Wayne Dyer calls "[breaking] it down into easily managed steps" (303) begins.

When our behavior revolves around resistance and judgment, we cement the certainty of closing our portal to the Energy of the Universe as well as increasing the likelihood of keeping it closed. Resistance and judgment hinder or even stop our spiritual growth.

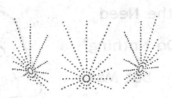

What Might Be Involved in a Personal Reality Intervention, the Makeover Everyone Requires?

We Are Best Served by Our Taking Note
of Our Intention and Our Behavior
and by Making Appropriate Changes or Responses.

Acting as a Witness by Monitoring Our Own Thoughts
That Are Not in Keeping with the Tao
Allows Us to Repeatedly Set Them Right
as We Move through Life, Lesson by Lesson.

In Time Many Lessons Are Learned.

Eventually,

We Feel the Need

to "Do Nothing"

but Make

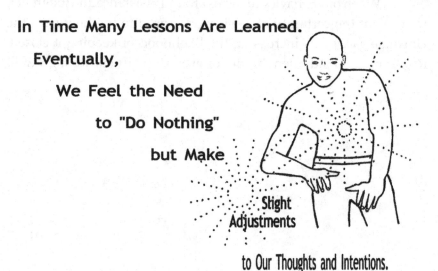

Slight
Adjustments

to Our Thoughts and Intentions.

Figure 64.2: Our Personal Reality Intervention

Our mortal body is only part of who we are, and it's our home while we are here on Earth. We each carry our own unique set of unlearned lessons that are fundamental to our success as we encounter our earthly training in the "School of Opportunity," our portal, the stage on which we get to choose the direction our life will take. I will refer to the lessons we need to learn as the Primer, or basic concepts that require our awareness, so we are able to progress to our next vibrational level. I believe that these lessons will be a part of the "easily managed steps" (Dyer 2007, 303) Dr. Dyer refers to in his essay.

As mentioned in the preface, another reason for using the word primer in the subtitle of this book is the truth held in its use as an acronym that stands for the basic and necessary change we need to make within ourselves—a Personal Reality Intervention (is the) Makeover Everyone Requires—PRIMER. It represents the idea that each person, on an individual level, needs to intervene in his or her own perception of reality by realizing how our learned responses short-circuit our life, and how releasing these preconceived ideas along with our painful memories opens us to the unlimited possibilities of new interpretations of reality. Each lesson has its own unique purpose, but the common thread throughout rests in the reality that these lessons occur in the now and represent the only time we have to make the changes we desire. The journey of our body will end, but the level of our spiritual evolution, the essence that we really are, is eternal. A real understanding of this allows us to begin to restructure our psyche. It also helps us to understand that only we are responsible for the decisions that control our lives, even when appearances suggest otherwise. The fundamental teachings of Lao-tzu in the Tao Te Ching form the primary and underlying structure for what I am calling a Primer.

Although Dr. Dyer refers to three steps to enlightenment in his essay on this verse, my commentary revolves around the last two. The above discussion leads to the second step. The gist of this step includes learning life lessons through "Tao-centered thinking" and "by being in the present moment" (Dyer 2007, 304). Where we are right now in life is our present moment, and conjointly our body, mind, and spirit are enrolled by default into the "School of Opportunity," that conducts continuous "classes" in the everyday-living classroom on the stage of life. An active and effective body, mind, and soul partnership promotes the understanding of these moment by moment life lessons, thus allowing progression lesson by new lesson. This present moment partnership is able to take us beyond what appears as the relational proximity of our mind to our spirit to the recognition of the Oneness of existence and the ultimate empowering of our intuition to represent the energy of our soul as our subtle guide.

This takes us to Dr. Dyer's third step to enlightenment, which is "getting out in front of big problems" (Dyer 2007, 304). How might we be able to do this? Are we to recognize guidance in the words of others, in happenings, in our inklings, or in whatever way we might identify our intuition? For many people, making decisions based on anything other than judicious thought processes would be ludicrous and folly. Nevertheless, we might begin by being consciously aware of our surroundings, our experiences, and particularly our feelings and responses as they exist within our performance on the stage of life. Having the awareness, for example, of some of the motives prompting certain aspects of our behavior may help us begin to realize the need to change some of our thinking. Right thinking facilitates wise decision-making. This process may begin to open us to our innate ability to recognize the flow of the energy of the Universe. This promotes creativity.

The energy of the Tao fills us and envelops us, much as the air we breathe surrounds us. Nature and all that it entails is in tune with this energy. Consider for example the unity demonstrated by a flock of hundreds upon hundreds of starlings, or a school of fish; they move with the synchronistic grace that presents the agility of a single-minded entity. Do we really know how they are able to do this? Is it a form of awareness and trust?

Our awareness might also help us get in front of life's problems. How much of each day do we spend being truly aware of our surroundings, of other people, of the meaning behind the words we speak and the words spoken to us, of the messages sent by our bodies, of the subtle flavors and textures of our food, or even of the physical presence of the driver we cut off in our haste? Our mind, often strained with a flurry of thoughts about work, home, relationships, and so on will regularly intercept what we consider intruding thoughts, further adding to our confusion. We feel increased pressure when we allow time constraints to impose on us, and our awareness of the present often becomes significantly squeezed into an almost nugatory or useless state. When decisions are made with a mind otherwise occupied, there is little likelihood of our being conscious of choices we can make that affect aspects of life that carry good and perhaps far-reaching reverberations for our lives. Therefore, we overlook things coming from the Love in our soul and instead rather respond to the fear in our mind.

Life's experiences interpreted by our thoughts stir up various aspects of fear within us. Lao-tzu tells us that in these circumstances "the sage does not act, and so is not defeated" (Dyer 2007, 302). We need to do nothing except surrender to these fearful thoughts and truly feel them—but not in a "woe-is-me" or an "I-deserve-this" fashion. Doing nothing could mean not acting out with resistance and/or defense. Only when we allow ourselves to experience feelings, rather than resist them, can we accept them. This acceptance is only that—acceptance; it does not necessarily imply that we like, appreciate, or condone what is happening. It could be quite the contrary. With acceptance, the darkness that fills us begins to be replaced by light, and the attributes that are found at the level of our soul, such as beauty, love, truth, and compassion start to unfold from their latent state.

When fear no longer fills us, we are able to realize that what truly completes us is Spirit. This consciousness allows us to demonstrate behavior most in keeping with a response from within and not a reaction driven by ego. It is when we begin to access the virtues held within our Spirit that we begin to recognize the deception our ego has so ruthlessly chiseled into our psyche. Trust in the Tao begins to erode fear's perceived power and slowly starts to crack the emotional and consequently, very, very powerful, constructs of fear that seal all access to the loving expressions of our Soul.

Living a life inspired by the Tao involves allowing our awareness and our thinking to serve us symbiotically. Lao-tzu tells us that the sage "learns not to hold on to ideas" (Dyer 2007, 302). Living consciously includes accepting life as it comes, thereby not allowing fear to permeate our Being. Life guided by decisions made through right thinking empowers us to move through life with growth as a priority. Part of being aware involves *observing* our actions through the spirit, which we are. I will describe it metaphorically as our spiritual "I," which has certain similarities to the "spiritual eye" as clarified by David Hawkins in *The Eye of the I*. He states that "the 'I' of the Self is the Eye of God witnessing the unfolding of Creation as Now" (Hawkins, *The Eye of the I* 2001, 10).

This places us in a position where we are able to analyze our performance using the rubric of the soul that has *love, caring,* and *compassion* among the main dimensions used to measure our performance. The lessons of life slowly educate us into the awareness that dramatic performances of the ego are not the answer. The lesson each experience teaches provides the necessary step to get us ready to live life by expressing the positive attributes of our soul. This truth empowers the promise presented in the systematic mastery of the *Primer* in the "School of Opportunity," by offering many chances to practice "getting in front of big problems" (Dyer 2007, 304). These messages or warnings keep repeating until we recognize them and learn the inherent lesson, allowing us to move to the next level.

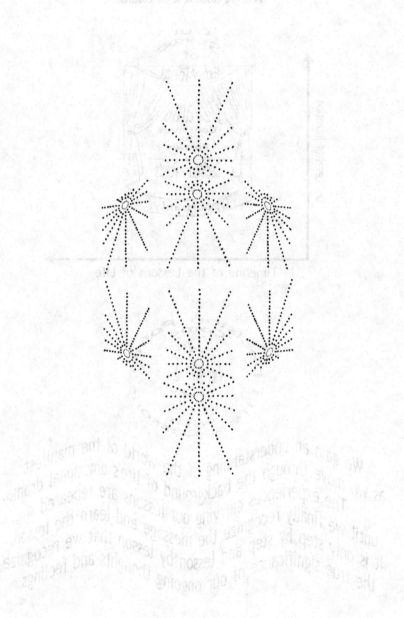

Every Moment Marks an Opportunity

(on Our Ever-changing Personal Stage of Transformational Potential within the Collective of Our Existence.)

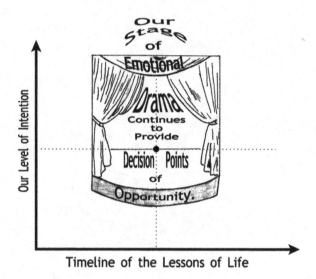

Our Level of Intention

Timeline of the Lessons of Life

We gain an understanding of the world of the manifest as we move through the background of life's emotional drama. The experiences carrying our lessons are repeated until we finally recognize the message and learn the lesson. It is only step by step and lesson by lesson that we recognize the true significance of our ongoing thoughts and feelings.

Figure 65: Our Moments of Opportunity

An Honest and Heartfelt Way of Life

65

According to Lao-tzu, nations are blessed when its leaders don't rule with "cunning" but instead "[blend] with the common people." He goes on to explain that those who "know they do not know . . . can find their own way" (Dyer 2007, 308). Wayne Dyer tells us that the phrase "I don't know" "is a symbol of strength rather than weakness" (310).

In the theater of our life, we allow the rules to be set by ego, and the drama takes place on a stage that we have set. For the most part the production is written, directed, and performed by us. All decisions are ours to make. It is up to us to determine how the roles played by others in our life will affect us. Both acceptance and responding within the goodness of the Tao allow us to move forward, but too much of the time during our performance on stage we feel the need to exercise control through the things we say and do.

A much-used strategy employed by ego is to seek knowledge and to use it to our advantage. Opportunistic maneuvering of knowledge and connections is used to influence others and to acquire money, power, and relationships; it has little or no redeeming value when all we hope for is personal gain. Our attachment to the outcome seems to be all that matters. Our thinking drives this underlying intention. When we don't allow ego to lead the way but instead approach life from our center and acknowledge that we do not know, our intentions are more likely to be heart-centered and focused on caring. In addition, without influence from the ego, our thinking is more apt to be ethical, upstanding, and principled. Thought evokes feelings, and feelings facilitate the flow of Universal Energy of a corresponding frequency. Heartfelt intentions that convey goodness prompt the Tao to be dedicated to responding with goodness.

If we do not resist our fear-based feelings about things present, past, or future and we consciously give ourselves permission to experience the associated pain and discomfort in any part of our body, we can then more easily release the feeling of psychological pain because we have experienced it, and we have survived. Our resistance no longer keeps the pain alive. When we realize that we do not know how we should live but we decide to live from the intention of being and doing good, our feelings and behavior come from the energy center of our heart and soul, and we open ourselves to guidance from the Tao. This allows for and promotes growth and healing.

At their root, our intentions are sustained by the thoughts that we allow ourselves to hold in our consciousness. Our sustained creation of a consummate picture in our mind of the circumstance we wish to manifest allows us to feel the sheer, undiluted emotions that are inherent to the experience.

Organization can be important, but we should not become attached to our step-by-step plans. Relax and release from the outcome. Our intentions, enveloped in and coalesced with the Energy of the Universe create our experiences. Do not assume that ego, through knowledge and manipulation, can successfully plan the events needed to bring fruition to our desires. It may happen but instead we should realize that it is not in anyone's control, including our own. Our ego works from the false assumption that systematic intervention is the only and best way to control outcomes. Learning from the past and making knowledgeable decisions as a result is the path to take when it aligns with the goodness of the Tao. Clinging to our desired outcome by worrying and watching for any indication that may prompt us to intercede leaves us in constant anticipation of failure. Too often, when we think we have the knowledge and personal ability to reach our goals on our own, we fail. Realization that all we can do is prepare the way by taking the right steps releases us from the burden and sets our frame of mind to the level of knowing that the outcome is already here. We then vibrate at the same level as the anticipated outcome. Moreover, we can now feel the emotions that will be experienced when our intentions are realized. Accepting that on our own we do not know what to do allows us to be tuned in and aware, so the all-encompassing Energy of our Universe, the Tao, can help guide our decisions.

We must also realize that during this time the Tao continues to take its cues from our innermost feelings and intentions that originate in our seemingly never-ending thoughts. This happens with or without our awareness. Everything is energy and energy is everything. Our body's energy system responds immediately with each change of focus in our awareness. If we rely solely on our knowledge to solve problems, plan our lives, and so on, *and* in addition we fret about the uncertainty of our plan of action to deliver the outcome to which we have become attached, our stressful thoughts will reflect our anxiety-ridden nature and override our wishes. The predominant feelings that germinate in the fertile medium of our awareness communicate with the Universe and through this interconnection attract the things we spend much of our time thinking about, including what we do not want.

We should feel good about the knowledge we have acquired. We also need to feel good about applying this knowledge in heartfelt, honest, and meaningful ways. However, following this we need to relax. We are energy; the Universe is energy; we are part of the Universe. Stay relaxed and trust; the Universe knows; therefore, we know. The answer lies in the Energy of the Universe, the Tao, which is available to us. When we have conditioned our thoughts to focus on the present while maintaining wholesome intentions, feelings spring up in our awareness, bloom, extend their radiant consciousness into the Universe, and attract corresponding circumstances into our lives.

The universe responds to whatever is at the hub of our intentions, and the feelings within the nucleus of our resolve extend into the periphery of our decision-making, thus attracting the essence of our thoughts into our lives. Awareness of the connection between our intentions and our lives provides direction to our choices. Our continuing consciousness of the intention that fuels our feelings and emotions allows us first to recognize and then to accept responsibility for our choices as well as choose the new direction that the intention powering our choices may need to take. Opportunity always rests with our choice, and choice is, always was, and will remain ours.

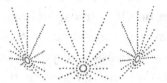

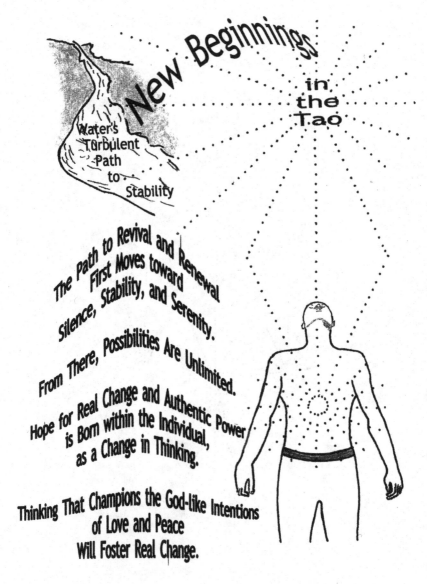

New Beginnings in the Tao

Water's Turbulent Path to Stability

The Path to Revival and Renewal
First Moves toward
Silence, Stability, and Serenity.

From There, Possibilities Are Unlimited.

Hope for Real Change and Authentic Power
is Born within the Individual,
as a Change in Thinking.

Thinking That Champions the God-like Intentions
of Love and Peace
Will Foster Real Change.

Figure 66: New Thoughts—New Beginnings

Authentic Power

66

Lao-tzu describes the sea as "king of a hundred streams" because of its humble position "below them." He tells us that the sage remains "low so the world never tires of exalting him" (Dyer 2007, 312). Wayne Dyer tells us that "for Lao-tzu, nature's great symbol is water." He goes on to advise that "when [we] emulate that element, [we'll] begin to see that judgment and exclusion have no place in the Tao" (313).

I would like to suggest other nuances as applied to water that might also symbolize aspects of our lives. The laws of the Universe serve as the source of energy that causes water to choose the shortest path to a place of rest. Like water, we too seek a peaceful state and try to do so as quickly as possible; but unlike water, our freedom of choice often lengthens our journey to peace. Comparable to our lives, moving water encounters obstacles and carries remnants of the contact as diversely sized fragments of debris, just as we carry many sorts of memories of the difficult experiences of our lives. This off-scouring carried by the water only begins to be released when the water reaches a more peaceful state. Less turbulent water allows the release of the load it is carrying; and similarly, a peaceful mind is more apt and able to forgive and set free any undesirable and damaging memories.

Water, with the force of universal attraction as its constant and unfaltering driving force, flows until it reaches a position of stability. As it experiences stillness, the turbid evidence of its previously agitated condition begins to abate; and the universal force of gravity dispels the cloudiness that veils its natural clarity.

This stillness can be compared to the serene clarity we might feel when we meditate. Although our humanness usually prevents us from meditating with dedication similar to the nonstop commitment inherent in the universal force of gravity, regular reflection allows us to reach deep within ourselves to a place of connection with our universal Source. It is often only here, in this place of calm, where we make the realization that the baggage of life that we carry does not reflect who we are. We experience a feeling of unburdened contentment as we release our woes.

Water flows in its search for balance. We too are in search of balance. Even while gravity is engaging water to seek a nethermost position, the water is exposed to our sun's reenergizing rays. This, combined with other contributory conditions, hastens the renewal of water's vitally important and life-sustaining role. Absorbing solar energy rekindles and animates its primacy as both an instrument in and a source of the life-sustaining support that is essential in the progression and advancement of all living things. We too must seek a place of silent tranquility and renewal to reestablish who we are in spirit by connecting with our Universe and confirming that real strength is not found in sham or posturing.

Authentic power only comes from change that originates from our level of intention. We can begin to do this by following the idea of Lao-tzu of choosing unpretentious behavior in all we do, which includes assuming a subordinate position. A prerequisite to this is the acceptance of life as it is by releasing our resistance to the things that are. This immediately removes many burdens from our heart. Love and peace need to be our motivating force. As we live our lives, we need to focus on the heartfelt intention of harmoniously reconnecting to the Source of all that is while allowing our minds to flow into the silence of connectivity and Oneness. Regularly giving of ourselves to others from a caring and considerate heart helps intensify our state of peaceful awareness. Making the most of the present by humbly living our intention, right now, connects us to the consciousness that is God. All things are possible through unassuming actions that are based on the Love that is God and done without the intent of publicity. The possibilities surrounding our intentions resonate within certain of the unlimited possibilities available through our boundless Universe. Reality as we know it is the manifestation of the resonance of these possibilities, yielding the synchronistic events that we experience as our lives.

Meeting life through a genuinely self-effacing and gracious demeanor works in congruence with a thankful attitude and an intention of sincere goodness, to reveal and bring to light authentic power that has its source within us

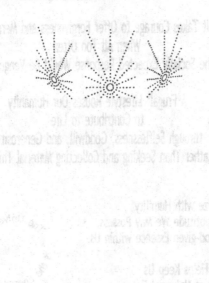

Our Personal Evolution Is Enhanced by Intentions That Model Universal Love.

It Takes Courage to Offer Forgiveness and Mercy,*
When All Too Often
the Socially Expected Response Would Be Vengence.

A Frugal* Lifestyle Rouses Our Humanity
to Contribute to Life
through Selflessness, Goodwill, and Generosity,
Rather Than Seeking and Collecting Material Things.

Recognize with Humility*
Any Personal Apptitude We May Possess,
As Fruit of the God-given Essence within Us.

This Helps Keep Us
in the Flow of Universal Energy,
Which Is the Source
of Any Competence or Mastery
We May Display,
including Leadership.

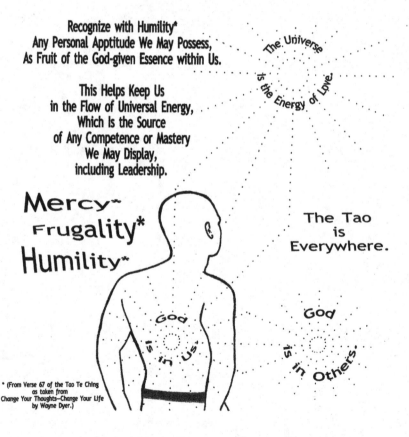

Mercy*
Frugality*
Humility*

The Tao
is
Everywhere.

The Universe
is the Energy of Love.

God
is in Us*

God
is in Others*

* (From Verse 67 of the Tao Te Ching
as taken from
Change Your Thoughts—Change Your Life
by Wayne Dyer.)

Figure 67: Living Our Treasures (Dyer 2007)

The Treasures of Life
According to Lao-tzu

67

In verse 67 Lao-tzu describes the Tao as "not something gained by knowing or lost by forgetting" (Dyer 2007, 316). Our Universe is vibrant, attentive, and responsive. In keeping with the Oneness of our Universe, whatever intentions our actions display come back to us. The Tao is the very essence of Love and exists as the Universe itself. Our Universe does not judge; instead, it continues to mirror varying scenarios of the same lessons we fail to learn, providing opportunity after opportunity for us to progress, as determined by our decisions. Our personal evolution is enhanced by intentions and actions that model and foster a universal love that is deep-rooted and sincere. We cannot escape the ego while living in the world of the manifest, but right thinking is able to direct our actions.

Lao-tzu embraces three very real treasures that help guide our thoughts toward living the Truth in our Universe. These are not riches according to the world of ego, where we are conditioned to live, but these treasures are beneficial, even vital, to the development of personal characteristics that allow us to recognize meaning in life.

What are these priceless treasures that Lao-tzu favors? They are *mercy, frugality,* and *humility,* qualities that are shamefully almost absent in today's power-seeking, materialistic society. Lao-tzu adds that these treasures foster the development of *courage, generosity,* and *leadership* (316). Sadly, too much of the world sees power as the treasure we need to seek. It is often measured by the amount of extra stuff we amass that we do not need and the number of lives under our direction. Too often little or no regard is given to the method we use to rack up these things or how we grab and keep this power. Treating people with *mercy* will result in a significantly different immediate outcome with differing and possibly evolving repercussions than treating people with cruelty.

Cruelty controls, but all the while it instills hatred, complete with what feels like an almost primal need for reprisal writhing beneath the surface, ready to erupt at the slightest opportunity. As with everything we do, we should not forget that retaliation is also a choice we make. The decision to feel the actual agony of unjust treatment and move through the process, painful moment by painful moment, instead of displaying rage, requires the absolute Love of the Tao, our true strength. Having the resolve of spirit to extend forgiveness, *mercy*, and even compassion to those who ruthlessly dominate, spawn suffering, or conspire catastrophe allows us to escape the very overwhelming compulsion to choose to do the same by vowing and seeking revenge. It takes boldness to move against the routinely accepted mores of a society. Offering forgiveness and *mercy* when the socially expected response would be vengeance is much more difficult to set in motion because we are moving against popular thought—and quite likely against the feelings created by our own conditioning. *Courage* is needed to help break the inertia inherent in this ongoing cycle of hate, and Lao-tzu says *courage* is fostered by *mercy* (Dyer 2007, 316). *Mercy* is able to unfold and spread when the acceptance of an offer of forgiveness creates feelings of what may be an unexpected hint of remorse in those answerable.

In our materialistic world, wealth is a major source of power, and our identity becomes entwined with a compelling and oftentimes forceful authority that is dependent upon money and the things it can buy. *Frugality* is seen as weakness. When the money is spent, when possessions are lacking, where is our identity? Furthermore, the comfort we feel in our identity comes to rely on personal possessions as well as the sense of power we get from having authority over others. When we lose positions of control and/or the excesses in our lives, at whatever level in society we function, the crutch we use to prop up our ego gets knocked out from under us; and with it, both our false identity and our flawed comfort level crumble. We need to realize that we have been treating life as a commodity and have been relying on hoarding and exploitation to sustain our identity. This is the first step in understanding that life is about *giving*. Living a *frugal* lifestyle rouses our humanity to contribute and communicate with life instead of greedily laying hold of as much as possible. We deserve the abundance the Universe supplies for us, but our dependence upon more than we need as a substitute for our lack of self-esteem simply leads to a completely insatiable greed. When living a *frugal* lifestyle, we still must tend to matters that are urgent as well as those that are important, but now there is opportunity for selflessness, goodwill, and *generosity* to grow and become a priority, and as Lao-tzu told us, *generosity* is fostered by *frugality*.

Releasing our identity from the grip of dependence upon things and circumstances allows an understanding of who we really are and what really guides us in our decisions toward displaying a *generous* spirit. Too often we become arrogant in our accomplishments, by foregoing *humility* and by expecting and taking full credit for our strengths. Really, our talents are gifts that we received as seeds from the Universe. A particular aptitude has its start as an essence within us that we choose to nurture; and its continued development and maturation in our life depends on our conscious awareness that the inspiration we continue to receive comes from the Universe, not from us. Unfortunately, with our too often ego-controlled attitude, we tend to take advantage of others, including friends, coworkers, and organizations. For this, we may feel little or no culpability or shame. Any form of exploitation or any type of mistreatment of any person, of any life form, or of any earthly resource all result from arrogance and judgment. Preying on others, whether for monetary profit or as a quick way to bolster our ego does not hasten the evolutionary process of our personal growth.

Gratitude should play a major role in our life and *humility* needs to be part of all we do. *Humility* encourages reverence for life and allows us to live in the Energy of Love through kindness, caring and consideration. A life guided by *humility* may elicit hints of appreciation shown by others and may infuse in them the urge, if ever so slightly, to emulate living the intention of Love, thus reducing the habituated need to enact personal defense mechanisms. Our position may now begin to combine *leadership* with *humility,* which Lao-tzu tells us are connected.

In his essay on verse 67 Wayne Dyer tells us "what genuinely successful people have learned before [us]." He states that "we're all instruments for Tao or God or whatever [we] call the energy that writes the books . . . and so on" (Dyer 2007, 319). The energy of Love in the Universe possesses authentic, ongoing power. Being conscious of this awesome power allows us to step free from old, familiar, and entrenched paths of behavior and sets in motion a new way of thinking that is encapsulated by practicing the character traits described by Lao-tzu as treasure (316). The treasures of the world are transient, but the treasures valued by Lao-tzu carry deep and lasting meaning. These precious attributes touch the intention we need to hold within ourselves in our approach to life, so we are able to feel the worth in every person and in all that makes up the whole. To repeat, when our heartfelt intentions are fed by thoughts that revolve around the "three treasures" of Lao-tzu that are *mercy, frugality,* and *humility,* the protection of Love lives and thrives at our center and releases the truth of who we are. This allows us to fill our life with the complementing outcome of living these "three treasures" that Lao-tzu describes as *courage, generosity,* and *leadership.*

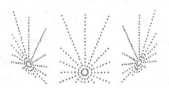

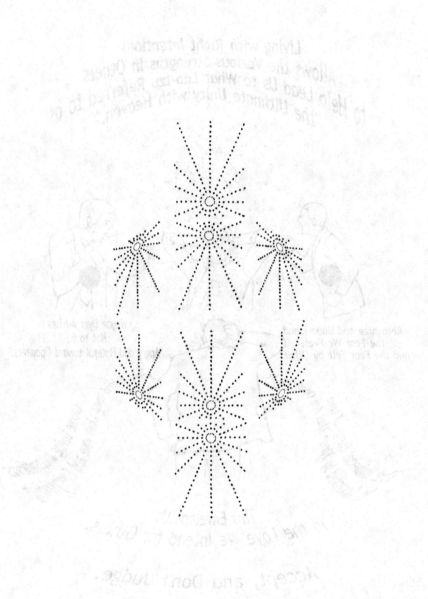

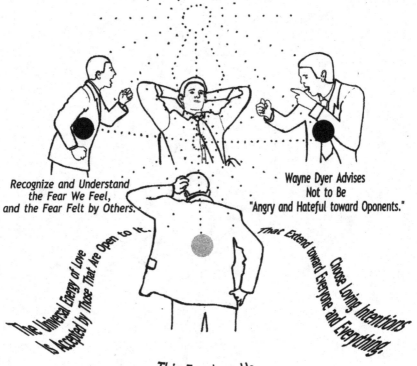

Figure 68: Living with Right Intentions

Power through Collaboration

68

In verse 68 Lao-tzu mentions "the virtue of noncompetition," which is "employing the power of others" (Dyer 2007, 322). We are all part of the same source. We are all connected; we all share in the same Oneness. Wayne Dyer advises us not to be "angry and hateful toward opponents" but rather to "see them as a part of [us] that's working to help [us] achieve excellence" (323-24).

The Tao is everywhere, this includes in us and in everyone. It follows that the thoughts of God (Energy) are also all around, in all places. We like to think that our thoughts can be separated into compartments and categorized as things favored and things not favored, but the reality is if we wish favor for ourselves and ours and at the same time judge others and strongly wish ill favor for them, the dynamic feeling of negativity harbored within our intention toward others is more likely to override, prevail as dominant, and serve to attract that contrary and obstructive intention toward ourselves.

Why might this be? We attract what our deepest thoughts intend despite where we wish our shallow reasoning might lead. This could be compared to surface water that yields to the universal force of gravity. Unfailingly, it is being pulled by this ubiquitous force as it applies to the inherent depth that is the essential characteristic of a hollow, gully or ravine. To continue this metaphor, we also attract whatever truly captures our deepest thoughts and feelings. Because the Universe simply resonates with our more potent and energetic thought processes, it does not assess, rank, or respond to our ego's way of wishing good for some while judging others. We can do the most good for all by consciously intending the best for everybody—yes, for everybody—thereby enlisting the good and highest qualities in others to coalesce with and nourish our intention. Having consistently favorable intentions for all in the only moment we have attracts goodness and ensures that we have a good relationship with life, despite the fact that it does not appear auspicious to our ego-controlled way of thinking.

In our everyday lives, recognize with understanding the fear that may be present in us and in others and show and feel the acceptance of ourselves, of all people, and of situations, by neither condemning nor condoning, while intending and demonstrating right behavior toward everyone, including ourselves. This allows us to acknowledge potential adversaries as equals, who experience similar issues and concerns to ourselves. The personal recognition of the Oneness of all is a shift in consciousness that fully supports us and opens our minds to the positive aspects of others. Being consciously aware of the good in ourselves and in other people can begin to repeat itself within the lives of those influenced by this loving action. People who carry within themselves a loving and trusting attitude may prompt the resonance of a similar attitude within others.

Anticipate the best, live in the present, and accept whatever comes as one step toward the best that God has to offer, since what God has provided was shaped by the choices we have made up to this moment. Choices guided by love harness the energy of others and keep us experiencing life's fullness. Many of us fail to see how what we call coincidence in our lives has a greater significance than what we like to give it. Our awareness of things as they happen, especially those that appear to be coincidence, can markedly influence our thought processes, our intentions, and our ultimate decision-making.

Coincidence is the primary focus of the book *The Spontaneous Fulfillment of Desire* by Deepak Chopra. With purposeful detail, he explores, develops, and clarifies what many of us consider a "web of coincidence in our lives" (Chopra 2003, 27). In the book he discusses how "to understand the connectedness or synchronicity of all things [in order] to choose the kind of life we want to live" (35). He states that "the ultimate goal of 'synchrodestiny' is to expand [our] consciousness and open a doorway to enlightenment" (260). In his discussion of what he calls the "fifth stage" of consciousness, he states that "part of [us] is localized and part of [us], being nonlocal, is connected to everything" (256).

I would like to compare the part of us described above as "connected to everything" to the energy that is accounted for and clearly and explicitly explained in The Seat of the Soul by Gary Zukav (Zukav 1990). He spells out that "when energy leaves [us] in any way except in strength and trust, it cannot bring back to [us] anything but pain and discomfort" (224). He goes on to say that the attributes of authentic power only manifest when we release our energy as love and trust. Zukav has an added and meaningful dimension to understanding the "Light of the Universe" by describing it as the energy of life that flows through us. Zukav explains that "a thought is energy or Light that has been shaped by consciousness," and he equates this to "creation." He explains thought as a nonphysical example of form and portrays us as "dynamic being[s] of Light" that "[inform] the energy that flows through [us]." I am intrigued with the insight Zukav reveals. He describes universal energy or "Light" as "entering at the top of [our] head and descending downward through [our] body." In my mind, this revealing and eye-opening clarification introduces a new awareness through his explanation that "[we] give that Light form . . . and are shaping the Light that is flowing through [us]." Zukav describes our thoughts, feelings and actions as "forms that [we] have given to Light" that "reflect the configuration of [our] personality, our space-time being." (105-06). Our state of consciousness determines how we think. Our thoughts affect how we interact with the Energy of Life within us. Ongoing thoughts produce our intentions. Our reality is the manifestation of these intentions. When we include the strengths we see in others within our intention, the energy we extend is saturated with "the higher frequency currents of appreciation, acceptance and love" (Zukav 1990, 128). According to Zukav, this allows energy and influence to radiate instantly from soul to soul (128).

We are responsible for our own reality, whether we realize it or not. Although the intent of the saying "God helps those who help themselves" was probably initially meant in a literal sense, I will also suggest that the actual work that needs to be done must be combined with meaningful day-to-day dedicated intention, meant for the good of all, in the direction of our area of interest for the promotion of good. The nucleus of our intent needs to be singular in its concern for the realization of good for others as well as for ourselves. Intentions that are split in the sense of *good* and *bad* lack consistency of purpose, and this cognitive dissonance will likely leave us in a frazzle, vulnerable to the circumstances that a lack of principled direction may attract. Wayne Dyer advises us to keep in mind that "whenever [we] say or do something that's harmful to someone [we] love, [we're] doing something to harm [ourselves]" (Dyer 2007, 325). Along with the good intentions that we feel surrounding the idea of being able to help others within our own area of interest, our intentions need to include forgiveness, trust, and healing. The issues we face in this world confront all of us. When more of us begin to collaborate in our shared goodness, perhaps we will be one step closer to what Lao-tzu describes in the last line of this verse as "the ultimate unity with heaven" (322).

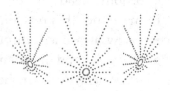

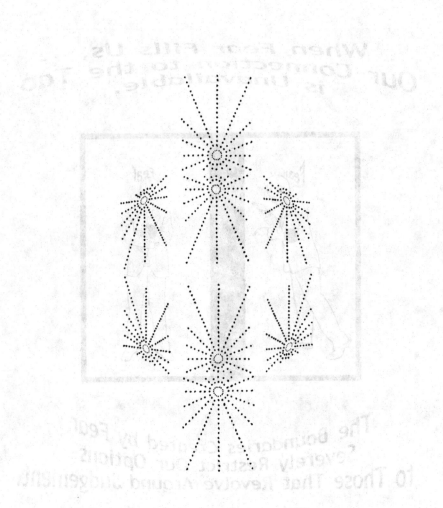

When Fear Fills Us,
Our Connection to the Tao
is Unavailable.

The Boundaries Created by Fear
Severely Restrict Our Options
to Those That Revolve Around Judgement.

Figure 69.1: Fear Creates Boundaries

Recognize Good
in Our Perceived Enemies

69

In verse 69 Lao-tzu reveals "there is no greater misfortune than feeling 'I have an Enemy.'" He goes on to explain that "when 'I' and 'enemy' exist together there is no room for [our] treasure" (Dyer 2007, 326). The use of the word *enemy* has become a "normal" way of categorizing many things, especially people. Unfortunately, it represents a disquieting concept involved in many scenarios, and consequently, in one form or another, the idea of *the enemy* proves to be an incendiary sticking point in most difficult or contentious issues. A change in thinking that would no longer demand that we classify a particular group of people or type of idea as an enemy is difficult to make. What would replace this thinking?

It is disheartening to realize that too many young children, already at the age that they enter the school system, have well-established ideas about friends and enemies. In addition, our personal conditioning, whether positive or negative, initiates the development of one story and another, which we may associate with the word *enemy*. Too often there is a story we cling to that captures much of our attention. If the treasure Lao-tzu spoke of in verse 67 is not central to us, whatever story is at the center of our focus, if continued, becomes our sustained intention and fills us. When fear, from almost any source occupies our thoughts and crowds out loving thoughts, we experience pain and discomfort.

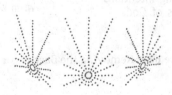

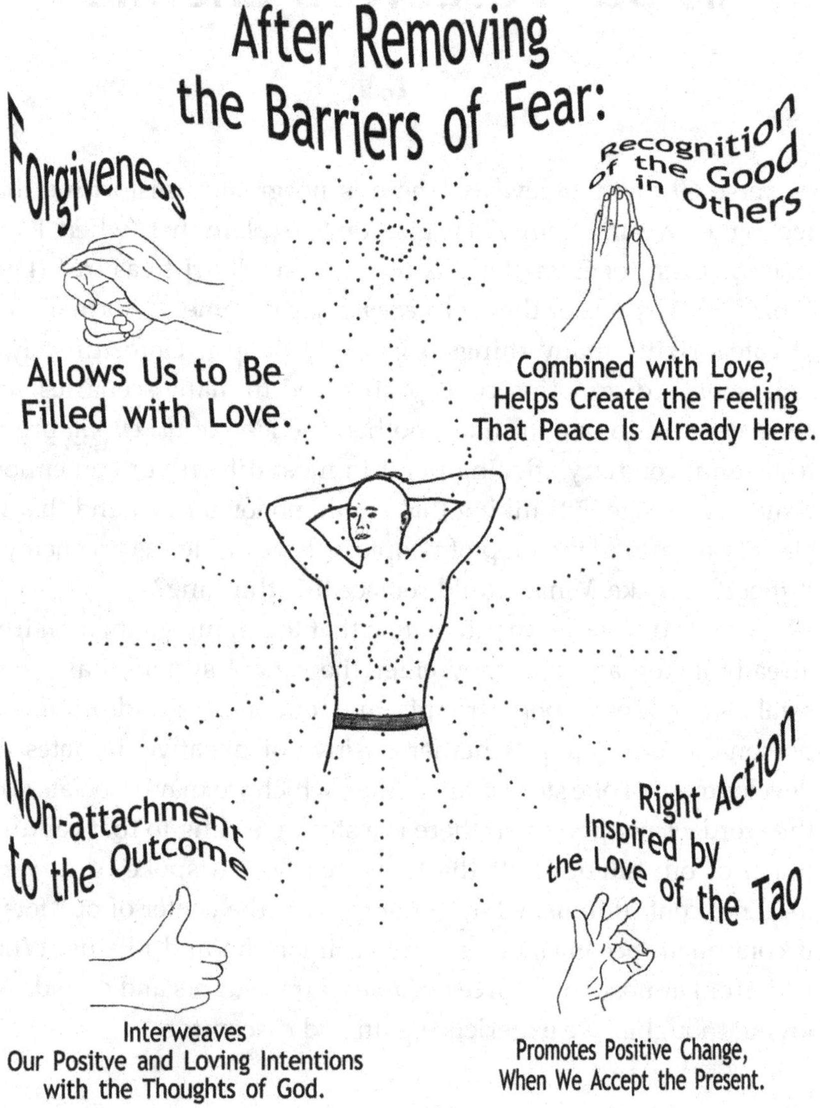

After Removing
the Barriers of Fear:

Forgiveness

Recognition of the Good in Others

Allows Us to Be
Filled with Love.

Combined with Love,
Helps Create the Feeling
That Peace Is Already Here.

Non-attachment to the Outcome

Right Action Inspired by the Love of the Tao

Interweaves
Our Positve and Loving Intentions
with the Thoughts of God.

Promotes Positive Change,
When We Accept the Present.

Figure 69.2: Removing the Barriers of Fear

Only love can replace fear and guard against its dominance in our life. Know that Love is the only truth. Judgment is not love. It does not bring peace no matter how valid our reasons to judge appear to our ego. Do not judge; lay down your defenses. It is in our favor not to allow righteous indignation to act as the motivation behind our actions. Accept and forgive; acknowledge all as equals, and look for the good in others. Know people for who they truly are.

Because of what we tell ourselves about the past, the present, or a situation yet to come, we project fear into our world. We have allowed these feelings to permanently occupy our mind and therefore fill the space within us. It can cause us to lash out at anything within our own understanding that even remotely represents "the enemy." The result is pain and darkness.

Only forgiveness, forgiveness for all, including ourselves, heals the ever-widening rift that exists in our minds between those we classify as an enemy and ourselves. Forgiveness ushers the restorative light of love into our lives and replaces the idea of separation with that of unity. Look peacefully upon others and do not label those with different views as enemies. This allows the space within us to be filled by the powerful energy of the Tao.

When we are filled with God's love, we are also overflowing with the feeling that peace is already here. Loving and peaceful intentions heal. Minds that share mutual thoughts of acceptance bring peace and healing. Minds that reject, judge, and separate bring disorder and darkness.

Recognition that we all share in the energy of the Tao (God) is the first step of our journey to understanding. For this truth to grow within us we need to live the realization that ongoing conscious awareness allows us to bring *to* mind and keep *in* mind the powerfully responsive energy in and around us.

What are some simple things that we can do to remind ourselves of the ongoing, everywhere presence of the Tao? We can be aware of the astounding miracle of life as it presents itself to us each morning and take note of the positive in the events of the day that follows. Let this remind us to appreciate Life's presence. When we think about an old friend, is it merely coincidence that we meet him or her within the next few days? Be aware! Slow down and appreciate the simple things we seem to take for granted. Enjoy the steps we take in life as we take them. *Right now* is our only connection to what is, and our awareness of the presence of the Tao in all that is helps us realize that we need to thank God for all we have and all we are able to do. Part of being thankful is feeling gratitude to our Source for our Life as we live it. We attract healing energy when this becomes a regular and conscious thought process. Doing this helps to consistently honor the present by acknowledging and appreciating the vital energy that presence holds. When the space within us that is designed to house the vibrant energy of the Tao is filled instead by fearful thoughts of an enemy or an equivalent form of fear, the consciousness of the Tao is shut out from revealing its presence within us.

Jesus said, "I am the way, the truth, and the life" (John 14:6, King James Version). In the book *A New Earth*, Eckhart Tolle explains that "the Truth is inseparable from who [we] are" (Tolle 2006). Truth refers to the "I am" or essence that Jesus is. This suggests that the Life in Jesus is the spiritual Truth of God. Therefore, Truth, Life, and the esse of Jesus are one. God is everywhere, so the spirit of God is also in us, just as it is everywhere else. We have life, so this indicates that we too are part of this Truth. The Life or Spirit, which we are, is Truth. This Truth is in us and we need to recognize this same Truth in all others.

Accept things as they happen, but exit situations that are toxic or a safety concern. Menacing people and situations are to be approached with care or even avoided, and in most cases it is best not to condemn anything or anyone as an enemy. It is also advisable not to attempt to control through fear or anger-driven actions. Situations handled through force or manipulation almost invariably turn cyclical, and the action is sure to be returned with an even greater negative intensity. Because many people feel that the perpetrators of hateful acts must be made to suffer an equal or greater consequence or counterattack, it requires great strength to allow understanding into our hearts. In the case of the judicial system, it must be respected and consequences must be handed down to people who are responsible for crimes. Recognizing Truth in a wrongdoer is challenging, partly because of our personal conditioning. It is made even more difficult because of public opinion. We may finally be able to start doing this when we gain the understanding that the motivating factor behind the wrongdoer's action probably lies in deep pain and suffering. Unfortunately, the action was caused by the painful fear he or she felt. This by no means excuses the action because each of us is responsible for our own decisions. It just puts a different face on the action. The choice was still made, and it remains difficult for most to understand. Slowly, change may begin to happen when society as a whole begins to realize the inherent danger lurking in action that results from fear. This may be a step toward breaking the cycle of retaliation as well.

Living consciously, as we recognize and accept the present for what it is, allows the energy of the Tao (God) to live and manifest through us. It might be refreshing to enjoy the simplicity of living life while doing nothing and allowing our decisions to be made for us. This of course, in a literal sense, is not possible. Furthermore, any idea of this sort may sound like naïveté, as non-action, or even "Pollyanna-like," but living a connected life can be precise and well-defined in its focus and will advance within its own timeline and master plan. On the other hand, the reality of daily living recognizes the challenge of using intuition inspired by love to choose our action, because in our ego-dominated world importance is placed on control, according to our perceived priorities and schedule. Consequently, to live a connected life we will need to recognize reminders from God to stay tuned to our intuition in order to resist the continual manipulations prompted by the ego. Ongoing conscious effort that promotes action that is not fear-driven or attached to a particular outcome empowers us to live our lives with Tao-centered responsibility.

Being detached from the outcome allows for the true immersion of who we are into the business of living because we are actually present in the moment and not simply focused on the future. Life involves choices, and inevitably all our choices direct us to our next choice point in life. Making wise choices, appropriate to where we are in our lives, interweaves our positive and loving intentions with the manifestation of consciousness, thereby creating the life we live.

See, know, and feel the Go(o)d in others as critically more significant than their views. People and nations choose to exert power over other people and nations for many reasons and in a multitude of ways, many of which are negative and arise out of fear. Circumstances like these result in anxiety, unrest, and many times things much worse, and cause the ego, whether at a personal level, a group level, or a national level to choose actions that are driven by fear. This fills all involved, as well as all onlookers, with fearful thoughts about an enemy. Reaction on both sides is then limited to things precipitated by fear and therefore to consequences unlikely to lead to peace. These situations shut out our internal energy source because the space within us is filled with fearful thoughts and not by the powerful thoughts of God.

However, when we recognize our perceived enemy by accepting the good (God) in them, we connect to our source of power by allowing ourselves to be filled with the Love of God. The material power that ego seeks is no match for inner strength. The question remains as to how we arrive at this inner strength. Too often we become entrapped by the fear we feel because we cannot see beyond it. We become mired within the subterfuge of our own confusing thoughts—thoughts about what we have been *told* to believe as the truth as well as what *we think* experience has taught us. This does not suggest that we are not able to learn from other people or that we cannot learn from our own history.

The problem lies in deciphering relevant information from what Iyanla Vanzant calls "deceptive intelligence." (Iyanla Vanzant is a well-established author and powerful spiritual teacher who made this reference in a web-cast that followed online after Oprah's Lifeclass 5 broadcast in the 2011 fall season on the OWN Television Network.) Because of the enclosed space of our thinking, our tired old thoughts that may have little or no relevance in our present circumstances keep reverberating in our minds, making them almost impossible to ignore. When we hear ourselves repeatedly saying things, we believe them. These deceptive directives need to be trashed to allow things to change.

Wayne Dyer reminds us in his essay on verse 69 that "[our] treasure is [our] peace of mind and [our] Tao connection" (Dyer 2007, 329). Releasing the past contributes greatly to our peace of mind, and this helps reveal our treasure. To paraphrase Oprah Winfrey, we need to open up to the idea that the past had to be the way it was for the present to be as it is. Only when this idea is accepted can our self-imposed borders begin to disperse, allowing us to break free from our entrapped thinking into the limitless expanse of all possibilities. When we forgive all, we release our confining thoughts about enemies. Forgiveness and the recognition of the good in others, allows us to be filled by the power of the Truth, the all-encompassing Energy of God.

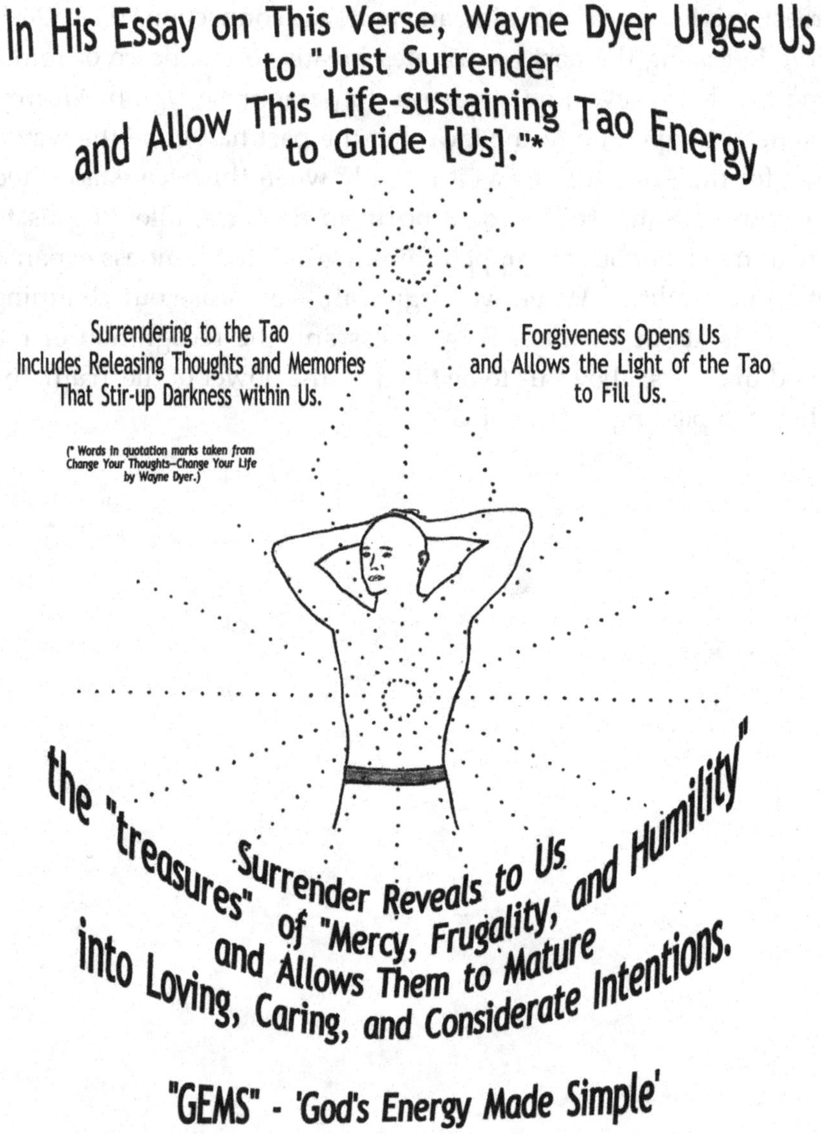

In His Essay on This Verse, Wayne Dyer Urges Us
to "Just Surrender
and Allow This Life-sustaining Tao Energy
to Guide [Us]."*

Surrendering to the Tao
Includes Releasing Thoughts and Memories
That Stir-up Darkness within Us.

Forgiveness Opens Us
and Allows the Light of the Tao
to Fill Us.

(* Words In quotation marks taken from
Change Your Thoughts—Change Your Life
by Wayne Dyer.)

the "treasures" Surrender Reveals to Us.
of "Mercy, Frugality, and Humility"
and Allows Them to Mature
into Loving, Caring, and Considerate Intentions.

"GEMS" - 'God's Energy Made Simple'

Figure 70: God's Energy Made Simple—GEMS (Dyer 2007)

Recognizing and Polishing Our "Precious Gems"

70

Lao-tzu begins verse 70 with "my teachings are very easy to understand and very easy to practice." He laments that people don't get the message and follows with, "yet so few people in this world understand and so few are able to practice" (Dyer 2007, 330). Too many of us do not realize and acknowledge that we are all a piece of the Tao. Despite our differing outward appearance, and the possessions we may or may not have at this moment, on the inside we are all spiritual jewels, or "gems" (330).

The Oneness of the world and Universe that we call home consists of the unlimited, ever-present mother Energy that prevails and allows for the unlimited, all-pervasive nature of the Tao, giving it total interconnectedness. It is simply a matter of feeling a conscious coupling to and Oneness with this omnipresence. This connection creates a real but unseen and impalpable conduit that might be thought of as an ever-outreaching and luminescent-like radiance that connects with the non-material paragon of Love within us. I would like to think that in one way or another, this might help to represent the *easy aspect* as understood by Lao-tzu. It may be helpful to think of GEMS as an acronym representing the idea of *God's Energy Made Simple.*

Emotions that surge from the bowels of our being add our humanness to the innate Tao-centered zeal that drives us toward our grounded, fulfilling, and life-sustaining aspirations. It is our choice to merge and coalesce our thoughts with the genuine "I" that we are at the center of these emotions. This reflects our true purpose and produces heartfelt feelings and actions that validate all life. On the contrary, we could allow our thoughts to be influenced by restricted thinking patterns often influenced by adverse and damaging life

255

circumstances that predispose our ego to lead us to make unwise choices, as well as to follow unwholesome popular opinion. This creates a state of dissonance between the whisperings within us and our thoughts. This undermines and diminishes life by restricting the flow of loving thoughts, thereby strangling the expression of our being. Allowing our thoughts to align in full congruence with our love-centered emotions creates peaceful feelings within our hearts, because our thoughts and emotions are in harmony with the thoughts of the Tao. These feelings are what we become and what we attract.

Simply stated, our thoughts, feelings, and intentions, no matter what they are, communicate. In Gregg Braden's audio presentation *Speaking the Lost Language of God* (Braden n.d., cd10), he summarizes the gist of the program in one sentence: "We must become in our lives the very things that we choose to experience in our world." In addition, he informs us that "Western science now suggests that we are bathed in a field of intelligent Energy. This field is everywhere, all the time. It links all creation; it responds to powerful emotion." He also calls this energy "the mind of God" (cd10).

The first chapter of *The Seven Spiritual Laws of Success* by Deepak Chopra is devoted to "the law of pure potentiality." Chopra explains that "pure consciousness is pure potentiality" and that "pure consciousness is our spiritual essence" (Chopra 1994, 9). He also refers to "pure consciousness" as the "field of all possibilities" (13). Gregg Braden calls it the "field of intelligent energy" (Braden n.d.). How do these ideas compare? I cannot speak for these accomplished individuals, but in my opinion the views vary in their intricacies but agree in their overall message.

There is a lot of fascinating material to process in Braden's genuinely substantiated discussion of the "lost language of God," but put very simply his findings appear to strongly support bona fide emotion and feeling as the critical connection linking our prayers to the Universe.

In *The Seven Spiritual Laws of Success*, Chopra states that "through silence, through meditation, and through non-judgment, [we] will access the first law, the 'Law of Pure Potentiality'" (Chopra,

The Seven Spiritual Laws of Success 1994, 18). He goes on to explain that we need to break the bounds of our "internal dialogue" to connect with the "creative mind" (which I will call "our mind in stillness"). At the same time he suggests we "create the possibility of dynamic activity" (which I will compare to our innermost intention) and allow it to move us "wherever the power of [our] attention takes [us]" (20-21).

To my way of thinking the basic ideas of Chopra and Braden, blended with the gist of the Tao, might be summarized as follows: we live in a world of all possibilities. The choices we make during what is often barely detectable moments of silent awareness may begin to move us to *feel the possibility* of what our active awareness *connects to* with realism. Living the recognition that we are part of the Oneness of our Universe allows easy but subtle access to the Tao, with constant opportunity to receive direction from our Source. This is possible because our origin is the very essence or Spirit of the Tao, and this means we are not separate from the immediate thoughts of God. We just need to be receptive to the hushed murmurings coming from within us. The Tao creates and honors life.

In his book *Inspiration*, Wayne Dyer reveals that "the fundamental truth each of us needs to affirm is: I am a Divine creation. All creation has purpose. I am here to be like God" (Dyer 2006, 54). When we honor the principles of life, our thoughts are like the thoughts of God. We come from the peaceful state of the Tao. Our thought patterns allow the development of our humanity to be guided by the Tao, in which and through which we experience life.

Heartfelt communication is the key to any relationship, and steady improvement during our lifetime is a worthwhile goal. Knowing how to commune with the Tao is what makes life truly meaningful. In his book *You'll See It When You Believe It*, Wayne Dyer tells us that "thought is real" (Dyer 2001, 59). In our dreams and in our waking thought-lives, we are convinced that our thoughts are real, as is strongly suggested by most everyone's experience. At times our thoughts evoke an almost instant response within our body, which is, of course, the function of our nervous system.

However, are we aware of all influences that may affect our nervous system?

The Tao is everywhere and the Tao is in us. The thoughts we feel in their fullness act as our vital mode of communication within the ocean of the all-powerful Energy in which we exist and of which we are a part. The personally determined paradigm of our existence forms the sum and substance of our past heartfelt intentions that are responsible for the life we are living right now. Thought has no limit; thoughts of beauty, thoughts of affirmation, and thoughts of love are clearly the most powerfully effective tools the Universe has to offer. To paraphrase Gregg Braden from his audio program *Speaking the Lost Language of God*, thoughts can be used to direct our emotions to create feelings that synchronize with the thoughts of God.

Wayne Dyer reminds us that in verse 67, Lao-tzu explained "God-realization in the form of the three treasures: mercy, frugality, and humility" (Dyer 2007, 332). In verse 70, Lao-tzu speaks of simply clothed sages as possessing gems within (330). Dyer refers to the great masters, such as Jesus, Buddha, and Mohammed and suggests these treasures are also held within them. (332). Because Lao-tzu tells us in verse 67 that mercy becomes courage, frugality becomes generosity, and humility becomes leadership, I would like to suggest that to accomplish this conversion, the masters have impeccably practiced and polished their "treasures" and represent the ultimate level of awareness and virtue to which we can only strive.

The comment by Lao-tzu that tells us that this idea is "easy to understand" suggests to me that all we need to do is realize that we are part of the consciousness that is God, experience the stillness that this consciousness represents, and feel the achievement of our needs prior to their arrival. I would like to think that we might be reminded of these simple ideas by thinking of the acronym **GEMS**—*God's Energy Made Simple*. It is also our responsibility to acknowledge these "gems" by feeling their presence in the form of practicing mercy, frugality, and humility. The more we hone these skills, the more polished our "gems" will become.

To paraphrase Dyer from his essay on this verse, he tells us that Lao-tzu's knowledge about how readily available these "gems" actually are probably increased the disbelief Lao-tzu likely felt as to why something so manageable was not embraced by more people. This simplicity is expressed in our heartfelt feelings that attract experiences of the same level of vibration, which is to say no matter the frequency at which we function, these vibrations will manifest in our lives again at a level of corresponding frequency. This, I believe, is also part of what Lao-tzu meant.

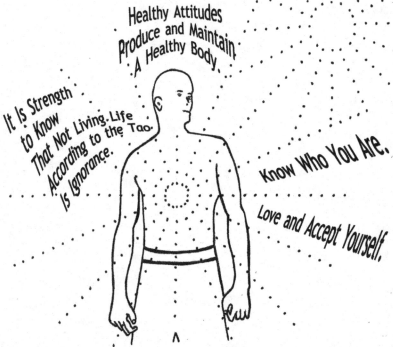

Knowledge about the Tao is Strength.
Strength Produces Right Thinking,
Which in Turn Produces Healthy Attitudes.

Healthy Attitudes
Produce and Maintain
A Healthy Body.

It Is Strength
to Know
That Not Living Life
According to the Tao
Is Ignorance.

Know Who You Are.

Love and Accept Yourself.

Feel Optimum Health
in the Vibrant Awareness
of All Possibilities in the Present
by Knowing and Living the Tao.

Figure 71: Healthy Attitudes

Trust in the "Knowledge" of the Present

71

According to Lao-tzu in verse 71, "knowing ignorance is strength" and "ignoring knowledge is sickness." He goes on to say, "Only when we are sick of sickness shall we cease to be sick" (Dyer 2007, 334). How might the "sickness" and the "knowledge" spoken about here be connected? In his essay on verse 71, Wayne Dyer helps clarify this confusing verse.

Perhaps we might compare the "ignorance" mentioned by Lao-tzu to not living life according to the Tao, and the "knowledge" about living a Tao-centered life might be seen as "strength." Therefore, Lao-tzu might be equating "ignoring" what we know about the Tao to "sickness."

"Sickness" could also be seen as unwise decision-making, because if we live our lives ignoring Tao-centeredness, the hard work we do for things of the ego may lead us to neglect and overwork our bodies, making us more susceptible to physical sickness since our body's energy is more focused on our ego's attachments than on our well-being. Not only does this block the connection to the Tao, it sets up and keeps in motion an ongoing and uncomfortable background noise of tumultuous thoughts that crisscross our minds in a frenzied attempt to accomplish the business of working toward our attachments using hard work alone. Since we are not tuned in to the energy of the Tao to make the necessary actions easy, we must expend much energy to reach our attachments.

If we truly believe that the things we want for our lives are already here, including our health, and release our attachment to these things, we are open to receiving God's love, and with that, our action becomes less stress-filled. This does not mean that we are not busy doing all the things required, but it does mean that the backdrop of frenzied feelings is gone and has been replaced by calmness and peace. This makes things easier because we can then be more aware of intuition that leads us to the next appropriate step. When our body is not under the near neurotic tension of needing to achieve things for the ego, we can release those attachments and give the *background* of our being *permission* to relax into the Tao.

In addition, Lao-tzu's opening lines might also be understood to mean that the *recognition* of poor thinking is knowledge and a powerful advantage, while *not* practicing right thinking causes suffering and sickness. What is within this knowledge mentioned by Lao-tzu that is so significant?

In *Gifts from Eykis*, a work of fiction by Wayne Dyer, Eykis shares many vitally significant truths about right thinking. Through the voice of this character, Dyer shares his "secrets of the universe." The last gift shared is that "there is no way to happiness: happiness is the way" (Dyer 1983, 179). In our ignorance (poor thinking), most of us spend much of our lives chasing happiness. Our chosen profession(s) may help us develop certain goals and pay our bills, which of course is a necessary thing, but too often the happiness we seek is circumstance and object dependent, so we experience what we interpret as feeling content only briefly, with much of the remaining time spent in distress striving to feel complete.

Part of this knowledge is realizing that real and lasting contentment does not have its source in money and things. It originates in our connection to the piece of God that we are. The fuel that powers these feelings of happiness is generated by right thinking. When thoughts dictate the need for society's symbols for happiness, real happiness persists in being out of our grasp. When thoughts remain in the moment, feelings about the past and the future should be entertained only long enough to determine if anything can be done to improve, correct, or apologize for a situation. Appropriate action can then be considered and chosen if deemed auspicious. If nothing can be done, the thought should be brushed off as unworthy of our attention.

Because the message is applicable to this verse, I have chosen to add a quote taken from a different translation of the last lines of verse 9 of the Tao Te Ching, used in the book *Invisible Acts of Power* by Carolyn Myss. As indicated on the front panel of the dust jacket, she is "an internationally renowned pioneer in energy medicine." The Tao quote reads, "do your work, then step back, the only path to serenity" (Myss 2004, 2). Where is the knowledge in this? Stepping back appears complacent and submissive; so what is the operating force? Could it be hidden in the attitude and belief we hold as we *step back*—a trust in the perspective that the present is pregnant with possibility? Carolyn Myss tells us that "it is about surrendering to divine guidance" (Myss 2004, 3). When we shut down our brain chatter, our intuitive sensitivities become more acutely tuned within our daily routine. This step of wisdom toward surrender calms our thoughts and attitudes.

In her book *Sacred Contracts*, Carolyn Myss quotes Jesus from Matthew 21:21: "All this and more can you do if you have faith" (Myss 2003, 233). How do these words correlate with the knowledge that verse 71 tells us not to ignore? Faith is a product of our thoughts, and our thoughts form our intentions. It is our intentions that help us develop our faith. Having the faith that the Universe (or God) will recognize the intention we truly feel within us can also be thought of as unparalleled knowledge. The bonus is that God or the Universe or the Tao (or whatever we call this all-powerful Energy) responds at the same frequency of the intention we feel within us. A clear relationship exists between our thinking and the things that manifest in our lives. This includes our feeling of wellbeing. This is invaluable knowledge.

The counsel Wayne Dyer provides through the fictional character in the book *Gifts from Eykis* adds significant explanation connecting knowledge to awareness. Another example from the book reads as follows: "Throughout history authoritarianism has failed to take hold where people were encouraged to think for themselves" (Dyer 1983, 152). Truly meaningful knowledge leads toward awareness and fosters our inner growth by promoting the evolution of our ideals, our purpose. Living our purpose through the Tao allows us to relax into living our intention.

A genuine understanding of the Tao makes clear the importance of our awareness of self and focuses our attention on an urgent need for individualized thinking and personal choice, instead of hollow and assumed thinking that is easily influenced by ego and popular opinion. Simply stated, our intuitive choices direct the flow of our lives, not choices made because of the fear of being judged by others. It follows as well that judging others has no place in a freethinking mind. This includes accepting things that are, rather than resisting what has already happened, by engaging in frantic behavior and futile thought processes in a bizarre attempt to change reality. This contributes further to the background noise within our thinking process. Confused thinking is an energy drain on our already stressed bodies. Knowing this appears self-evident, but our ego relishes the replay and repeated revision of our "should have" scenarios.

Panicked pursuit toward any particular person, thing, or contrivance leads nowhere, while a Tao-centered approach allows the release of attachment to the wish, while feeling the contentment its materialization brings. This requires the relaxed acceptance of things as they are. The same acceptance applies to many things we do. We may accomplish tasks, perform rituals, or peel our potatoes in one particular way, but the acceptance of multiple approaches in doing things relaxes tension between and among individuals and groups that do things differently.

When the Pharisees asked Jesus when the kingdom of God would come, Jesus replied, "The kingdom of heaven is within" (Luke 17:21, KJV). This emphatically reinforces the idea that at our center we are Love, and to quote Wayne Dyer, we are "a spark of God." This is the knowledge also offered by the Tao. It is up to us to transform it into experience. We need to live our lives by loving and accepting ourselves, while remembering who we really are. Living in present awareness allows us to be a representative of this knowledge to everyone.

I believe it is the opinion of Lao-tzu in verse 71 that being aware of and living the knowledge of the Tao leads to a healthy life, free of sickness. Why might this be so? Instead of being held hostage in the unease of performing for the ego, the energy of our body is able to relax into our purpose, thereby allowing us to feel the good intentions we have for ourselves and for all others. This predisposes us to attract from the Universe the same goodness that we project, but perhaps in a form that we may not expect, yet conforming to the choices we have made. This may include good health, healing, and general well-being.

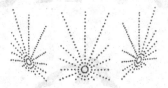

Figure 72: In Awe of the Truth

Living in Awe of the Truth

Lao-tzu begins verse 72 by informing us that our feeling "a sense of awe" is needed to avoid disaster. He also clearly states that feeling fear prevents "a greater power" (Dyer 2007, 338) from arriving. People have been seeking to explain "a greater power," or in other words the *truth* of our existence, for probably as long as time, as we know it, has existed. What is the truth of our existence? Is this truth being sought, a part of, or *the* reason to feel the awe spoken of by Lao-tzu? Where can it be found? How does it reveal itself and to whom? When does this happen and under what conditions?

Many questions like these have been asked throughout history with ever so many answers. The result has been the formation of a variety of religions and beliefs, many of which represent the idea of God, and can help connect us to the Truth, but unfortunately are also tied to their root in ego. They make up many of the religious organizations, sects, and belief systems that we know today.

Does it follow that there are as many gods as there are religious beliefs? Alternatively, is only one of the belief systems correct? If so, which one? Is truth only released to those who are born into or select the *right religion* and abide by its rules and rituals? It hardly seems fair, realistic, or at best even plausible that God would think this way. Why would an unbiased God select one group over another? The omnipresence of God presided over the evolution of all species, including the different races within the human grouping. Logic precludes the idea that following this, God would select a set of parameters decided by one particular group or organization and its ego-based system over another ego-based system. In my opinion, this simply defies the sensibilities of what we might consider to be a caring and unbiased God.

All races originated from nothing, which is the Source we all share. In addition, all races, representing all religions and no religion, will return to this same Source. Unfortunately, in most instances, the experiences of life allow our thoughts to become absorbed by the selfishness of ego, and these self-serving thoughts attempt to convince us that we are something we are not. We grant permission to our thinking processes that promote the idea that we are separate. Thus, it is our thoughts that keep us from being in tune with our Source.

So where is the truth we are seeking in all this? Simply stated, the Truth is everywhere—absolutely everywhere—within our Universe. The utter magnitude of this reality is without boundaries. The intricacies of the workings of our universe and the world in which we live have been the subject of great minds for hundreds upon thousands of years. Many have been searching for these answers. Could the answers lie in the Truth that all of us seek? Might it be that the knowledge needed to unravel the Truth would also provide the answers scientists need to explain certain aspects of the workings of our Universe? One report on what I interpret as an important step in this direction was strikingly emblazoned in capital letters on the front cover of the July 23, 2012 issue of Maclean's magazine that decisively trumpeted a prophecy about the revelation of the Higgs boson, (a particle first proposed by Peter Higgs, theoretical physicist, in 1964), as "THIS CHANGES EVERYTHING." Revealing and enlightening comments from theoretical physicist Lawrence M. Krauss are included in the ensuing article written by Kate Lunau and Katie Engelhart titled *Unravelling the Universe* (Lunau and Engelhart 2012, 40-47) within the same issue of the magazine. The authors of the article tell us that there are those who refer to this discovery as the "God particle" (47) but Krauss is quoted as simply but succinctly describing the "Higgs boson" as "it's beautiful." He goes on to briefly comment on the discovery of what the authors of the article refer to as the "Holy Grail" (42) of physics by saying, "The fact that empty space is endowed with these properties—that what appears to be empty space endows particles with mass. Apparently, nothingness is responsible for our existence" (47). Krauss is the author of the book *A Universe from Nothing*.

The miracle of life, the marvel of the revelations of science, the spectacular beauty of our Earth, and the puzzling and unexplained happenings of life are all too often ignored and taken for granted instead of viewed in awe. Our odyssey from Source to human experience and back to Source presents us with many lessons to learn about the role we play in the workings of our universe. We can appreciate the togetherness or Oneness with which our Universe operates, as well as accept our part in it, or we can resist inclusion within the pervasiveness of this all-powerful energy and make important life decisions within the limits that fear imposes on us. It is only when we feel the awe of our existence, instead of fear, that we experience Truth. A deep feeling of reverence, awe, and appreciation at the wonder of the workings of our Universe attracts this same all-powerful energy, Truth, into our lives.

In his essay on this verse, Wayne Dyer comments on the great significance of "the metaphor of nature" (Dyer 2007, 341) used by Lao-tzu in the Tao Te Ching. Dyer supplements the message within the metaphor with a quote from a thirteenth-century Catholic monk, Meister Eckhart, who said, "God created all things in such a way that they are not outside of himself" (Dyer 2007, 341). Dyer adds further clarity by citing John 15:4-5, part of which reads, "Just as a branch cannot produce fruit unless it stays joined to the vine, you cannot produce fruit unless you stay joined to me" (341).

We are part of all this. The plan of our Universe is perfection. Unfortunately, our ego sees perfection without the powerful energy or light of God shining upon, or guiding our course of action, moment by moment. That being so, ego sees perfection as relying solely on thought derived action, which leads to showy displays designed to extol praise upon the accomplishments of ego. This is the false perfection of the ego.

Our true self, our Being on the other hand, is perfect. What's more, we are perfect; we are whole; we are complete. We need nothing but to accept ourselves as we are. The gifts we have been given at birth and beyond, no matter the circumstances, suffice. To fulfill our ultimate mission in life, we need to do no more than remain open and alert to the illuminating intuition coming from the Energy of God that exists everywhere, including within us. Responding and acting according to this guidance allows the power of God to permeate our lives. This is living in awe of the Truth.

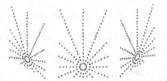

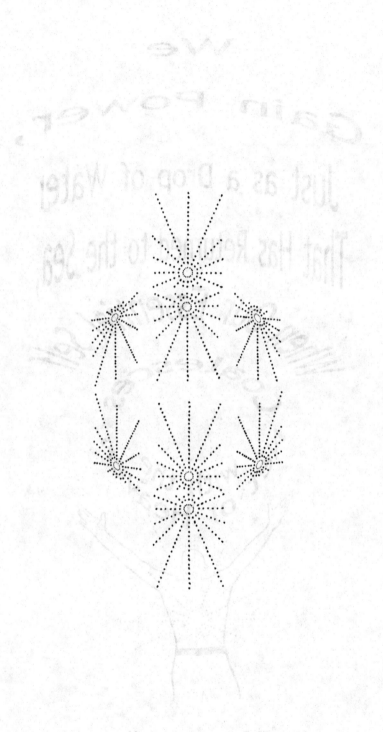

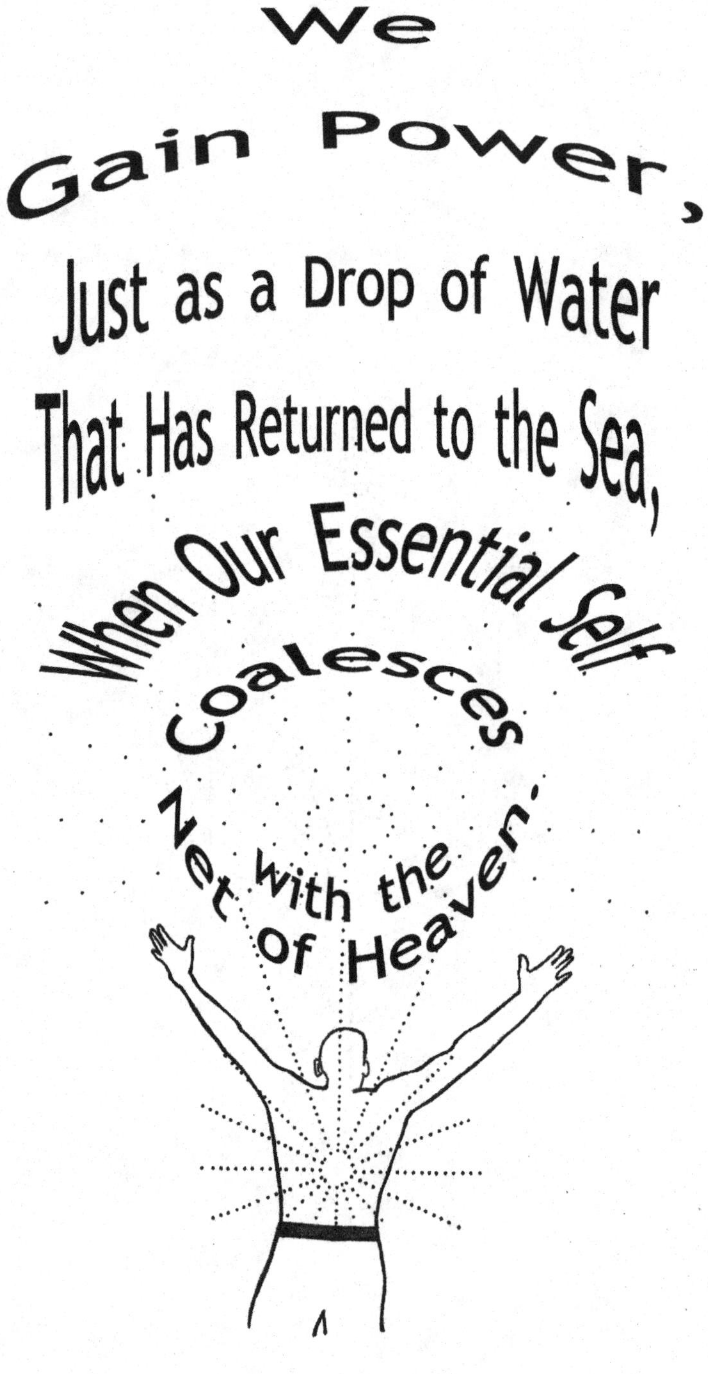

We

Gain Power,

Just as a Drop of Water

That Has Returned to the Sea,

When Our Essential Self

Coalesces

with the

Net of Heaven

Figure 73: Coalescence with the Net of Heaven

Invisible Energy— the Net of Heaven

73

In verse 73 Lao-tzu tells us that bold actions "sometimes benefit and sometimes injure." He continues to explain that heaven conquers "without striving," gets answers but "does not speak," receives everything needed but "does not ask," and accomplishes all on schedule but "does not hurry." He concludes with the all-inspiring statement that "[the] net of heaven catches all" (Dyer 2007, 344); and in my mind that means it leaves nothing out. Wayne Dyer begins to clarify the again paradoxical words of Lao-tzu by telling us "that the way to heaven is to eschew bold actions and remain cautious" (345).

I will begin by saying that this commentary will equate the net of heaven of which Lao-tzu speaks to the Truth we all seek. Instead of following the ways of the ego, our needs can be met by seeking Truth and living according to the natural rhythm of the Universe, which is nature's way and our inherent way. Who we really are, our natural being, is buried under layer upon layer of conditioning that makes us forget our true existence. Fortunately, the net of heaven allows us opportunity to use the four seemingly unrealistic ways that Lao-tzu tells us heaven uses to accomplish without the commonly used forces of the ego. Instead, in our quest for ego's wants, we often resort to incessant striving, harsh demands, and manipulative speech, as well as repeated and strident requests that are acted out by us, sometimes with the frenetic urgency comparable to a pack of hungry wolves consuming a fresh kill. Much too often we appear to be primed to believe that we need to get what we can before it is gone.

Rather than resorting to force, we need to open ourselves to Truth. Many have identified Truth in various ways in the past.

Wayne Dyer quotes John Keats (1795-1821) from the poem "Ode on a Grecian Urn" in Dyer's book *Wisdom of the Ages*. Keats equates beauty and truth in his well-known quote by stating that "all [we] need to know" can be succinctly represented by the statement "beauty is truth" and "truth, beauty" (Dyer 2002, 84). Wayne Dyer sees beauty as the silent Truth within us. To carry this to a discussion of the Tao, Truth can be seen as representing the Oneness that we all share. The part of the Truth—the Tao—that we are is our connection to what Lao-tzu calls the net of heaven.

Also in his book *Wisdom of the Ages*, Dyer includes the biblical quote, "As you think so shall you be" (Dyer 2002, 197). According to the quote, it is the invisible part of us, *thought*, that determines the nature of our physical existence and experience. How can something that has no physical form carry such heavy responsibility? Furthermore, how might this be involved in connecting us to the Truth?

Later in the same book, Dyer calls attention to another poet, E. E. Cummings (1894-1962), whose poem "here is little Effie's head," about "empty-headed Effie" reveals more about the significant and momentous power of thought. How we think is vital to our being able to place our trust in the net of heaven. In the poem, Effie's thoughts were filled with the emptiness enlisted by the predominant intent generated by six words Cummings calls crumbs: *may, might, should, could, would,* and *must* (Dyer 2002, 233). Dyer tells us that releasing these words from our thinking process is vital to our growth (in very primary and fundamental ways). He suggests that detaching from the use of the words may and might sets us free us from our permission-seeking behavior. Removing the words should, could, would, and must from our vocabulary serves to liberate us from our habitually tenacious attachment to what are often life-inhibiting expectations assigned to us by others, despite our *not* having made that decision within ourselves (233). It also frees us from feeling we need to follow the pack. Although it may be difficult to remove these words entirely from our way of communicating, when these six words no longer *command our thinking*, our true calling can begin to manifest. We no longer feel forced to act on the controlling thoughts originating from implanted fear.

In keeping with the idea that our thoughts interact with one another to produce our intentions and help form our connection to the Truth, the net of heaven, I will again refer to the following reference taken from *The Seat of the Soul* by Gary Zukav. As previously mentioned, he reveals that "not all forms are physical. A thought, for example, is a form" (Zukav 1990, 105). This does not agree with our conventional concept of form. Zukav explains that form is created from energy and is shaped by consciousness. He goes on to clarify that our consciousness affects how we think, feel, and act. Consciousness, thinking, and feeling all play a crucial part in our lives and obviously do exist, but they are intangible. Only the actions that result, from these *untouchable forms* of form can be perceived. Our personality is an outward expression of this *form*. The nature of our personality, guided by our intentions, gives direction to what we experience. I would suggest that the net of heaven as expressed by Lao-tzu represents the same source of energy that Zukav is describing. It is worth repeating that he says "[we] are shaping the Light that is flowing through [us]." He goes on to explain that we give this energy the *form* of *thought, feeling,* and *action* (105-07).

Zukav clarifies further by describing that "intentions shape Light" and "set Light into motion." He tells us that it is our intentions that "create [our] reality" (110-11). I suggest that our intentions lead us to the possible scenario that we have chosen, because the things we experience and the events of our lives are filtered through our mindset as determined by intention and promoted through intuition. Our intentions help to fine-tune our perception of intuition so we will be more likely to notice, and respond to, opportunities that will help manifest the intentions we feel. Our intentions act as the central guidance system for our lives.

Also in the *Seat of Our Soul*, Zukav reveals that true power lies in "the deepest source of our being" (26), which is consciousness; power does not rest in the things of the world, such as force, striving, and manipulation, all powered by the impatience of ego. The controlling forces of ego don't give us power. Power lies in the awareness that affects our thinking. If we allow love and trust to provide the focus of our intention, it is more natural for us to "respond to life's difficulties with compassion and love instead of fear and doubt" (Zukav 1990, 127-28). These intentions are more likely to come from the heart than from the mind.

Zukav's explanation of energy flowing through us, directed by our personality, is an empowering concept. It adds an interesting and dynamic dimension to Lao-tzu's view of the net of heaven. Our intentions give direction to this energy as it flows through us, and when we realize that who we really are is a piece of this energy, our intentions are more likely to be focused on the thoughts of God than the wishes of the ego. We accomplish greater things using the relaxed way of nature as opposed to the demanding structure of the ego.

Approaching life's situations from the beautiful and peaceful place within us—our place of Truth—is only possible when we allow our mind to be still and our intention to be one of love. Connecting to the Truth is our coupling to the net of heaven. Honor each coupling, or near coupling, by being present and living in the awareness that the net of heaven is the invisible and untouchable Energy of the Universe, which also *forms* the intangible within us, our true self. When our vagrant thoughts are subdued, our awareness of who we are can coalesce with the invisible Energy net of heaven, even if only for a moment.

Frequent quiet times and meditation allow our invisible self to connect more readily with the net of heaven, thus permitting it to provide our lives with the things of life we need, without using force. The "net of heaven catches all" (Dyer 2007, 344) that we require for a healthy and happy life.

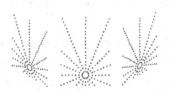

Awareness of the GAP Connects who We Are Directly to Our Source While We Are Living.

Figure 74: Awareness of the Gap

Awareness of the Gap

74

In verse 74 Lao-tzu asks us to understand and accept that all things change. He adds that if death is not feared "there is nothing we cannot achieve" (Dyer, *Change Your Thoughts—Change Your Life* 2007, 350). Just as the miracle of life is a product of our Source, death is part of the renewal cycle of life and is of the Source.

According to Lao-tzu, it is not our place to play the role of "the lord of death" (350). For selfish reasons the human race has been tyrannizing others, using death and the fear of death in what seems like increasingly more and more violent and unspeakable ways. As stated by Wayne Dyer in his essay on this verse, the tool of renewal and creation was designed by our Source to happen "in accord with nature, not performed as an ego decision" (352).

What might it be that Lao-tzu recognizes in death that if not feared allows us unbounded accomplishment during life?

In his book *Power, Freedom, and Grace*, Deepak Chopra asks the eternal questions of "Where did I come from?" and "What happens to me when I die?" (Chopra 2006, 62) A clue in understanding the message of Lao-tzu may be seen in Chopra's answers, as paraphrased in my brief account that follows. He tells us that we did not come from anywhere because we were always here and that nothing happens when we die because we do not go anywhere. Of what significance is this information?

Typically, we consider our brain as simply the generator of our thoughts. Contrary to this, Chopra compares our brain to a telephone. When the connection between the receiving device, the phone, and the transmitter is lost, communication is stopped, but the components involved do not go anywhere (62-63). In the case of death, the neural communication network of our brain has stopped its function as our connection to the "mind field," but the life force, the soul that we are remains "everywhere and nowhere," in the words of Deepak Chopra (Chopra, *Power, Freedom, and Grace* 2006, 64). This provides us with another way of viewing the concept of death.

How are the ideas that we hold about life and death developed? These ideas become part of our worldview. In *Life after Death*, Chopra describes our worldview as being constructed of three layers: energy, beliefs, and structure (Chopra 2006, 233). All our experiences consist of vibrating energy of varying frequency. Since our beliefs affect our behavior, our experiences, and our beliefs work in concert to produce the life we lead. As we live our lives, it is always our choice whether or not to make decisions that maximize our personal growth and personality development. Our personality provides the structure with which we approach all aspects of our lives, including the regulation of our approach to life and death. Our perception serves as a filter and works together with our personality to organize our lives. We use our brain as a judgment center in defense of our beliefs. As we move through life, our decisions may or may not lead us to a broadening understanding of life. Greater consciousness leads us to change our beliefs as well as renews our system of judgment. This, in turn, fosters new experiences.

In his essay on verse 74, Wayne Dyer tells us to "move from wanting to see permanence in [our] life to realizing that *all* things change due to the nature of this being an ever-changing world" (Dyer, *Change Your Thoughts—Change Your Life* 2007, 351). One purpose life serves is to provide opportunity to reorganize our thought processes to facilitate living life according to the Tao. This involves change.

Chopra advises us to recognize that "all viewpoints are valid" and not to "defend an 'I am' that [we] know is just temporary" (Chopra, *Life after Death* 2006, 233). He encourages us to focus on "transformation rather than defending the status quo" (233). Thus, as we live our lives on Earth, aspects of our personality can be transformed, providing our thinking leads to good decisions.

Also in *Life after Death*, Chopra explains that "thinking, the basic operation of the mind, organizes reality to make sense. The universe does this physically" (Chopra, *Life after Death* 2006, 200).

He clarifies this through example by making a comparison between the significance of the *spaces* between genetic material and "the void, where *something* is arranging random events so that they are meaningful" (200). Later he explains the intrinsic and vital purpose of these spaces by stating that "the gap is the reference point, the stillness at the heart of creation, where the universe correlates all events" (247). This is profound.

In his book *Getting in the Gap*, Dr. Dyer discusses the idea of "making conscious contact with God through meditation," which is also the subtitle. He tells us that the Oneness of our Source cannot be divided, just as the light from our sun and the silent voice of God cannot be divided (Dyer 2003, 5). An ancient Zen observation quoted by Dr. Dyer states that "it's the silence between the notes that makes the music" (12). He explains that the function of the gap is creativity.

Our brains keep producing/receiving thoughts at random or at will, and rarely do we acknowledge a moment of silence between thoughts. Arriving at these gaps between thought and taking that moment to make a connection to the Oneness that is God, is what Dyer is teaching us in *Getting in the Gap*. It is in these gaps where creativity thrives.

Later in *Life after Death*, Chopra expresses that "what happens when we die remains a miracle," and subsequently tells us, "Science supports the claim that the field is capable of creative leaps and endless transformation" (Chopra 2006, 237). He then reminds us that "without death there can be no present moment, for the last moment has to die to make the next one possible" (248).

Is death our *ultimate gap* that exposes our "I am" to the all-powerful creativity of the universe? In *Power, Freedom, and Grace*, Chopra reveals to us that "through death we recreate ourselves at every level" (Chopra 2006, 69-70), and he soon follows this statement with further revelation, where he makes known that "the transformation after death . . . is just a change in the quality of attention in consciousness" (72). Does recognizing and knowing this open us to receiving the ultimate power within the gap, right now, in the present moment? Does a connection to the gap kindle the all-encompassing and guiding force of Nature and cause it to expand within us, displace the dark fear of death, and supersede and restore it with the light of all things possible?

When our worldview accepts a new way of organizing our thoughts regarding the concept of death, to include phrases such as "recreate ourselves," and "a change in the quality of attention in consciousness" instead of focusing on the commonly held idea of "a movement to some other place and time" (Chopra 2006, 72), it allows us to live our lives consciously, within the framework of the Tao, without resistance to what is, and without fear of death. According to Lao-tzu, when we don't fear death, "there is nothing we cannot achieve" (Dyer, *Change Your Thoughts—Change Your Life* 2007, 350).

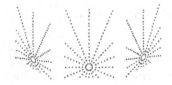

Figure 75: Forgiveness Allows Freedom

Forgiveness and Trust

75

In this verse, Lao-tzu mentions over-taxation and authoritarian control. These things evoke stress and fear. I will focus on these feelings without addressing any particular cause. Frequently, lack of or loss of control over our lives prompts fearful thoughts.

    Gifts from a Course in Miracles, edited by Frances Vaugan and Roger Walsch, states, "all [our] misery comes from the strange belief that [we] are powerless" (Vaughan 1988, intro 1995, 244). A feeling of powerlessness can trigger many emotions, perhaps including hatred of those deemed responsible. Among other things, facing difficult circumstances may lead us to thoughts of helplessness. Not knowing what to do or where to turn for direction may leave us feeling uncertain and without purpose. In her book *Sacred Contracts,* Carolyn Myss suggests that "most of us would probably admit that changing our lives for the better—as well as helping other people—is part of the reason we are on Earth" (Myss 2003, 39).

    Wanting to help others and ourselves is one thing, but knowing about an effective way to start can be quite another. *Gifts from a Course in Miracles* suggests that forgiveness is the way to begin helping ourselves and others. "Those [we] do not forgive [we] fear. And no one reaches love with fear [at their side]" (Vaughan, 75). In addition, it clearly unveils that the world we are in "is a world of illusions" and that if we don't forgive, we "are binding [ourselves] to them" (76). Later this book discloses, "Until forgiveness is complete the world does have a purpose" (182). Forgiveness is an ongoing process of reminding ourselves to let go of the past. According to a quote by Oprah from her second Lifeclass on the Oprah Winfrey Network in the fall of 2011, "Forgiveness is giving up the hope that the past could be any different." She tells us that this way the past cannot hold us hostage.

Once we are no longer held hostage, we can begin to plan our strategy and act on it, in an attempt to begin to change our circumstances. David R. Hawkins, in his book *The Eye of the I,* provides advice on how to handle negative situations. We are "not to try to eliminate the negative but instead to choose and adopt the positive" (Hawkins, *The Eye of the I* 2001, 67). Seeing the positive in circumstances that on the surface appear negative may require massive action, often involving life-changing decisions on our part that may create the shift our lives may need. Part of the strength that is required for such an undertaking may be found in the trust referred to in the following quote from *The Eye of the I.* "Place faith and trust in the love of God, which is all forgiving, and understand that condemnation and fear of judgment stem from the ego" (65). When we recognize and accept that who we are is a piece of the Tao, not our ego, we can more easily access the feeling of forgiveness together with the acceptance of circumstances. This provides us with a place of calm in which to allow our trust to grow.

In addition, we develop trust in ourselves when we recognize, and then avoid, strictly ego-based decisions. Making wise decisions also may help us to trust in those that we have chosen to be a part of our lives. *Gifts from a Course in Miracles* "teaches us that whatever [we] accept into [our] mind has reality for [us]. It is [our] acceptance of it that makes it real" (Vaughan 1988, intro 1995, 24). This of course applies to those of us in charge as well as those of us who look to others for direction. Wayne Dyer reminds us about the importance of our trust in those under our charge, and how it "will lead to their trusting themselves *and* the wisdom that created them" (Dyer 2007, 359).

Lao-tzu concludes this brief verse with the understanding that our awareness must move in the direction of trust. I would suggest that this trust include the following: trust in the oneness of the process of life; trust in the unifying power of our Universe; trust in that our forgiveness of others, and ourselves, promotes our personal freedom; and trust in our connection to and oneness with the Mind of God.

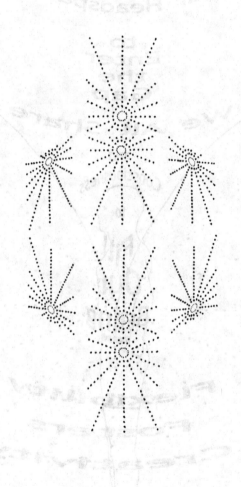

Flexibility

Our Allows Headspace
to
Enter
the
Gap
We All Share
and
Consciousness
to
Fill
Our
Being

Flexibility
Fosters
Creativity
to
Blossom.

Figure 76: Flexibility Fosters Creativity

Live within the Flexibility Offered by the Gap

76

In this verse Lao-tzu compares the flexibility of life to the rigidity of death. Wayne Dyer's essay on this verse relates rigidity to the need to always be right (Dyer, *Change Your Thoughts—Change Your Life* 2007, 362).

In his book *The Sky's the Limit*, Wayne Dyer discusses the tendency of authoritarians to categorize the world into people and things hated and people and things loved (Dyer 1980, 108). Many people lead rigidly domineering lifestyles that stem from an overbearing, ego-dominated personality. Moreover, like Dyer writes in his book *Real Magic*, we feel convinced that change is impossible because we think only genes, family, culture, and chemistry control our personality (Dyer 1993, 218-21). Also in the aforementioned book, but in direct opposition to this common way of thinking, he reassures us that "[we] can change in a moment when [we] become a spiritual being first and a material being second" (233). This provides the confirmation many of us may need to realize that there is life beyond our rigidly controlled and hectic modern lifestyle.

In *The Sky's the Limit* (Dyer 1980, 184-85), he suggests that a way of living similarly to the spontaneity often experienced in childhood is a much-favored lifestyle over the unbending manner many of us display when exercising dominance over others. He goes on to quote apostle Paul: "Love does not insist on its own way" (111).

In *Pulling Your Own Strings*, Dyer teaches us that "being creatively alive requires suspending as much of [our] rigidity as possible" (Dyer 1979, 215). When we live increasingly more from spirit than from the material, the rigidity imposed by the finite nature of our materialistic desires becomes less and less important to us. We gradually become aware of the exceedingly transient nature of the reward offered by *ownership*, compared to the deep and lasting joy and contentment that comes with consciousness, the ongoing recognition and acknowledgement of who we really are. Our level of awareness is the essential variable determining our flexibility or lack thereof.

A quote by David R. Hawkins in his book *Power versus Force* emphasizes the importance of our knowing who we really are by reminding us that awareness is connected to living a principled life. "An individual's level of consciousness is determined by the principles to which one is committed" (Hawkins 2004, 279). Adding more significance to this idea, he goes on to say, "injury to man's 'spiritual eye' has resulted in dimness of moral vision and blindness to truth" (280).

Likewise, it is blindness to the consequences our rigidity has on others, as well as on ourselves, that keeps the ego trained on things such as being right, judging others, and inflexible thinking. Not only does this egotistical behavior leave a very poor impression on those we may be trying to put down, it also may appear ill-mannered or worse to those we are attempting to impress. In addition, these actions tend to lock us into ego-based thinking patterns, with rewards strictly limited to momentary pride and temporary happiness unequivocally tied to a need for ongoing winning performances, as seen through the eye of ego.

To paraphrase Chopra from his book *The Ultimate Happiness Prescription,* he reminds us that while being right gives us a moment to take comfort in being able to gloat, it does not bring "true happiness." Furthermore, he explains that because "right is whatever conforms to [our] perspective," we are a "cocreator with God," but he also points out that if we relentlessly feel we always have to be right, "the opposite happens" (Chopra 2009, 75).

If we persist in this type of behavior, our brain activity will be in rapid fire as we encourage thoughts around our ego's need to win. The more frequently we can give up the need to be right, the less chatter and noise our mind experiences. It is then by conscious choice that we can select the quiet space of love and forgiveness to bring us happiness and move in the direction of detachment from the need to finish first. Alternatively, we can follow our ego in its fear-driven agenda and live with the incessant yattering of our mind telling us all the things we should have done, the things we should not have done, and the things we should do now. The level of distraction this addiction to being right stirs up in our minds is self-inflicted.

There are many ways of doing things. Most ways are no better than most other ways, only different. Wayne Dyer quotes an old proverb in his essay on verse 76, part of which states, "The way doesn't exist" (Dyer, *Change Your Thoughts—Change Your Life* 2007, 363). It follows that no personal or group way of living can be followed as the single, best answer.

Chopra suggests that we surrender—not to a person but to the "path." The "path" is something all of us share, and yet it may be different for all of us. To follow this path, we dedicate ourselves to this shared space, not to the personal space of individual ways, schemes, or targets that any of us might have. Chopra explains that this takes our ego out of the picture and continues to explain that "[our] focus shifts to the space between [us] and the one [we] love. This is the gap between ego and spirit" (Chopra, *The Ultimate Happiness Prescription* 2009, 82).

Our awareness of this gap moves us in the direction of our path, resulting in much less of the upsetting mind twaddle that embezzles our happiness time and time again. When our mental energy is not hijacked by ego, we are more likely to direct this energy to peaceful thoughts that come from a place of calm acceptance and are parallel to the thoughts of God. Our actions are more likely to be congruent with the thoughts of those we love, and when the consciousness from comparable sources of love unites, increased energy levels may elevate our awareness. We are now much more likely to live our life with flexibility.

Figure 77: Giving

Giving
from a Place of Surplus

77

The seventy-seventh verse of the Tao speaks of giving from a place of surplus—giving of the fullness of the Tao to all, including those living in deficiency and need. The giving described here includes the giving of material things as well as the sharing of the full and complete resonance of our being with those around us.

In *Reinventing the Body, Resurrecting the Soul*, Deepak Chopra tells us to "offer yourself first." He explains that "'yourself' means the real you" (Chopra 2009, 247). He goes on to remind us that when we present our "imitation" self as we act out our roles in society, there is the "expectation of a return" for the gifts we give. The false confidence we feel that is built of the external trappings we cling to and the beliefs we carry is an "illusion." His recommendation is to offer strength to those in need by "[aligning our] spirit with the weak," by offering "the wholeness of spirit" through the heartfelt and earnest gesture of the opening and sharing of ourselves to others (248). Later he explains that living an abundant life is not about faith or religion, nor need it be about being materialistic. "It is about trusting the flow," and, he says "that wholeness doesn't have holes in it and never leaves a void" (251).

In the book *Invisible Acts of Power*, Caroline Myss includes stories she requested from readers "about their experiences with grace and life-changing acts of service" (Myss 2004, 4). One contributor talks about the gift of caring companionship. The person wrote, "She taught me that love asks no return and when you extend yourself to anyone, Jesus is there beside you" (256). Caroline Myss concludes this section with the words of Jesus taken from James 2:14-26. Here is a portion of that quote (Myss, *Invisible Acts of Power* 2004, 256-57).

> If a brother or a sister is ill-clad and in lack of daily food, and one of you says to him "Go in peace, be warmed and filled" without giving the things needed for the body, what does it profit? So faith by itself without works is dead .... You see that a man is justified by works and not by faith alone .... For as the body apart from the spirit is dead, so faith apart from works is dead.

It is clear through these words of Jesus that faith and works must function in tandem to be truly beneficial when we are giving of our surplus.

In his essay on this verse, Wayne Dyer tells us that the word surplus "actually symbolizes *much more*" (italics added). He goes on to say that, "Whenever you see deficiencies . . . make your own surpluses available" (Dyer, *Change Your Thoughts—Change Your Life* 2007, 366). When the offering of our surplus of the necessities of life—and *much more*—is done with warmth and caring to those in need through the open and heartfelt extension of our true being, these acts are a unifying connection to the limitless power and abundance of the Tao.

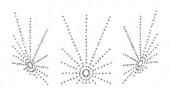

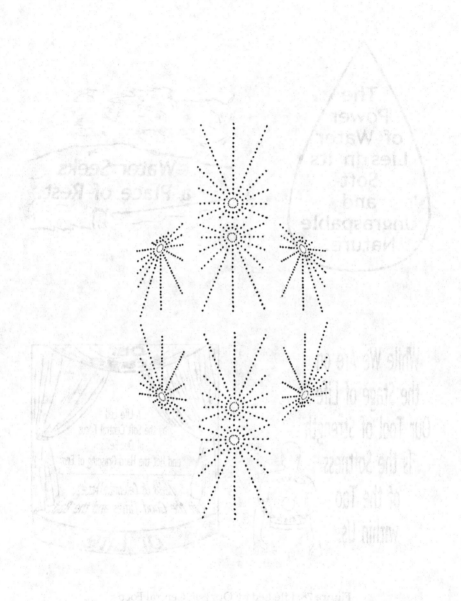

The Power of Water Lies in Its Soft and Ungraspable Nature.

Water Seeks a Place of Rest.

While We Are on the Stage of Life Our Tool of Strength Is the Softness of the Tao within Us.

Our Stage

A Life Led by the Soft Central Focus of Our Being and Not the Hard Grasping of Ego

Helps Us Celebrate! Accept. in the Good Times and the Bad.

of Life

Figure 78: Life Led by Our Soft Central Focus

Living
from Our Place of Softness

78

In Dr. Wayne W. Dyer's comments on verse 78 he notes the frequent reference to water by Lao-tzu in the Tao. These comparisons to water encourage us to assume the softness of water as our tool of strength, instead of the harshness of egoism that seems to be the ego's choice. All things—water and humankind included—originate from the same Source. Water readily follows the prompting of the force of gravity, and the cyclical nature of water allows it to keep renewing its liquid state while fulfilling its vital role of life support on Earth.

Wayne Dyer informs us that "Lao-tzu reiterates three themes" that represent "the true characteristics of water." A very brief summary follows. The first is that water can "overcome . . . by yielding." The weak appearance of water is discussed next, with the conclusion that "the weak overcomes the strong." The final point that water cannot be permanently damaged because it is reconstituted when it returns to Source emphasizes the value of returning to source for renewal. Lao-tzu suggests that we parallel these attributes in our lives (Dyer, *Change Your Thoughts—Change Your Life* 2007, 370).

Might an even closer look prove helpful in strengthening the correlation that Lao-tzu draws between the action of water and the workings of our lives?

Gravity is the force responsible for pulling water steadily closer to a place of rest. Although gravity pulls water toward rest and stability, water also encounters obstacles along the way. Perhaps corresponding to the constant pull of gravity is our endless desire for happiness that almost continually pulls at the choices we make that determine the direction of our lives. Although, most of the time we do not recognize what we are really searching for, the joy we seek is also a place of rest, a state of (spiritual) contentment.

In his book *Unlearning the Basics*, Rishi Sativihari discusses the Buddha's "four noble truths." In his discussion of the second truth, *tanha*, or "thirst," he reveals the yogic myth, which "teaches us that tanha is the dualistic desire of an empty subject to possess completing objects (Others), to escape or destroy depleting objects (Others), and to ignore inert objects (Others)" (Sativihari 2010, 36). He compares "Others" to something negative to be eliminated (29). To briefly paraphrase, he is saying that we seek to fill our emptiness with certain "Others" that we see as a source of pleasure. Because we cling to these things as the source of our happiness in life, the yogis, or spiritual practitioners, saw them as something to escape from or avoid. We see "depleting objects" as causing us pain and as something to steer clear of, or destroy; and "inert objects" hold no value or importance to us, so we feel indifferent and emotionless toward them and seek anything but . . . so we ignore them (32-35).

He continues by making it very clear that the overpowering need that we have to fill our emptiness with objects, money, or people *is not real* despite our being convinced that it will make us feel whole. He reiterates this by relating that the "samsara" or stories created by our minds "to foster the illusion that the objects we are pursuing are real, permanent, and will completely and forever satisfy our needs" are a myth. He later reveals that this type of thinking "is the foundation of ordinary consciousness" (37). It appears to follow that the constant direction we take from the ego, to some extent, might be compared to the constant pull gravity exerts on water. According to Sativihari, ego allows us to flourish, but only to a certain degree. Gravity also allows water to gain power or "flourish" by giving it direction to unite as a unified mass of moving energy. The comparison here seems to be that ego promotes the development of our life-skills, which can be used to direct our energy, while gravity unifies water's energy. Sativihari also reminds us that ego not only promotes "our flourishing," but also is "the root cause of our greed, hatred, indifference, and injustice" (Sativihari 2010, 38-39). Similarly, the erosive force of moving water may be the cause of immediate environmental destruction including loss of life, but at the same time the consequence of nutrient relocation has the potential for future benefit. It appears that the force driving our behavior and the force propelling water both yield consequences of positive and negative import.

Could there be further parallel between the behavior of water and the behavior we display as induced by our mental struggle for happiness? When water falls to Earth, it is often not *content* to linger at its position of impact. Likewise, we so often are not content with the impact of our circumstances on our lives. Water responds to gravity as it diverts the recently arrived raindrop by either pulling it into thirsty soil as future life support, or by pulling it over impervious surfaces, ever leading it toward and contributing to its ongoing cyclical rebirth. While this is happening, the energy-rich portion of the water rejoins its gaseous origin. The laws of nature lead water around obstacles that obstruct its purpose and cause it to completely avoid the areas totally unrelated to its sole purpose, which is finding a solid basin that leads to quiet stillness, further energy absorption, and regeneration.

Because we yearn for happiness, we too are not content with our situation; the stories we create support the idea that the only way to be happy is to attract certain people and things into our lives that we think will fill the hollow we feel inside. These may prove to be obstacles that present lessons to be learned, thus allowing us opportunity to change paths, as water does in the face of obstacles. We too, will avoid whatever hinders our progress or has no significance to our goal, and favor that which we feel will fill us, by following the stories fabricated in our minds. To repeat, according to Sativihari, these stories have become "interwoven into the very structure of ordinary consciousness" (Sativihari 2010, 41).

On water's downward trek to lower ground, gravity automatically pilots it around obstacles to have it fill the hollowness in its path. We frequently allow the ego aspect of our personality to serve as our automatic pilot generating thoughts, ideas, and stories that promote the *belief* that objects will fill our hollowness. Our mind tends to respond spontaneously, especially in familiar situations, by following story patterns developed according to the success level of past scenarios. This can be a good thing when we learn from our mistakes, but it may also keep us from growth.

Water uses gravity to reach its level of stability while ego uses pride and greed to grasp at the hope of a stable level of happiness. Both are limited by the parameters of their function. Hard surfaces will temporarily hold water back, but with time, the soft nature of water works to eke out a new channel of release. Just as it may take time for the softness of water to find a new passage where none existed before, it is a process for us to recognize that the hardened ways of our ego-driven behavior are not going to really lead us to the joy we seek. This is because we are not the rigid ego that developed the character that we have come to believe we are. We are spirit, and as water is soft, who we really are is also *softness*, an indescribable essence or energy; we are not the story-generating ego of hardness that we think controls us. Just as gravity continues to act on water while its softness works out a new path, once we realize that we are not the ego that created our character, whether it is hard or soft, we can choose to exhibit the softness within us, when we realize that we really are an indefinable softness.

In *Unlearning the Basics*, Sativihari refers to the psychologist Adrian van Kaam as suggesting "that a key existential choice that we make in life is the choice of what our *central mode of existence* will be." He goes on to explain that "the peripheral modes then derive their shape, color, and meaning from that central mode" (Sativihari 2010, 125-26).

We might say that water's central purpose is to work with Source to find serenity at its lowest level while both supporting life and continually surrendering to the evaporative power of Source for escape and regeneration. Lao-tzu suggests we live our lives in ways comparable to the way in which water behaves.

We can choose to live our lives with right conviction by acknowledging who we really are by both surrendering to and reconnecting with our Source. If our central purpose, or "central mode," as it was referred to earlier is to promote goodness, our actions will support this lead and we will offer our support to others. As water chooses its path according to the prompts received from obstacles it encounters, we, as well, can choose to be attentive and to act on the subtle yet powerful prompts provided for us by our life experiences throughout our allotted time on the "Stage of Life," so generously provided by our Source. The choice to behave with the softness of water is ours alone. Doing this simply means living life with the intention that we surrender to the softness of the part of the Tao that we are and that we be open to the guidance it offers in helping us through our experiences. This way, through good times and bad, we are listening and responding to the sometimes clear but most often hushed "whisperings," as Oprah would describe them, that come from the part of the Source that is in us.

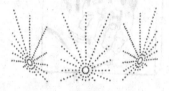

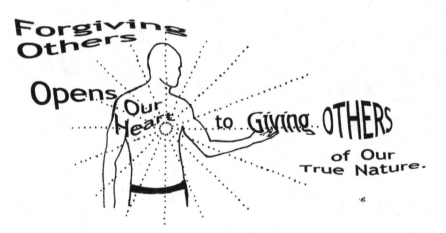

Arguing Because of Our Illusions about Others Grips Us With Fear

Forgiving Others Opens Our Heart to Giving OTHERS of Our True Nature.

When We Give Love, Life's Fullness Is Opened to Us.

Figure 79: Offering Love

Arguments, Forgiveness, and Giving

79

The all-out disagreements we have with others frequently originate in the separate and independent illusion we each have of the other person. From either person's point of view, these conflicts are unlikely to be easily resolved because the illusion held by the ego of the other will likely remain. Compromise from both sides is required, but in the event of undeniably toxic relationships, estrangement may be necessary.

Lao-tzu suggests that we extend acts of kindness favoring our dissenter without presuming he or she will do the same for us; this may not be an easy thing to do. Disparaging comments raise our level of fear and tend to make us feel weak and vulnerable. This increases the likelihood of our using an indignant riposte as a defense mechanism because it is often easier to lash back in anger than to contain ourselves in the knowledge of who we are. In addition, many times it has become a conditioned response because many of us have been taught not to allow others to take advantage of us. This concept definitely has validity. We are the ones, after all, responsible for taking charge of our personal rights. Hopefully we are able to do this through firm but respectable behavior that rests within the parameters of the Tao. The sharing of our Tao-centered nature in circumstances that are otherwise not conducive to showing care and concern may have the effect of turning a situation around, simply through a giving heart that will not accept abusive treatment. Giving of ourselves in these circumstances is very difficult, so it needs to be a distinctly conscious choice.

How can we even begin to restore calm to our overactive brain and bring ourselves to the place of quiet awareness that is needed? Here are several thoughts that may help, as taken from

Gifts from a Course in Miracles edited by Frances Vaughan and Roger Walsch: "If you attack error in another, you will hurt yourself." "Every loving thought is true. Everything else is an appeal for healing and help" (Vaughan 1988, intro 1995, 65). These two quotes suggest that retaliation is harmful to us and that extending anything but love toward others is a plea to be rescued.

In times of argument, we usually attempt to prove ourselves right and the other wrong. Our ego feels obligated to vindicate itself of blame by placing fault on the other person. The previous quote clearly tells us that fault-finding indicates the need for "healing and help."

"Lift up your eyes and look on one another in innocence born of complete forgiveness of each other's illusions" (75). This quote, also from *Gifts from a Course in Miracles*, indirectly promotes the idea of acceptance of and giving freely to others. To be meaningful, giving must come from the heart. Hearts filled with resentment have only resentment to give. When we forgive others for the illusions they carry about us, our hearts are set free and we are able to see them in a new light. We are now able to give of the warmhearted goodness that has *always been* within us. This warmth can be shared, because forgiveness of others and ourselves has opened our hearts. Lao-tzu tells us that "to the giver comes the fullness of life" (Dyer, *Change Your Thoughts—Change Your Life* 2007, 374).

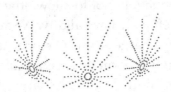

Figure 80: Melding Intention with Purpose

Simplicity and Contentment

80

In verse 80 Lao-tzu focuses on the importance of living a simple, contented life. Living simply usually results in a more relaxed lifestyle. Simple living as opposed to a life of stress could be compared to separating the things we really want from the things we actually need. In his book *Soul to Soul*, Gary Zukav talks about "artificial needs" and "authentic needs." He explains that artificial needs are used to create an impression on others for the purpose of influencing them in our favor. He also explains the "fundamental fear" shared by all of us, the feeling of "not being worthy of life." He describes "the frightened parts of [our] personality" as having what I call a "pernicious" need for gathering more and more stuff "to make ourselves feel safe, worthy, and lovable." We also feel that wealth and possessions make us more powerful, but "authentic power requires that [we] distinguish between [our] artificial needs and [our] authentic needs." Lao-tzu advocates a simple lifestyle and this idea fits nicely with the advice given by Zukav "to [set our] *intention* to create harmony, co-operation, sharing and reverence for life" (Zukav, *Soul to Soul* 2007, 288-89).

Wayne Dyer quotes Carlos Castaneda in Dyer's book *The Power of Intention*: "*Intent* is a force that exists in the universe" (Dyer 2004, 4; italics added). Dyer tells us that all of us, and everything, has a connection to this undetectable force or energy. He elaborates by saying that "this field is home to the laws of nature, and is the inner domain of every human being. This is the field of all possibilities, and it is [ours] by virtue of [our] existence" (135). When what we contribute to our world is in harmony with our intention to do "good," we live a more complete and meaningful life. It is built into the simplicity of our awareness of this concept. The strength of this simplicity lies in "a field of energy that flows invisibly beyond the reach of our normal, everyday habitual pattern" (6).

It is the good intentions that we have while living our life plainly and without embellishment that will resonate in harmony with the goodness of the Tao. Lao-tzu encourages us to be content with the basics, as they will fulfill our needs, but our ego rouses us to pursue things like wealth, pleasure, power, and more. Wayne Dyer reminds us that when we make our life only about pursuing these things, we "miss the purpose of living." He also suggests that "in a sense, thoughts about [our] purpose are really [our] purpose trying to reconnect to [us]" (150-51). This is an intriguing concept. I would suggest that our level of awareness helps us to decipher thoughts prompted by the desires of ego, from thoughts that fill us with the contentment of realizing our true purpose.

Each of us is able to share his or her personal talents in a creative way unique to us when we simply live in harmony with the Tao by living the purpose of our lives. We do not need expensive, over-the-top materials and products to express our inspiration and feel fulfilled. Happiness does not necessarily follow a wealthy or even an extravagant lifestyle, and depending upon motivation, an affluent lifestyle does not necessarily foster resourcefulness that is an overall benefit to society. Of course the converse is also true. The wealthy and affluent can live life with the heartfelt intention to be a benefit to society through the charitable and worthwhile actions they take that benefit humanity.

Creativity and contentment within the parameters of goodness, as set out by the Tao, can happen at any economic level of society, but the key is that it contributes to the joy and development of the individual and that of society, while employing, as well as facilitating, eco-friendly processes.

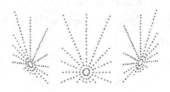

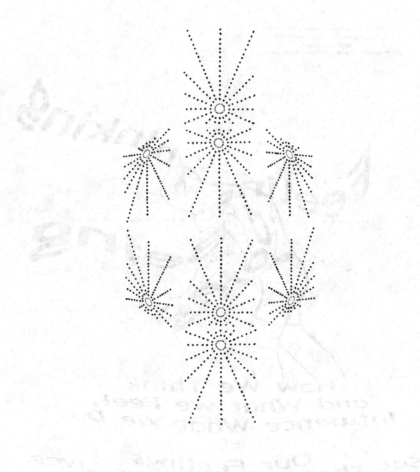

Live with
"Being, Feeling, Thinking, and Doing"
in Congruence.

The above section in quotes is taken from
The Ultimate Happiness Prescription
by Deepak Chopra
(This includes the same words labelled in the drawing below.)

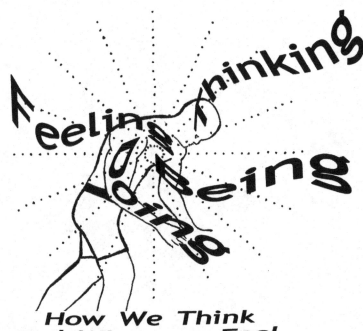

Figure 81: Living in Congruence

Living in Congruence with Consciousness

81

Like verse 1 of the Tao, verse 81 uses circular statements for emphasizing the Truth of the Tao as being the essence of all there is while at the same time confirming that it is nothing. It is our conscious connection to the nothingness of the Tao that supports us and provides what we need through our consciousness, which in turn directs our behavior.

Deepak Chopra, in *The Ultimate Happiness Prescription*, explains that "consciousness . . . functions to create change at four fundamental levels: being, feeling, thinking, and doing" (Chopra 2009, 109). The quotes in the following paragraph from verse 81 describe actions that can be looked at as representing in near perfect congruence the levels of being, feeling, thinking, and doing as referenced above.

When our consciousness represents the Truth at our center, "true words" are what we reveal through our *thinking*, if we allow it to be guided by the essence of our Being. Yet according to Lao-tzu, these "true words" cannot express the beauty of the Tao. When we *feel* complete in ourselves, what we *do* is affected by our connection to the "virtue" of the Tao. We do not "look for faults" in what others say and do, and our tendency to argue is greatly reduced. When we *feel* there is enough to go around, we enjoy giving to others and have little desire to "accumulate anything" because we receive all we need to feel fulfilled through the conscious connection we have with the Tao. How we choose to be is directly affected by a feeling of completeness in ourselves. When we know we are complete we enjoy just *being* and *doing* what is right; we do not think about "faults," and just as "heaven does good to all" (Dyer, *Change Your Thoughts—Change Your Life* 2007, 382), we too should make that our goal.

311

Also in the *Ultimate Happiness Prescription*, Chopra tells us that "pure being leads to the highest level of feeling, and the highest level of feeling creates the highest level of thinking and doing" (Chopra 2009, 111). In my opinion, in this last verse of the Tao, the concepts addressed by Lao-tzu reflect higher-level thinking.

In his book *The Biology of Belief*, Bruce Lipton, a cellular biologist, presents his research that has led him to make the statement that "we are not victims of our genes, but masters of our fates, able to create lives overflowing with peace, happiness, and love" (Lipton 2008, xxv). He also firmly believes that according to this "New Biology," "the fully conscious mind trumps both nature and nurture" (xxvii). He reports "that every protein in our bodies is a physical/electromagnetic complement to something in the environment" (159). Are our heartfelt feelings part of the environmental agency that gives direction to life?

Lipton uses an analogy that compares our body to a TV set. When our body dies, it compares to a dead TV that no longer displays a picture. He tells us that the image does not die because "the death of the television as a receiver in no way killed the identity broadcast that comes from the environment." He goes on to say "that [our] identity, [our] 'self,' exists in the environment whether [our] body is here or not."

He continues by telling us that this analogy is not complete. He now compares our body to a Martian rover equipped with "cameras," "vibration detectors," and "chemical sensors" to relay information back to Earth. "The NASA controller interprets the information" and sends appropriate directions back. Similarly, we interpret our experiences on Earth in a particular way and within the parameters available to us, we are able to choose how we respond or react.

Our thoughts and our intentions serve as the medium for the message we are sending. The Tao promotes the acceptance of all. Can controlling our intentions to include the acceptance of everyone and everything as they are allow us the control, which Lipton discusses? (Again, as stated in verse 64 and elsewhere, this does not mean we condone it; we just accept it as being so at this moment.)

Is this finding of Lipton suggesting that we can become "masters of our fates," a science-based explanation of the central message of Lao-tzu in the Tao Te Ching, which originated about two thousand five hundred years ago?

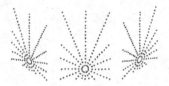

Afterword

What Quantum Physics Tells Us about Our Origins and How We Should Live is the newspaper-like heading subtitle of the book *God is Not Dead*, by Amit Goswami, PhD. This dust jacket commentary by Deepak Chopra immediately reminded me of the title of the book *How Should We Then Live?* by Francis A. Schaeffer. Chopra describes the book by Goswami as "an excellent argument for nothing less than the existence of God" (Goswami 2008, cover). What makes this particularly significant to me is the connection to the comment I made in the preface of the book you are now reading that pertained to the book *How Should We Then Live?* As stated there, reading Schaeffer's book in 1978 prompted me to continue to search for a rational and equitable answer to the posed question. It has been the focus of my reading, off and on, since then. When I finally decided to put my thoughts down on paper, I used the chosen translation and the analysis of the Tao by Dr. Wayne W. Dyer as the foundation for my endeavor. The Tao in itself provides the answer as to how we should live, but I have chosen to use Dyer's interpretation of the Tao together with a compilation of compatible as well as congruent ideas from various sources to position what I consider the crucially essential pieces of a connecting bridge that I feel may direct us to the answer of the all important question as to how we *should* live.

Scientists are only beginning to understand how our universe works. We are also living at a time when we are beginning to realize, even further, our part in these workings, although these ideas do have an earlier origin. One of these sources is Max Planck, (1858-1947), and he is quoted by Gregg Braden in his book *The Divine Matrix* as saying "science cannot solve the ultimate mystery of nature. And that is because, in the last analysis, we ourselves are . . . part of the mystery that we are trying to solve" (Braden 2010, 3). "Recent discoveries reveal dramatic evidence that Planck's matrix—The Divine Matrix—is real" (Braden 2010, back cover). Might the "answer," as we understand it today, exist in the form of many analogous explanations that share a common thread? I have attempted to consolidate some key concepts using the Tao as both the consolidating structure and the basic message. Braden also quotes insight from the philosopher Kierkegaard (1813-55), regarding "shattering [our existing] paradigm." "There are two ways to be fooled. One is to believe what isn't true; the other is to refuse to believe what is true" (Braden, *The Divine Matrix* 2010, 37).

How does the Tao and the other material I have included in this book correlate with quantum physics? Amit Goswami presents the concept that "Jesus's God and the quantum-consciousness God are one and the same" (Goswami 2008, 278). He addresses the issue that "popular Christianity posits God and the Spirit as separate from us." Many of us believe that this is where the two ideas seem to part ways, but Goswami asks, "If God is truly separate from us, then how can we receive God's guidance and love?" (279) Quantum physics, according to Goswami, finds that "God is not separate from us; God is indwelling in us, in our unconsciousness. Consciousness is the ground of all being, which includes us." He also reports that "the concept of non-locality . . . implies that you and I are connected without any signals through space and time . . . our connection through consciousness transcends space and time." He reminds us of the words of Jesus on this topic: "The kingdom of God is everywhere, but people don't see it." Goswami goes on to say that we cannot point out any particular place for it (Goswami 2008, 279-80).

Amit Goswami describes "spiritual enlightenment" as being "steadily situated in quantum God-consciousness." He believes that Buddha reached the last stage of enlightenment and reports that the accounts about Jesus revolve around the words he said and the miracles. These miracles suggest that "Jesus acted from the quantum self or what in Christianity is called Holy Spirit" (281-82). Goswami quotes Matthew 5:48, where Jesus says, "Be perfect, therefore, as your heavenly Father is perfect." To Goswami this suggests that "Jesus himself attained perfection, and he encouraged people to do the same" (Goswami 2008, 284).

Goswami asks what happens when people have completed the "death-birth-rebirth cycle." He says they are completely "transformed" or "liberated." He continues by saying that scientifically, the "quantum monad[s]" of these "fully perfected patterns of living" "should be there in potentia available for future use." He suggests that a quantum monad can be invoked as a spirit guide. "A Hindu has . . . Krishna or Shankara, a Buddhist has Buddha, a Jew has Moses, a Moslem has Muhammad, and a Christian has Jesus" (Goswami 2008, 287). This leaves us recognizing the need to have respect for these ways of organizing religious belief.

To my way of thinking, this all ties in with the Tao; the energy of the Tao is everywhere and in everyone and this does include those of any faith or belief system. Because the Tao is in everyone, those of no faith or religious system are also included. This means all have contact with the Source of all there is, no matter if he or she believes it. As we so decide, the road we take to get there varies, and that is okay. We all have the choice to show respect to the Tao, our Source, our God, or whatever other term of reference we use. We are free to do this in our own personal ways, which might include our religious practice and custom, or it might not. When seen from this perspective, proving that the group to which we belong is right and others are wrong is no longer an issue of division. Our *recognition* and *acknowledgement* of belonging to *the group of Oneness*, to which *everyone* belongs, removes the implicit group requirement of judging one group against another.

Consider certain strategy used in business. Compare getting very much caught up in the details of our own belief system to the common business mantra of KISS: *Keep It Simple, Stupid*. Too many confusing details on the workings of a product or an idea being sold clouds the understanding of the big picture, which prevents the crux of the matter from being seen, let alone being understood. The heart of the belief system is lost in defense of the details.

However, please do not misinterpret. Understanding the development of one or more of the major world religions or belief systems can be a good thing. It is particularly so when seen from the position that any one system is only one among many, and it, together with others, may allow us to see God (the Tao) within ourselves and in everyone. When the details of any single belief system blocks the Goodness of the Tao (God), the simplicity of the big picture fades out of our personal view because all that can be seen in our mind are the details of that belief system as being the only option.

This *does not* suggest that every strange, disconnected, or questionable collection of ideas about a god are worthy of honor in this way. It does, however, mean that the Tao *is in everyone,* even if his or her ideas do not coincide with the reality of the Tao. The real issue at the core of this discussion is our thoughts. When the thoughts, feelings, and intentions at our very Being do not comply with the Goodness that is the Tao, a shadow of darkness completely obscures our Light.

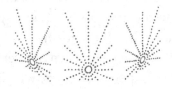

About the Author

With a modest upbringing and supportive parents, Daniel Frank completed his teacher training at the age of eighteen and started his nonstop forty-two-year teaching career the following year. He acquired his BA and BEd while working full time. In January of 1978, his interests led him to a course offered at the local secondary school based on the book *How Should We Then Live?* by Francis A. Schaeffer, a "theologian and philosopher . . . [with] forty years of intensive study of humanism and Christian truths." It stirred something within him to search for more answers to the question asked by the title of Schaeffer's book. Although many of the authors he has read to date have contributed to the view of God he holds today, Dr. Wayne W. Dyer tops the list.

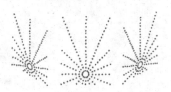

Works Cited

Aurelius, Marcus. *BrainyQuote.com*. 2012.
    http://www.brainyquote.com/quotes/quotes/m/marcusaure1
    48753.html (accessed February 11, 2012).

Braden, Gregg. *Speaking the Lost Language of God*. Niles, IL:
    Nightingale Conant.

—. *The Divine Matrix*. Hay House, Inc., 2010.

Chopra, Deepak. *Life after Death*. New York: Harmony Books, 2006.

—. *Power, Freedom, and Grace*. San Rafael, CA: Amber-Allen
    Publishing Inc., 2006.

—. *Reinventing the Body, Resurrecting the Soul*. New York: Harmony
    Books, 2009.

—. *The Seven Spiritual Laws of Success*. San Rafael, CA: Amber-Allen
    Publishing, New World Library, 1994.

—. *The Spontaneous Fulfillment of Desire*. New York: Three Rivers
    Press, 2003.

—. *The Ultimate Happiness Prescription*. New York: Harmony Books,
    2009.

Colton, Charles Caleb. *BrainyQuote.com*. 2012.
    http://www.brainyquote.com/quotes/quotes/c/charlescal120
    3963.html (accessed Feb 11, 2012).

Confucius. *BrainyQuote.com*. 2012.
    http://www.brainyquote.com:/quotes/quotes/c/confucius104
    563.html (accessed February 11, 2012).

Dyer, Dr. Wayne W. *Being in Balance*. Carlsbad: Hay House Inc.,
    2006.

—. *Change Your Thoughts—Change Your Life*. 1st ed. Hay House, Inc.,
    2007.

—. *Getting in the Gap*. Vancouver: Raincoast, 2003.

—. *Gifts from Eykis*. 2002: Quill, 1983.

—. *Inspiration*. Carlsbad: Hay House, Inc., 2006.

—. *Pulling Your Own Strings*. New York: Avon Books, 1979.

—. *Real Magic*. New York: Harper Paperbacks, 1993.

—. *The Power of Intention*. Carlsbad: Hay House Inc., 2004.

—. *The Sky's the Limit*. USA: Simon and Schuster, 1980.

—. *Wisdom of the Ages*. New York: Quill, 2002.

—. *You'll See It When You Believe It.* New York: Quill, 2001.

Goswami, Amit. *God Is Not Dead.* Charlottesville, VA: Hampton Roads Publishing Company, Inc, 2008.

Hawkins, David R. *Power versus Force.* Carlsbad, CA: Hay House, 2004.

—. *The Eye of the I.* W. Sedona, Arizona: Veritas Publishing, 2001.

Jampolsky, Gerald G. *Love is Letting Go of Fear.* Berkeley, CA: Celestial Arts, 2004.

King James Version. *Holy Bible.* Nashville: Crusade Bible Publishers, 1973.

Lipton, Bruce H. *The Biology of Belief.* Carlsbad: Hay House Inc., 2008.

Lunau, Kate, and Katie Engelhart. "Unravelling the Universe." *Macleans's*, July 23, 2012: 40-7.

Myss, Caroline. *Invisible Acts of Power.* New York: Free Press, 2004.

—. *Sacred Contracts.* New York: Three Rivers Press, 2003.

Newland, Guy. *Introduction to Emptiness.* Ithaca, NY: Snow Lion Publications, 2008.

Sativihari, Rishi. *Unlearning the Basics.* Somerville, MA: Wisdom Publications, 2010.

Schaeffer, Francis A. *How Should We Then Live?* Old Tappan, NJ: Fleming H. Revell Company, 1976.

Tolle, Eckhart. *A New Earth.* New York: Plume, 2006.

Vaughan, Frances and Roger Walsch, eds. *Gifts from a Course in Miracles.* New York: Tarcher/Putnam, 1988, intro 1995.

Zukav, Gary. *Soul to Soul.* New York: Free Press, 2007.

—. *The Seat of the Soul.* New York: Fireside, 1990.